SHE BRUSHED
HER LIPS ACRO[...]

"I love you, Jacob, just as you are. I don't expect you to conform to some rigid pattern that doesn't suit you. If my 'differentness' causes you embarrassment, I'll understand if—"

He brought her mouth to his again, kissing her deeply. "Shut up, Desirée," he whispered, sliding his body over hers. "You're my dream lover...." He kissed her again and again until she was heedless of all else but him—heedless of the fact that the moon beyond the bedroom window was in the last triad of its cycle.

It was the time of the waning moon—a time when all things had to end to fulfill their beginnings. The waning moon: the sum of the whole, the symbol of all things seen and unseen, of all that had gone before and was yet to come....

ABOUT THE AUTHOR

Ruth Alana Smith is constantly experimenting with unusual themes and story lines. In *Spellbound*, Ruth's fifth Superromance, she once again stretches the bounds of category romance and challenges readers with insights and questions. Interestingly enough, Ruth, a devoted wife and mother of two, insists that her everyday life in Pasadena, Texas, is anything but unusual. She even admits to being a homebody at heart!

Books by Ruth Alana Smith

HARLEQUIN SUPERROMANCE

Ruth Alana Smith
SPELLBOUND

Harlequin Books

TORONTO • NEW YORK • LONDON
AMSTERDAM • PARIS • SYDNEY • HAMBURG
STOCKHOLM • ATHENS • TOKYO • MILAN

Published May 1989

First printing March 1989

ISBN 0-373-70356-2

PROLOGUE

HEAVEN—THE ASTRAL PLANE—OR WHATEVER ONE MIGHT PREFER TO CALL THE REALM BEYOND MORTAL CONSCIOUSNESS.

"GUARDIAN ANGEL SECOND-GRADE, Alistair Mackey, report to the Fisherman at once!" The summons blared over the loudspeaker.

The snoozing angel's eyes immediately flicked open and he sprang into motion. Jumping off the bed and into his boots, Mackey grabbed his tunic, silver wing insignia and grungy hat, then dashed lickety-split down the sunlit corridors.

"What now?" he muttered to himself, skidding around the final turn of the glass-enclosed maze. "I've been faithfully tending to me duties."

Suddenly the silver wing insignia he'd lopsidedly pinned to the robe's lapel glowed bright red and registered a mindful beep. The ruddy-faced Mackey grimaced, donned his beloved bushman's hat, and affixed the leather strap beneath his unshaven chin. He knew full well that the Fisherman would make mention of his nonregulation attire, but he felt naked without his trusty hat. Cocking it just a fraction so it sat smartly over a sandy-colored brow, he knocked on the appropriate door and awaited permission to enter.

"Come in, Alistair," a resonant voice commanded.

With a jaunty strut, the apprentice angel stepped into his superior's domain and offered a chipper greeting. "G'day, mate!"

The Fisherman smiled, then gestured for Mackey to come closer. "I see you still have the need to embrace material reminders from your past."

Mackey grinned sheepishly. "I suppose you could say that I'm a creature of habit, Fisherman. Wearing me hat is the same as you sportin' that shiny halo. Besides, I miss the Outback. The hat, well, it's got the smell of crocodiles and ale about it and every now and then I take me a big, deep whiff, just for old times' sake. I can't see the harm in it."

"Neither can I, unless, of course, your reasons for refusing to adopt our celestial dress code are not purely inspired. Perhaps your nonconformity is more a matter of defiance than preference?" The Fisherman gave Mackey no chance to refute the rightful assumption. "I sense in you an almost desperate desire to cling to the familiar. Could it be possible that you still do not fully accept your assignment as a permanent one?" The Fisherman's eyes were filled with wisdom and kindness.

"That may be, mate." Mackey shoved his hat back from his sun-baked forehead and scratched his scalp. "To tell you the truth, I think there's been a mix-up. I know you blokes don't make many mistakes, but for starters I wasn't ready to check out down below. I was in me prime. Fit as a fiddle, I was. Of course, I understand the Almighty didn't require my piddling consent," he respectfully submitted. "What baffles me most is what an old croc poacher like me is doing in Heaven. Just between us, I don't really think I belong here." The last words Mackey said in a conspiratorial whisper.

The Fisherman's smile broadened. "Our master does not make these decisions lightly. There is a divine purpose in your assignment. Trust me, Angel Mackey."

The Aussie demurred to the higher authority with a humble nod.

"The reason I sent for you is that I was alarmed by what I discovered when scanning the daily printouts. Since I only review them once a week, I was unaware that one of your charges on earth is undergoing great spiritual trauma. Why have you not apprised me of this disturbing development?" the Fisherman asked.

Uh-oh! Mackey cringed inwardly. His fudging was going to be a source of contention between him and the Fisherman once more. "Which charge might that be?"

"The fact that you need to ask only confirms what I had hoped was not true. You've been neglecting your duties again, Angel Mackey. How can I impress upon you the importance of the responsibility you carry? Souls on earth are at stake and these frequent excursions you take to Cloud Nine are becoming a problem."

Alistair stared ashamedly at the marble floor.

"Come see for yourself the havoc of which I speak." The Fisherman spread the computerized graph on a podium for the ex-croc poacher's inspection. "Look here…and here…and here." He pointed to a series of erratic fluctuations. "It's apparent that this soul is in dire need of personal surveillance and guidance."

Alistair searched for excuses. "Could be mere glitches—a computer malfunction, perhaps. I'm not meaning to sound sacrilegious, but I don't put a whole lot of faith in your miraculous microchips. You see, I'm a man of instinct. That's what made me a near-legendary poacher in the Outback," he bragged. "And, begging Your Eminence's pardon, it's me own sensory system I choose to rely on whenever danger lurks about. Dependable it is, too. Prickles the hair on the back of me neck, it does."

The Fisherman saw through the rationalization. "All the more reason for you to travel down below and evaluate the situation personally," he countered.

Mackey checked the name on the top of the sheet. *Jacob Ryan Malone.* His idol. Keeping tabs on him was almost as exciting as tracking crocs. What a life he lived! Why should he be discontented? The man must be daft.

"I feel an interference, Angel Mackey—another force at work," the Fisherman worried aloud. "Prepare to make a trip to earth. Do nothing but observe, then report back to me with your preliminary findings."

"Yes, Fisherman," the Aussie obediently replied. But before he took his final leave, he made one itty-bitty request. "Would it be all right if I was to wear me hat below?"

The Fisherman sighed. "You're invisible on earth, Angel Mackey. Wear it if you wish."

Mackey beamed. "I appreciate it, mate. G'day."

CHAPTER ONE

BOSTONIANS WOKE to a record-setting chill factor on the morning of the first Tuesday in February. The date also happened to mark the occasion of Jacob Ryan Malone's closing summation in a civil suit that had received a great deal more local media attention than it deserved. Part of the reason for the exaggerated interest was that the defendant in the case was a wealthy and prominent local businessman. The other part was that Malone himself was a celebrity of sorts.

Only the very rich and/or the most influential could afford the services of Malone and Van Cleve, Attorneys at Law. Though their exorbitant fee was restrictive, the outcome of any case they undertook was practically assured in favor of their client. Their reputation was such that it had become somewhat of a status symbol to be championed by them. They were the Gucci of legal eagles. However, it was Jacob Malone who received most of the acclaim since it was he who was the brilliant orator, the impassioned showman, the one who actually argued the more sensational or ticklish cases in court. Adeline Van Cleve kept a low profile. She was the partner with the aptitude for tedious research. More often than not, it was her shrewd mind that devised the legal arguments by which to set precedents.

As Jacob sat in his plush office overlooking the Charles River, sipping coffee and studying the notes he'd prepared for his summation, his concentration waned. It didn't matter a whole hell of a lot because he seldom kept to a predetermined format when addressing a jury. He relied more on gut instinct—on what he perceived in the jurors' eyes or surmised from their posture as he approached the box. That sixth sense he possessed always provided the perfect angle by which to sway a jury. Often he had completely reversed his psychology at the last moment—chosen some alternate recourse or an unorthodox appeal—and it was the subtle switch in tactics that ultimately led to a judgment in his client's behalf. It was a tricky balancing act, but sometimes it was only by virtue of his flexibility and unconventionality that Malone gained an all-important edge in an iffy case.

The ritual of coming into the office early and psyching himself up before wooing a jury was a little bit habit and a whole lot of presummation jitters. As well, the token appearance never failed to reassure his partner, who was a born worrier. According to Addie, every new case was a potential disaster that threatened the firm's credibility. Each time they represented a new client she would claim that this was the fatal one—the unwinnable case that would surely be their undoing. Armageddon lurked just around the corner. The day before a trial date was the worst. It was then that Addie lost all of her objectivity and professionalism, not to mention her confidence.

"We're going to lose. It'll take a miracle to pull this one off," she'd fret. "And you can wipe that patronizing smirk off your face, Jake Malone. I know what you're thinking. Here she goes again. Gloom-and-doom Addie is venting her insecurities. Okay, I admit that so far my fears have proven to be unwarranted, but it's different this time, Jake. I really do have a strong premonition of an upset. I tell you, it's highly probable the judgment will go against us. We're going to look like incompetents, and once the tide starts turning, it won't be long before Malone and Van Cleve will be reduced to chasing ambulances for a percentage of some poor lamb's misery.

"Where are you going? Fine. Fine! Just waltz out on me. I know you've pressing matters on your mind—never mind that the law practice we've worked so hard to establish could soon be out the window. What's her name? Where is she listed on the social register? Doubtless, she's some South Hampton yuppie who's into sushi and crystals. Just do me one favor and make it an early conquest. I'd hate for you to miss your own execution tomorrow."

Such was a typical Addie pep talk before any given court appearance. She was a born pessimist.

A faint smile broke out on Jacob's swarthy face as he continued to think about his semineurotic but sharp-witted partner. Addie had a near-genius IQ, and an amazing single-mindedness when it came to the law. Whenever they represented a new client, she lived and breathed the case, as if only it and nothing else were vital to her existence.

Jacob perceived her modus operandi as similar to the Lamaze birthing method, since both involved concentrated effort and some major sweating. He'd heard more about the natural-birth process than he'd cared to when his brother had attended classes to prepare for his sojourn into fatherhood. For months it had been virtually the sole topic of conversation between the two of them. That was when Jacob had first begun making the comparison with Addie; it was a means of relating on a personal level to what the hell his brother was constantly babbling about.

Yeah, thought Jacob, if or when Addie ever decided to produce kids rather than induce verdicts, she would be a natural. Whenever a case drew to a conclusion—as this one was about to—and her initial pride in the accomplishment had worn off, she experienced the same kind of pain as Jacob believed a new mother must undergo. Postpartum blues was how he teasingly described Addie's after-trial condition. "Hey, cheer up," he'd kid her. "It won't be a month before you'll become impregnated with another cause. Then, you can revel in those familiar brain contractions—rejoice in the low back pain you invariably suffer when huddling over your precious legal precedents. You'll have that bloom to you again, Addie. Nausea, insomnia, paranoia. It'll be grand," he'd predict with a wink.

There was more than a grain of truth in his chiding. There were times when their partnership took on many of the same characteristics a marriage did during Lamaze training—times when they worked better jointly than separately. Every now and then an especially complex or sensitive case came along and it would make sense for them to pair up. Jacob could remember more than one sticky situation when either their imagined insecurities or supposed inadequacies warranted a collusion of effort and expertise. Not that Addie wasn't capable of arguing a case in court—as long as it was cut-and-dried litigation and did not require showmanship. Similarly, Jacob was well and able to prepare his own briefs, as long as they didn't entail extensive research. He simply didn't have the patience for referencing mounds of legal texts.

Yes, Jacob mused, vacating his chair with a lazy stretch of his tall frame, he and Addie were a good team. They had made quite a name for themselves in Boston and had more money than any pair of thirty-five-year-old lawyers should, in all modesty, boast of. He owned two of everything—houses, sports cars, sailboats, motorcycles, Arabian thoroughbreds, Renoirs and Rolexes. He also had a coterie of adoring and desirable women at his beck and call. For several years the sweet fame, fine possessions and endless variety of beautiful ladies had sufficiently soothed his inherent restlessness. Lately, though, the seeds of discontent were again beginning to stir deep within him. It was more than just boredom with material things; it was an internal dissatisfaction.

His green eyes narrowed as he strode to the window and braced a shoulder against the tinted glass. Why did he feel so restless? Why over the past few months had he begun to question the morality of the law he practiced? He found the case he was working on particularly offensive. It kept eating at him, day after day, bit by bit, like a colony of termites gnawing away at a foundation.

Jacob fished a gold toothpick from his pocket. He used it as a substitute for the cigarettes he'd kicked a year ago. Hell, he reasoned to himself, it was his job to champion those who paid his fee. It was not his responsibility to pass judgment on a debatable issue. That was the jury's job. Everyone was entitled to representation under the law. The rich and powerful were no less entitled than the common folk. Yet the rich and powerful could better afford lengthy litigation and brilliant legal counsel. There were, in effect, two distinct sets of justice at work in the good old U.S. of A., based on one's financial ability to wage legal battle. Sure it was discriminating, but that was the present system. So why should he be bothered by the immorality of accepting fat fees for performing a necessary function within the system? If he didn't, someone else would. It was that simple.

Or was it, he wondered.

He shrugged and glanced over at the notes on his desk. He knew his client, Desmond Bower, had rigged evidence in his own favor, and that stuck in Jacob's craw. He didn't just suspect it; Bower had actually confirmed it. Jacob had no qualms about fighting dirty—he'd done so many times when the occasion had called for it. He did, however, have one rule to which he strictly adhered: dirty tactics were okay—*as long as they were within the parameters of the law.* Bower had overstepped the limits in rigging evidence, but Jacob had realized this too late. By the time he'd confronted his client about the suspected tampering, the deed had already been done. He was then caught in a dilemma about professional ethics and personal morality.

He could have withdrawn from representing Bower then and there, but it would have been messy. There was the matter of confidentiality to consider. Any and all statements made by a client to his lawyer were considered to be privileged information. Jacob was bound by ethics not to disclose the details—even incriminating ones—of a case, the same as a priest was sworn by oath to keep sins revealed in the confessional confidential. To do otherwise would be a violation of trust. And if Jacob, a prominent attorney, had withdrawn from a controversial case at the eleventh hour under some vague pretext, a great deal of negative speculation would have been provoked.

Such a maneuver could conceivably have slanted public opinion against Desmond Bower, and it could most certainly have been argued upon appeal that, in a very broad sense, Jacob's severing of his services had somehow affected the final judgment. At that point Bower would probably have used his vast influence to bring about Jacob's review before the Bar. Though the slimeball's chances of succeeding at having Jacob's license pulled would have been slim next to nil, to someone like Bower the end result was secondary to getting even. Jacob had dealt with a score of Bower types during his career. He knew the demigod mentality of power brokers. If Bower had considered himself double-crossed, he would have become obsessed with discrediting, harassing and generally undermining the culprit—namely the firm of Malone and Van Cleve.

"So you had—and have—no choice but to follow through," he concluded aloud, deftly rolling the gold toothpick from one corner of his mouth to the other. "Paint Bower as a second Mother Theresa in the eyes of the jury and get him off the hook, no matter how much you personally dislike the sorry son of a—"

"God! I hope you aren't planning to include that crudely phrased character assessment in your closing remarks." Adeline donned a grim expression as she closed the office door behind her.

"I might." Jacob refrained from meeting her eyes as he reseated himself behind the desk.

"Please, Jake, I'm already sweating this case enough as it is. Spare me your warped sense of humor this morning, will you? I know you're not fond of Bower but, fortunately, that's not a criterion for our representing him. I did your homework for you. Now all that's left is for you to go in there today and wow 'em with one of your gifted oral dissertations." She ensconced herself in one of the two leather chairs arranged opposite his desk.

He wanted to tell her the truth about why he wasn't fond of their client, but he knew she'd only develop a case of the hives and become even more insistent that

he do nothing—positively, absolutely nothing—to incite the wrath of Bower. Addie was good at inventing
crises, not at withstanding the pressure when they actually materialized.

Jacob neatly folded his notes and slipped them into
his inside coat pocket along with the toothpick. "I'll
do real good, Miss Addie. I'll save the day for Desmond Bower's company and somehow manage to
preserve the integrity of Malone and Van Cleve in the
process," he said with detectable cynicism.

The tension ebbed from her face a bit. "Good.
That's precisely what we must accomplish."

"At any price?" he pressed.

Her clear blue eyes assessed him for a reflective
moment. "We've had this same discussion at least six
times in as many months—each time we take on a new
client, as a matter of fact. It's becoming a bad habit.
What is it with you lately?"

He shrugged off the touchy question. "I don't
know. Maybe I'm burned out or something. I keep
having second thoughts about the fairness of the system."

Addie sighed, leaned back and unbuttoned her pin-
striped navy jacket. "I don't understand this sudden
preoccupation with the system. It exists. It has it's
flaws but, as the saying goes, it's the only game in
town. So you play it to the best of your ability. It's
what you devoted years of your life learning how to
do." She sat forward again. "It's what pays for all
those fancy toys of yours." Leaning back once more,
she added, "Let me attempt to put this into perspec-

tive for you one last time. You provide a service. In return for that service you receive compensation that subsidizes a six-figure bank account and makes you irresistible to your fawning harem.''

It amused him that she always managed to inject something about his love life into the conversation. ''You're avoiding the issue as usual,'' he returned smoothly. ''Somehow you've reduced a lofty matter of conscience to a sleazy matter of hormones. You're developing some bad habits of your own. Maybe I should reverse the question and ask what's with you?''

Jacob was a master at turning the tables on a person. It was what made him so outstanding in a courtroom. Addie shifted her slim weight uncomfortably within the chair, recrossed her legs and adjusted the hem of her skirt a discreet inch over her knees. ''Nothing. I didn't realize you were so sensitive about your overactive hormones. I'll try to refrain from mentioning them again.'' She sounded half sincere.

He wasn't fooled for a second. Addie did not approve of his life in the fast lane. She even more strongly disapproved of his many women friends. He hadn't figured out yet if she coveted his life-style or if she was jealous of the interests he cultivated outside of the law practice. It never occurred to him that she might harbor deep feelings for him. Addie was a competent business partner, and the only other light in which Jacob would ever regard her was that of a sister—a lovable and necessary nuisance. Anything more was unthinkably incestuous. There were those with whom one was familiar, and those with whom one was intimate. Addie definitely fell into the first category.

Assuming his big-brother persona, he said goadingly, "And I'll try not to make reference to the lack of yours."

She stiffened visibly, slanting him an icy look. "Those second thoughts you're having may, in fact, be a symptom of burnout—physical, not mental. Lacking in oneself and pacing oneself are two entirely different things. Of course, I wouldn't expect you to appreciate the distinction."

He flashed her his most rakish grin. "That's a word you throw around a lot—*expect*. You're always saying you don't expect this of me and you certainly wouldn't expect that of me." Jacob's tone was smooth and easy as he went about collecting his attaché case from atop the wall-length bookcase and his topcoat from the closet. It never ceased to surprise Addie how lithely he moved for such a large man. "You forget, Addie, that I had a Jewish mother. I could write a dictionary with a hundred and one interpretations of the word *expect*." He glanced down at the Rolex Mariner on his wrist before delivering one of his famous zingers. "I have generally found that when someone so strongly professes not to have any expectations of another, the exact opposite is true." He was thoroughly enjoying making Addie squirm. A telltale trace of crimson colored her alabaster cheeks.

Addie had no immediate comeback with which to counter his insightful claim.

Satisfied that he'd struck a raw nerve, he bridged the awkward silence looming between them with a beguiling wink. "Well, it's showtime, Miss Addie. How do I look?"

Grateful for the reprieve, she brushed aside the silky locks of blond hair framing her face and perused his impeccably dressed person. He was tall, dark and, though not exactly Tom Selleck material, definitely intriguing in a coarse kind of way. His six-foot-three-inch frame was muscular, but not too much so, and his hair was dark, the texture of sable. He had an olive complexion, penetrating eyes that reminded one of jade gemstones, a Michael Douglas cleft in his chin, a sensuous mouth and a strong nose that was rightly proportioned to his angled face. Though Addie wasn't blind to Jacob's flaws, his charisma was such that one tended to overlook the obvious and see only what one imagined him to be. "You look impressive," she finally said.

He tweaked her chin, then strode toward the door.

She sat admiring him.

Jacob paused, and turned back toward her.

"I know what time court convenes and, yes, I intend to be there. Aren't I always?" she assured him. It wasn't that she was psychic; she had merely anticipated his question. In the five years they'd been partners, he had never failed to inquire if she planned to be on hand for his summation, and she had never failed to comply.

Jacob nodded, then left Addie to ponder what it was that she actually did expect to derive from a partnership with him.

THE COURTROOM WAS packed by the time Addie arrived. She made her way down the aisle, through the swinging gate, and mustered a confident smile for Bower's benefit as she seated herself at the table.

"Hear ye, hear ye, all those who have business before the Commonwealth of Massachusetts, step forth and be heard. Court is convened, the honorable Judge Judith Crawford presiding," the bailiff announced.

The black-robed judge took her place on the bench. "We heard counsel for the plaintiff's closing argument at the end of yesterday's session," she said. "Therefore, it is now your turn to address your final remarks to the jury, Mr. Malone. Please proceed."

As Jacob stood and approached the jurors' box, an expectant hush fell over the gallery. He was a commanding figure—sure of himself and equally sure of the outcome. "Good morning, ladies and gentlemen of the jury," he said pleasantly. "I'll try to be brief since I'm aware of your proximity to the heating vents and do empathize with your uncomfortable position. I'm sure it's quite literally like being on the hot seat."

Everyone chuckled.

He was off to a good start—suave and utterly charming in his self-assurance. Jacob cleared his throat and began his summation in earnest. "My esteemed colleague, Mr. Hanson, would like for you to believe that my client is a heartless slave driver whose crimes against humanity could be likened to those of Simon Legree. Though I enjoyed *Uncle Tom's Cabin* as much as anyone, I'm aware that it's a work of fiction. And so is the image Mr. Hanson presented of my client a work of fiction.'' Jacob glanced over at the plaintiff's table, taking note of the nondescript fellow sitting beside the opposing attorney. The man was acutely ordinary—an eight-to-five average Joe who foolishly thought he had a legitimate grievance and wanted his day in court. Well, he was about to become a disillusioned average Joe. He was about to find out it really didn't matter that he'd been swindled out of the monetary compensation he justly deserved, that within the narrow confines of the law and without concrete proof to the contrary, the three long years he'd spent developing a revolutionary software package had no value. He'd been duped by the ''big boys'' and now the big boys' gun was about to blow his rightful claim to pieces.

Jacob's dramatic pause had stretched beyond what Judge Crawford thought reasonable. ''You promised us you'd be brief, Mr. Malone,'' she reminded.

For a split second, Addie thought Jacob looked disconcerted, but he quickly collected himself. She sipped from her water glass, trying to appear casual when, in truth, Jacob's odd behavior had tripped her body's alarm signals. Her hand shook slightly as she replaced the tumbler on the table.

''I'm sorry, Your Honor. My imagination gets away from me occasionally. I was mentally picturing the plaintiff chained and shackled to a desk, being bullied by my client into producing technology that would transform the textile industry. And if that in itself were not a heinous enough deed, counsel for the plaintiff further contends that my client, Mr. Bower, mentally abused this poor, pitiful subjugated soul by dangling false hope before him—promising a lucrative share in an enormous bounty, should he be successful in his high-tech endeavor. It's an interesting conjecture Mr. Hanson puts forth. It has all the ingredients of high melodrama. It would play well on a New York stage but has not one whit of impact within a Boston courtroom. It's an absurd supposition, a contradictory hypothesis, at best. And yet—'' he addressed himself directly to the jury ''—it is precisely what my colleague would like you to believe of Desmond Bower.''

Jacob turned and pointed to his client. ''He wants you to believe that this man misled and exploited an employee, that he knowingly and under false pretenses encouraged that employee to slave and sweat over a project for three long years while having no intention of letting him share in the profits from such a project.'' Jacob's eyes made contact with Bower's. ''Why would he do that?'' he asked, letting his hand drop to his side with a theatrical flair. ''Why would a man in Desmond Bower's respected position conspire to cheat a loyal employee out of a small, really inconsequential portion of a veritable fortune and leave himself vulnerable to the charges he and his company face here today?''

Jacob's expression became stony as he continued to stare at the arrogant power broker seated next to Addie. *Because he's a greedy, scheming opportunist who'd cheat his own mother out of her welfare checks if he thought he could get away with it,* Jacob silently fumed. Bower had done exactly what the plaintiff had accused him of. He'd encouraged his employee to develop a software package under the pretext that he would share in the increased profits if the novel idea stood up in testing. When it had, Bower had arranged for an outside consulting firm to claim otherwise— that the concept was not feasible as originally designed and had to be revised and adapted through extensive research and testing. Since Bower's company had underwritten all the expenses to refine the concept into a workable package, and since a representative of the consulting firm had sworn under oath that the plaintiff's prospectus would never have produced the desired results as it was first conceived, and since the supposed agreement between Bower and his employee had taken place in private without benefit of witnesses—

"Mr. Malone!" was the somewhat exasperated call from the bench. "You seem to keep losing track and leaving sentences dangling in midair. You're trying my patience, sir. Court will take a short recess, during which time I strongly suggest you consolidate your points and be prepared to make them." Judge Crawford banged the gavel, then made a brusque exit into her private chambers.

A murmur rippled through the gallery. Jacob stood stunned. Addie's inner alarm system was now on full alert.

Desmond Bower made no pretense of hiding his annoyance. "What the hell is going on? He's making me look worse than the opposing attorney."

"Everything's fine, Mr. Bower." Addie put forth a supreme effort to appear unruffled—as though Jacob's embarrassing lapses were a common occurrence. "My partner knows what he's doing. he's leading up to making his point."

"Well, tell him to get to the damn point quick. He's making an ass out of both of us. I'm not paying him thousands of dollars to stutter and stammer."

Desmond Bower's blood pressure had to be out of sight, Addie thought distractedly. Even his ears were scarlet. "I'll have a word with him," she said, rising.

"Have three words with him," Bower suggested. "Tell him to get it together."

"Get it together," Addie repeated dumbly. "Yes, sir, I'll tell him," she said, scurrying to privately confer with Jacob.

"What in the hell do you think you're doing?" she whispered. "Bower is fit to be tied. He wants you to make your point pronto. Criminy, Jacob, get it together and stop your nonsense this instant."

He offered no excuse for his bizarre behavior. "I couldn't care less what the guilty SOB wants."

"Dammit, Jake, that's for a jury to decide, not you. Whose side are you on anyway? Lest you forget, it was Bower's signature on the sizable retainer check we deposited. This is hardly the proper time or place to go off on some kind of tangent and make a social statement. It ain't like the movies, Jake. You're not Al Pacino and this isn't *And Justice For All*. So, for heaven's sake, will you please just sum up and let's get the heck out of Dodge while the gettin' is good?''

Her plea struck its mark. "Okay, Addie. I don't need you to remind me of my priorities. I know which side my bread is buttered on. Go baby-sit Bower and assure him that I'll get his broad butt out of a tight crack." For the first time, he raised his eyes from the floor to hers and she could plainly see the frustration seething within him. "I said I'd do it and I will. But I don't have to like it."

Judge Crawford reentered the courtroom and Addie took her seat at the defendant's table.

"Did you get Perry Mason squared away?" Bower grunted beneath his breath.

She nodded while searching her handbag for the trusty roll of antacid tablets she never left home without.

"Are you ready to continue, Mr. Malone?" Judge Crawford inquired.

"I thank the Court for its indulgence," he replied. "And, yes, Your Honor, I'm ready to proceed."

"Then do so," Judge Crawford decreed.

Jacob strolled toward the jurors' box, unbuttoning his tweed suit coat and nonchalantly leaning an elbow on the wooden railing. "I apologize for my earlier preoccupation during the summation. I'm afraid I got carried away with the image Mr. Hanson projected of my client, as I'm sure many of you did. It's only natural to wonder if it could be possible that some feudallike arrangements still exist in our supposedly free society. It's only natural to wonder if perhaps the plaintiff was taken advantage of by a ruthless employer. We want to be fair in our judgment and our inclination is to give every possible consideration to the party whom we perceive to be the underdog. In this instance, that is clearly the plaintiff, for he is dependent upon Mr. Bower for his very livelihood and it is within Mr. Bower's power to strip him of that financial security on a whim.''

The textile tycoon wasn't sure he liked his attorney's tactics any better the second time around. He fidgeted within the straight-backed chair. Addie crunched two more antacid tablets.

''So,'' Jacob drawled, ''It's understandable that you might view my client as a tyrant who not only has the power to exile the plaintiff to a bread line, but who could also swindle him out of monies directly gained from the software program in question. Already your opinion has been slanted by underdog sentiment. Now I ask you, is that fair? Are you not prejudiced against my client strictly because he happens to be in a position of authority—the 'big, bad boss.' How many of you relate to the plaintiff's subservient situation? Are you dependent upon another for a weekly paycheck? How many of you secretly resent it and are slightly inclined in the plaintiff's favor?''

Slowly he scanned the faces of the jurors. On some he could see it; with others he could sense it—they were uneasy with the thought he'd implanted. ''I am not accusing you of being blatantly biased. I am only suggesting that any one of you could be uncon-

sciously influenced. Fortunately your personal feelings have no bearing on the decision you must reach.
Yes, fortunately, our judicial system makes allow-
ances for the human factor that filters into each and
every grievance that is aired in a court of law." He
paused before continuing.

"You must make your decision based solely upon
the facts presented and the legal interpretation that
governs those very same facts. Therefore, your decision should be quite clear. Mr. Hanson has presented
no witnesses to substantiate his client's claim that he
and Mr. Bower had a gentleman's agreement concerning the sharing of revenues that might or might
not be accrued from the as-yet-untested technology.
However, my client, Mr. Bower, has presented expert
testimony that the plaintiff's project proved unwork-
able, and would require major funding and consider-
able research to develop properly. The end result was
vastly different than the original concept. In other
words, ladies and gentlemen of the jury, the plaintiff's novel idea was a dud—a bomb—a washout."

Jacob turned and pinned the nondescript fellow
with a steely gaze. "Yet the plaintiff expects to be
compensated for a germ of an impractical idea merely
because my client is an easy target—an easy mark—a
ready prejudice to exploit."

"He did it. He stole my idea. I just want what's due
me. I'm not exploiting anybody!" the average Joe
protested, jumping to his feet. "You're twisting it all
around. Why are you doing this to me? My only crime
was in trusting that sneaky sack of—"

Judge Crawford whacked the gavel on the bench. "The Court will not tolerate any further outburst of this nature. I will find your client in contempt if you do not control him, Mr. Hanson."

At his lawyer's insistence, the perturbed fellow grudgingly sat back down.

Jacob swallowed the bitter aftertaste left in his mouth and continued. "Yes, I say exploit!" he reiterated, facing the jury once more. "Because everyone wants to see the underdog win. We all just love it when the small Davids of this world bring the Goliaths to their knees—when the 'big bad bosses' get theirs." He paused for dramatic effect.

"However—" he stretched out his words "—disagreeable it may be, the truth is that Mr. Bower has not been proven guilty of wrongdoing during the past few weeks. His only offense was being in a position of authority and, sadly, it is that very same envied position that makes him vulnerable to such ridiculous claims as we've heard in this courtroom today. The plaintiff has no legal grounds for his suit. You can come to only one reasonable conclusion. You must find in favor of the defendant and dismiss the plaintiff's claim as invalid. I thank you for your patience and attention, ladies and gentlemen of the jury." He demurred to them with an ever-so-slight bow of his dark head, then retreated to his table with a curt, "I rest my case, Your Honor."

Judge Crawford smiled indulgently before addressing herself to the jury. "You have, I believe, fully heard both sides of the issue. It is now your duty to retire and deliberate until such time as you can render a true and just verdict. I have previously charged you with your legal obligations. Court is adjourned.'' With yet another bang of her gavel, Judge Crawford ended the morning session and the jury filed out.

"Well, well, well . . .'' Bower sounded like a broken record. He slapped Jacob on the back. "We certainly got our point across. Troublemakers like that little weasel will think twice about suing the hand that feeds them. You were outstanding, Malone. You had me worried there for a bit, but you came through like gangbusters.''

"I wouldn't ice down the champagne just yet, Mr. Bower. There's still a minor technicality you're over-looking—like the jury having to find in your favor.'' Jacob shrugged off the other man's repugnant touch and busied himself with gathering his papers.

"I think their decision is a foregone conclusion. I'll buy us lunch someplace nearby. No sense venturing too far. I'm sure this whole sordid mess will be settled satisfactorily within the hour,'' Bower predicted.

Jacob snapped shut his attaché case and shot his client a murderous look. "I'm sure Miss Van Cleve will enjoy sharing lunch with you. I'm afraid you'll have to excuse me. I've suddenly lost my appetite.'' He sidestepped Bower, gave the gate an angry shove and left it swinging on its hinges as he stalked out of the courtroom.

"He's a moody one, isn't he?'' Bower scowled and straightened his tie.

"But a very good lawyer, sir," Addie quickly returned, glossing over Jacob's flagrant insult. "I, on the other hand, am ravenously hungry and would be delighted to have lunch with you," she lied. Her stomach was doing somersaults. She was positively queasy with nerves.

As DESMOND BOWER had predicted, it wasn't long before the jury reached a decision. They'd deliberated for all of an hour and a half before finding in the defendant's favor. It took Addie a few minutes to extricate herself from their exonerated client and by the time she did, Jacob was nowhere in sight. She finally caught up with him back at the office. She'd expected him to be in a foul mood. What she hadn't expected was to walk in and find him packing up a few personal belongings.

"What's this?" she uttered bewilderedly.

"I'm taking some time off. As of now, consider me on an indefinite leave of absence," he explained.

"Oh, come on, Jake," she pooh-poohed. "Don't you think you're taking the Bower case a bit too personally?"

"You're damn right I am," he admitted, flipping the latest issue of *The New Yorker* into a cardboard box. "Bower rigged the evidence, Addie. If you don't believe me, just ask him. He likes to boast about it. He railroaded that poor fella and we helped him do it. That makes me feel worse than low." Jacob stormed around the office, collecting various articles and chucking them into the box. "I don't like being an unwilling accomplice to a hatchet job. And, yeah, I tend to take it personally.''

Addie put a staying hand on his arm. ''It happens that sometimes we defend people who are guilty. It's the ugly side of the business. You knew it when you made a choice between starting a lucrative private practice and becoming a civil liberties activist.'' At the stubborn jut of his chin, she let her hand slide from his arm, retreated around the desk and sank into a chair. ''I can see by your attitude that nothing I say is going to make any difference. You're bound and determined to sulk about this. So, all right, go off somewhere and make peace with yourself. I suppose I can manage without you for a week or so. Just so long as you promise to have your head screwed on straight when you return.''

''You're not listening to me, Addie. I said I was taking an indefinite leave of absence. What that means is that I plan to get into my car and just start driving with no set purpose or direction.'' He polished off a canned soft drink and tossed it into the trash.

''What you're taking leave of is your senses! You can't just head off into the wild blue yonder and leave me to handle things around here all by my lonesome. You have an obligation to the firm and our clients.'' Her eyes grew wide as he slung his topcoat over a shoulder and picked up the cardboard box. ''I can't argue the tricky cases in court. You know I can't,'' she wailed. ''Don't you dare desert me, Jacob Ryan Malone. I'll never forgive you. I swear I won't.''

"Sorry, Addie. I'm up to here with everything." He indicated his measure of disgust by placing a hand to his Adam's apple. "I've got to have some space. It's more than just a restless mad. It's as though something is drawing me. I don't know what, but I sense its presence and it's tugging at me. Pretty weird, huh?"

"God! You really have lost your mind," she said with a resigned sigh.

He walked around the desk, leaned down and pecked her cheek. "I assure you that my mental faculties are intact. It's my soul that I fear I'm dangerously close to losing. I'll be in touch, Addie."

"Sure, sure, drop me a postcard from time to time." She was too stunned to argue. He was almost out the door when she called after him. "Silly as it sounds, I feel like a jilted wife. I didn't *expect* this from you, Jake."

"I know. Neither did I."

CHAPTER TWO

ON THE EVE of Candlemas, a full, bountiful moon glowed in the heavens above Marblehead. One sole figure had braved the fierce February winds and frothy spray of the Atlantic to celebrate the Grand Sabbat. The pilgrim seemed impervious to the harsh elements and the intermittent flashing of a lighthouse beacon as it swept over the rocky Massachusetts coastline. Beneath the ermine-trimmed hooded cloak, a pair of dark eyes fixed upon the opal sphere overhead. The beholder's gaze was unwavering in its awe and singular in its intent. Shortly a melodious voice called out to be heard above the roar of the breakers pounding the boulder-buttressed shore.

"When Rome ruled all the world, 'tis said,
Dear Venus, Hearts of men you led
To love, the great delight of life
With spell of beauty, not of strife.
Your power's still undimmed, I know,
To me true love in life now show.
Bring love to me on wings of sound,
Let happiness and joy abound.
With every act and thought of mine,

Let me attract my love divine.
Now quickly bring my love to me,
And as my will, so mote it be.''

Three times the chant floated out over the churning
ocean and wafted up into the heavens. Confident that
the plea would be given special consideration on this,
the feast of the waxing light, when seeds that will later
sprout and grow begin to stir from their dark sleep, the
pilgrim retreated from the high precipice and disappeared into the foggy recesses of the peninsula's interior.

AS LEGEND WOULD have it, the first settler of Marblehead was a fisherman who came across the bay from
the colony at Salem and lived in a large hogshead on
the shore of what would eventually be called Peach's
Point. As superstition would have it, however, the
township's roots were deeply entwined with the ancient traditions practiced in the sister colony of Salem
and which, in 1692, were declared to be acts of her-
esy. It was Salem that became infamous for its witch
trials and hangings, whereas Marblehead became re-
nowned for its marvelous harbor, sleek clipper ships,
prosperous merchant princes and the fierce patriot-
ism during the revolutionary war.

The quaint township still retained much of its rich
colonial character in the present day. The rocky cliffs
that surrounded the harbor—from which the town
derived its name—still guarded the shore; the Atlantic waters were still fished for cod and trapped for

lobster; two privately owned castles still cast their fairy-tale shadow; and monuments to Georgian architecture still bordered the winding streets.

Lafayette House, the edifice whose corner section had been removed so that an illustrious general's carriage could pass in the narrow street, had been preserved and restored, as had been the residence of the first general of the Marines, John Clover. He, with his amphibious regiment of Marblehead fishermen, had rowed Washington and his men across the Delaware and led the advance at the Battle of Trenton. The "Old North" church also remained, as did Fort Sewall, a fortification with guns and barracks that had once protected the frigate *Constitution* as it fled British men-o'-war.

The people of Marblehead treasured their heritage and took great pains to safeguard it. Of course, a few new enterprises had developed through the ensuing centuries, such as three of the oldest and best-known yachting clubs in America. Their presence had turned Marblehead into a major resort area where sailing and tourism flourished. The town was a strange blend of tradition and progress, of seventh generation Marbleheaders and yuppies. And there was one—just one—stout building, located on the fringes of the historical district known as the Old Town, that was rumored to have ties to the days of kinship with Salem. The two-story, dark red-frame Georgian structure with its slate-blue trim had years ago been converted to provide shop space on the lower level and living quarters above. Over the main entrance to the shop hung a sign that read, The Magic Herb Hut—Desirée Warren, Proprietress.

When it came to the subject of Desirée Warren, there existed three schools of thought among the citizenry of Marblehead. One's view of her was usually shaped by how long one had resided within Marblehead. The distinction between the townsfolk was as follows: true, dyed-in-the-wool Marbleheaders whose family tree went back seven generations or more; those who had migrated to Marblehead in the last few decades and permanently resided in the small community; and those who paid taxes in order to maintain a second home on the peninsula and who were often referred to as "weekenders" by the locals.

As it happened, the three diverse opinions held of Desirée Warren were, at the very moment, being expressed in the Mug and Muffin Shoppe, situated kitty-corner from The Magic Herb Hut.

"Will you look at that! I don't believe it." Patsy James, a permanent resident, craned her neck to get a better glimpse of the activity taking place across the street.

"What don't you believe?" Marilyn Estes, a weekender, asked, stopping midsip of her coffee and casting an offhanded look beyond the frosted bay window panes.

"I just saw Heather Braxton slip inside that Warren woman's shop. I'm shocked speechless." Patsy daintily dabbed at her red nose with a tissue. "Oh, I wish this cold of mine would leave me."

"I don't understand. Why would someone patronizing the herb shop upset you so?" The newcomer was genuinely baffled.

"Everything upsets Patsy," Archie Hooper chimed in. He owned the Mug and Muffin Shoppe. Six days out of every week for over fifty years he had awakened at 3:00 a.m. in order to prepare his muffins. It was a family tradition; the Hooper name dated way back. There was even an eighteenth-century mansion in town that had once belonged to a Royalist ancestor of his. "Colds. Witch tales. You name it," he muttered while clearing off an adjacent table.

"Witch tales?" Marilyn Estes parroted, suddenly very interested in the conversation.

"Archie's being his usual sarcastic self," Patsy said with a lift of her red nose. "He thinks I make too much of a fuss over the Warren woman. Unlike some people around here, I don't just shrug off the possibility that she's a bona fide witch."

"Really? How interesting!" Marilyn gurgled. "I mean, I knew everyone acted odd whenever her name was mentioned, but I'm afraid I never paid much attention to what was being said. So tell me the story on her. I'm just dying to hear. More coffee, please, Mr. Hooper," she requested as the shopkeeper passed by.

"If you listen to Patsy's version, you'll be believing the woman rides a broomstick and puts hexes on people," Mr. Hooper warned, shuffling off to get the coffeepot.

Patsy shot him a disgusted look, then returned her attention to spreading a generous layer of butter between the warm halves of a blueberry muffin. "Archie can scoff all he wants, but you haven't heard him out-and-out deny my claim, have you? No. And furthermore, he won't. The old-timers are too darn tolerant of the Warren clan, if you ask me. You see, they go way back, too. Desirée's grandmother and mother were admitted witches—confirmed heathens. They didn't even have the common decency to mask their unholy practices."

"You've got to be kidding." Marilyn was truly intrigued. She inched her chair closer.

"Hardly," Patsy snorted. "I wouldn't kid about something that caused me unbelievable misery in my younger days. It's hard for me to talk about it even now." Patsy sniffed into her tissue.

"Oh, I'm so sorry if I've brought up a sensitive subject." Marilyn treaded carefully, though she was fairly tingling with morbid curiosity.

"It's all right. It was a long time ago that it happened. Fifteen years and three days to be exact. That's when my husband Steven left me. Just packed up his things and walked out on me and the children."

"How awful," Marilyn commiserated.

"Yes, well, it wasn't his fault," the older woman hurried to add. "He wasn't himself when he did it, you see. He'd been acting strangely for days prior to his leaving." Patsy gazed off, the pupils of her eyes becoming pinpoints as she contemplated the red and slate-blue building across the street. "It was all her fault. She put a curse on him."

"Who put a curse on him?" the weekender prodded. "You certainly don't mean Desirée Warren. Fifteen years ago she'd only have been a mere child."

"I was referring to Desirée's mother. She was the one who did it. Chelsey Warren cast a spell over my dear Steven and he was never the same afterward." Patsy looked across the table at her breakfast companion. "Make no mistake about it, that one was truly a witch in every sense of the word," she said bitterly.

"Goodness gracious," was all Marilyn could manage to sputter.

Fortunately Archie arrived with the fresh pot of coffee. "Speaking ill of the dead again, Patsy?" he said in a ho-hum fashion as he refilled their mugs. "Patsy's been nursing a grudge against Desirée's mother for years. Not a word of what she's spouting can be proved."

"Neither can it be disproved," Patsy rebutted. "And don't you dare stand there and contend that Chelsey or her mother before her weren't professed witches."

"Didn't say that," he gently corrected her. "I was merely clarifying the fact that nobody—not even you—knows for certain what made Steven run off. Could've been that Chelsey had nothing to do with his disappearance from town," he suggested.

"Hmmph! I know what I know, Archibald Hooper. I was married to the man for over seven years. He loved me dearly. Adored me, in fact. We were blissfully happy together," Patsy told the weekender. "Everyone was always commenting about how we reminded them of a pair of lovebirds.'' She sighed wistfully.

That was not exactly how Archie remembered the marriage. Patsy was constantly whining and nagging Steven to get off his lazy duff and make something of his sorry self, and he was always sneaking away from her at every opportunity, usually to drink a few brewskies down at the tavern and flirt with the barmaids.

"She bewitched him, all right," Patsy was prattling. "What other explanation could there be? No man in his right mind would leave as good a woman as me," she stated flatly. "Chelsey Warren had eyes for Steven from the moment we arrived in Marblehead. It was shameless how she followed him around, flaunting herself and trying to lure him away from me and his faith."

Again, that wasn't exactly how the old shopkeeper recalled the scenario. Actually it was Steven James who had followed Chelsey Warren around town like some kind of panting mutt nipping at her heels. The man had been hopelessly smitten with Chelsey, but she'd never given him so much as a second glance.

"When Steven did not succumb to her feminine wiles, it infuriated the woman. There's only one thing worse than a woman scorned and that's a witch whose wicked advances have been shunned. She conjured up a spell and struck my husband witless with it. Probably something to do with toads and lizards and roaches and such," Patsy ad-libbed.

This was a new twist to the tale. Archie had never heard the bit about roaches before.

"Yuk," Marilyn croaked, imagining the repulsive creatures and shuddering.

"Horrible, isn't it? To think that poor Steven had no inkling of what evildoings were soon to beset him. One day he was as normal as you and I; a few days later he was a zombie. He up and quit his job, offering no explanation whatsoever. Then he marched into the house, packed his belongings and abandoned me and the kids without so much as a fare-thee-well. Now you tell me if that's not queer, especially when the two of us were so devoted to one another."

"Well..." The "weekender" didn't know precisely how to respond. It was definitely strange behavior on the part of Patsy James's long lost spouse. Yet the spell theory that Patsy had expounded could just be a jilted wife's invention. After all, she mused, anyone in Patsy's embarrassing position might be tempted to fabricate a wild excuse in order to save face. Nevertheless, Patsy's talk of witches and hexes was a little far-out. "Uh, it does sound a bit bizarre," Marilyn answered, trying to be tactful.

Patsy detected the skepticism in her voice. "You're not convinced of what I say," she said with a wounded look, holding up a staying hand when Marilyn Estes opened her mouth to speak. "Don't bother to deny it. I've had plenty of practice at reading people's faces when I tell them of the vile fate my husband suffered at Chelsey Warren's hand. You think I'm crazy with grief or perhaps just generally mad. Well, I can assure you that I'm neither," she declared most emphatically. "You and Archie may have your doubts but I am not deluded in the least. I'm thoroughly convinced of my suspicions. Chelsey Warren bewitched my husband. It's a fact—a fact I'll still be claiming on my deathbed."

"Now don't go working yourself up into a state, Patsy. You've a right to your opinion, same as the rest of us." Archie wanted to put a quietus on Patsy's witch lore before she spooked poor Mrs. Estes from the premises.

"I sure do," she said huffily, shifting her focus from him to Marilyn Estes once again. "I understand how you might scoff at the notion of a witch living in our midst. You're new to the area, my dear, and haven't yet learned about Marblehead's ties with the Salem legacy. I'd venture to say that you've read very little on the subject of witchcraft. Since the days of the burnings in Europe, the Craft has not been practiced in public. Its secret rituals are handed down within families and covens. Is it so preposterous to believe that the dark power was passed on to Desirée? I think not," she concluded, not giving her entranced audience a chance to respond.

Patsy continued in between nibbles of her muffin. "And here's another tidbit for you to mull over. Ever since the Warren matriarch first came to Marblehead in the early twenties and purchased the house across the street, only women have resided there. Not a soul in this town can remember there ever being a male around the place, at least not until recently, when Desirée's financial straits forced her to start taking in bed-and-breakfast boarders. Yet somehow generations of female Warrens have come into being. Very peculiar, don't you think?''

"A bit," Marilyn admitted.

"I tell you something else," Patsy clucked. "Witches are more common than you think. They look the same as anyone. They don't wear scarlet letters or go around announcing who they are and what they do. They mostly conduct their sacrilege in private. So how would you know whether or not a neighbor dabbled in the Craft?''

"I suppose a person couldn't know for certain," Marilyn conceded.

"I've been inside that shop across the street—not until after Chelsey died—you understand," Patsy quickly added. "I just wanted to see for myself what sort of pagan paraphernalia was displayed on the shelves. Herbs, my foot," she spat. "There are evil charms and love potions, the devil's roots and elixirs, magic bells, books and candles. It's all there—curses and spells for sale. Why, do you know, she's even posted a warning at the counter. Shoplifters will be hexed, it says. Now I ask you, how much more blatant can you be?'' she asked, once again not pausing for an answer. "When I spied that sign, I stopped dead in my tracks, I tell you. Eerie and unholy is what that place is! A blemish upon this Christian community.''

"Oh, that's a bunch of hooey, Patsy." Archie had reached the end of his patience. "First off, Desirée inherited the house and shop. It's her livelihood.

What's more, unlike her mother and grandmother, the girl doesn't profess to be a witch. So, where's the proof in your accusation?''

''The proof is in the fact that she's never out-and-out denied her pagan ways, either,'' Patsy stubbornly argued.

''She doesn't have to. Isn't anybody's business what her religious beliefs are,'' Archie insisted.

''Religious beliefs!'' Patsy hooted. ''Oh, that's a laugh.''

''For your information, Wicca is indeed a serious religion,'' Archie pronounced. ''It predates Christianity—goes all the way back to the Stone Age and fertility rites. In those days folks worshiped the moon because its cycles had a direct bearing on the hunting and planting seasons. The elements—earth, wind, water and fire—all had a part to play, too. So our early ancestors gave 'em their proper due. It makes a lot of sense when you think of—''

''I don't need a lecture on the origins of Wicca, thank you very much.'' Patsy brushed aside his commentary, searching busily in her purse for correct change and her car keys. ''To my mind, those who dabble in the Craft are heathens who have made a pact with the devil.'' She got up from her chair, collected her coat with its imitation fox collar and bundled up. ''That's why, just as soon as I am made the next president of the Women's Old Town Beautification Society, I intend to initiate a petition for the removal of that eyesore across the street,'' she announced.

"I just joined the Beautification Society myself a few weeks ago," Marilyn Estes put in. "I thought nominations for officers weren't until next month."

Archie Hooper looked amused.

Patsy James looked discombobulated. "Er, well, that's true, but it's practically a foregone conclusion that I'll be the next president. I mean, just *everybody* knows it."

"I didn't know," the weekender submitted most humbly.

"Like I said, my dear, it's understandable since you're relatively new to the town." Patsy cast the young Mrs. Estes a tight smile, then glanced at her watch. "I had no idea it had gotten so late. I have a zillion errands to attend to. It's been so nice, Marilyn. We must get together again real soon." She bent and kissed the air beside Marilyn's cheek. "Toodle-loo, Archie."

He shook his head and offered a limp wave as she scurried out the door. "Patsy's a real character," he muttered, more to himself than to Marilyn Estes. "Want a warm-up on your coffee?" he offered.

Marilyn declined with a shake of her head. "I would like a minute more of your time, if you can spare it," she requested.

"Sure," he obliged, settling in the chair Patsy had vacated.

"I know it's silly, but after all the talk about Desirée Warren, I'd really like to hear your impression of the woman. Call it idle curiosity, if you like."

Archibald Hooper was not surprised at the request. Folks were always drawn by the mysterious. Marilyn Estes was no exception.

"Well," he drawled, tilting the chair back on its hind legs and fixing his gaze on a cluster of muffin crumbs left on Patsy's deserted plate. "It's true what Patsy claims about Desirée's kin. I knew the grandmother and mother personally and I'm here to tell you that they were both of Wicca mind." He paused for a second. "Since I've been old enough to reason for myself, I've thought of witchcraft as something that grown-ups invented to fill children with wonder and dread and keep the more curious and daring ones in check. Make no mistake, Mrs. Estes, neither Chelsey nor her mother were ugly crones with warts on their noses who went about snaring disobedient children and making midnight snacks of 'em. No, they didn't fit the stereotype. They were lovely ladies. Genteel and exceptionally beautiful." His eyes and voice assumed a hazy quality for a moment, and then he mentally shook himself. Regaining his former clarity, he resumed.

"What I said about Wicca being a very old and credible religion is true. The Warren women were members of an exclusive sect—a sect that worshiped nature but whose rituals were twisted into something grotesque due to ignorance, fear and intolerance. The early witches were healers and astrologers. That's how come they put so much stock in their herbs and heavenly signs. They were respected in their villages. Actually being a witch was one of the few occupations by which a woman could elevate herself in those days. Wives and nuns were at the bottom of the barrel. They were regarded almost the same way as cattle—chattles of men. Prostitutes fared some better. They earned their own living but weren't respected much. It was the witches that held a bit of power and prestige.''

"If it was as honored a profession as you say, what happened to suddenly change attitudes toward witches?" Marilyn was impatient for Mr. Hooper to impart every morsel of knowledge he possessed about the pagan cult.

"Simply put, it was gossip that altered the course of history and doomed the witches, Mrs. Estes. The same kind of unfounded gossip that went on in here earlier. It began as a trickle of hearsay, then mushroomed into hysteria. That's when the persecution Patsy spoke of started in Europe. Witches were hunted down and methodically exterminated. It's guessed that nearly nine million in all were put to death. Wild accusations about the Wicca cult spread like the plague, but the stories were mostly untrue," he added.

"Surely there must have been some basis for the epidemic indictment of them—some shred of truth? I mean, people don't just make up such outlandish tales without something having triggered their imagination first." Marilyn had no idea why she was pressing the point. For the sake of debate, maybe? Or perhaps because she found it genuinely distressing that thoughtless gossip—of the kind that she herself had engaged in less than an hour ago—could cause such anguish for so many.

"There's usually a shred of truth behind any sort of malicious talk. But it's a certainty that when all is said and done, the facts will be misconstrued. Yes, the witches celebrated Sabbaths at night in the woods and believed in faeries, but the feasts were not the orgies that were later described. Witches didn't worship the devil or do his handiwork. The gruesome tales told about 'em was mostly poppycock, invented by men of the church because they feared the power of the Craft and wanted to banish its influence forever. So they charged the witches with foul crimes, and later enlarged their accusations to include those who were not of the Wicca sect but feebleminded or otherwise unfit, and once the poor souls were accused, even though falsely, they were as good as condemned."

"It sounds very similar to the atrocities committed against the Jews during the holocaust," Marilyn commented.

"I'd say that's an apt comparison." Archie sighed deeply, then continued. "Witches were tortured, hanged, or burned throughout the Western world. It was wholescale madness. So you can see why Wicca followers went underground."

The weekender nodded.

"I'm giving you a crash course on the subject of Wicca in the hopes that you won't nurture a preconceived notion of Desirée Warren before you've even met the woman. There's been a whole lot of that done in this town."

"Obviously," Marilyn agreed. "But you still haven't answered my question, Mr. Hooper. What's your honest-to-God opinion? Is she or is she not a witch?"

He smiled and eased his chair upright. "Heck if I know for certain one way or the other, Mrs. Estes. Desirée is a shy person. Keeps to herself quite a bit. She's been that way since she was a child. I suppose it's only natural for people to avoid unpleasantness whenever they can. Desirée knows how some folks feel about her. When people shun a person enough, he or she soon gets the message, unless they're dense or uncaring, which Desirée isn't. I can tell you this much. I believe her to be a good person. I've never known her to do anyone harm. Whether she's a witch or not, I really couldn't say." He pried his stiff bones away from the chair and straightened his bibbed apron. "Furthermore, I don't really care," he added by way of a postscript. "Can I get you anything more, Mrs. Estes?"

"No, thank you, Mr. Hooper. I appreciate the candid talk," she replied, gathering her wrap and leaving a generous tip before exiting the Mug and Muffin Shoppe.

Involuntarily her eyes were drawn to the red-frame structure across the street. *Why not?* she mused, setting out to satisfy her curiosity once and for all. A bell tinkled overhead as she entered the Herb Hut.

"May I help you?" a pleasant voice inquired.

"Ah, no," Marilyn stammered, pretending to be absorbed with the shop's contents. "I'm just browsing."

"Look all you like," was the gracious response from the proprietress.

When she thought it was possible to get away with a circumspect look, Marilyn braved a peek over her shoulder at the woman seated behind the counter. The first thing that caught her attention was the gorgeous mane of red-brown curls Desirée Warren possessed. She had enough hair to crown three heads. The sherry-coloured tresses tumbled past her waist—a virtual cornucopia of satiny ringlets. Marilyn next noted how petite the woman was. She was perhaps only an inch or two over five feet and quite clearly weighed less than a hundred pounds, a fact that was apparent in spite of the loose-fitting Shaker sweater she wore. Her skin was the same shade as the ivory-colored sweater, and smooth and flawless. But the most fascinating feature about the woman revealed itself when she lifted her gaze and caught Marilyn in the embarrassing act of staring at her. Her eyes were most unusual—a startling lavender-blue with flecks of gold, almond shaped, and fringed by dark, lush lashes.

Realizing she was gawking, Marilyn feigned a coughing seizure and averted her head.

"Would you care for a sip of water?" Desirée asked.

"No, no," the flushed weekender croaked, backing toward the door. "That won't be necessary." She coughed again for good measure. "A tickle in my throat is all. It happens now and then," she babbled, reaching for the doorknob. "A breath of fresh air will fix me right up. Good afternoon," she bid the proprietress before dashing outside onto the shoveled sidewalk. She turned to see Desirée Warren watching her from behind the shop's window. Gulping a few whiffs of cold air, she acknowledged the woman's unnerving presence with a nod, then proceeded across the street to her car.

She felt foolish. Worse than foolish, as a matter of fact. She felt petty and ashamed of herself. Desirée Warren had not behaved strangely. No, it was she—Marilyn Estes, the impressionable newcomer—who had acted ridiculously. She vowed to adopt Mr. Hooper's tolerant attitude rather than Patsy James's bigotry. As she started to climb into her station wagon, Marilyn was seized by another impulse. She paused, turning and glancing back toward the red-frame shop. The attractive young woman was poised in the doorway—still pensively watching, almost as if she anticipated some further reaction on Marilyn's part. The newcomer smiled self-consciously, then offered a timid wave. The proprietress returned the wave—also rather warily, Marilyn thought—then retreated inside the shop and shut the door. In the years ahead, Marilyn would often think back upon her first meeting with Desirée Warren and wonder why it was she felt an immediate and unusually strong sensitivity toward the woman.

IT WAS LATE, almost closing time, when Jacob Malone came upon Archie Hooper's establishment. A snowstorm had swept into Marblehead along with the evening darkness. "It's becoming a near blizzard out there," Jacob said by way of greeting as he whisked into the shop on a gush of arctic wind.

"Uh-huh," Archie concurred, setting aside the broom he'd been sweeping the floor with and surveying the stranger from head to toe. "I'm afraid I'm about to close up. A cup of coffee to ward off the chill is the best I can offer."

"Just directions to the closest lodging will do." Jacob brushed flakes of snow from his dark hair.

"Well, let me think." Archie mulled the stranger's words over. "You're asking for the closest lodging, eh? Not the best nor the cheapest, but the closest."

"That's right," Jacob replied. "I've been driving around in circles for hours in this blasted snowstorm. I just want the name of the nearest place where there's a warm bed to let for the night."

Archie sucked in his cheeks, then nodded. "Well, I guess that would be right across the street at The Magic Herb Hut. Miss Warren owns the place and she furnishes clean lodgings and a decent breakfast for a fair price."

"That sounds fine. Thanks for the recommendation," Jacob said wearily.

"Uh-huh, glad to have been of service. We pride ourselves on being hospitable here in Marblehead." Archie retrieved his broom and returned to his sweeping.

AT A TABLE in a dimly lit corner of the shop, Desirée
Warren turned the gold-leafed pages of a dusty volume and stroked the Birman cat huddled on her lap.
Suddenly both her eyes and hand stopped, and she
dismissed the ancient voice on the page for the one in
her heart. Almost trancelike, her small hand eased
shut the leather-bound volume and her polished fingertips moved to the sandlewood candle, snuffing out
the flame. The Birman perked its slate-gray tipped ears
and looked up at its mistress.

"He's come, Mew-Sinh. I can feel it. He is very
near."

She engaged the cat's eyes—eyes that were identi-
cal to her own—almond shaped and a startling shade
of lavender-blue with flecks of gold. "My God! Mew-
Sinh. We did it. We've summoned up my deepest desire."

CHAPTER THREE

THE OLD GENTLEMAN at the muffin shop had given Jacob an excellent lead. The lodgings he'd recommended were quite satisfactory and the proprietress, Miss Warren, was unbelievably accommodating. There was none of the usual hassle of securing a room for the night—no tedious registration, no payment in advance, no credit approval required. The woman simply invited him in from the cold, and then promptly escorted him through the darkened interior of what he presumed to be a replica of a nineteenth-century apothecary shop.

Wearily he'd followed her up a steep flight of stairs to a cozy room that contained a four-poster bed with crisp sheets and a downy quilt turned back in welcome. He really hadn't taken much notice of the proprietress, except to observe that she was a wisp of a woman and not much of a talker—a trait that, in his exhausted state, he'd found inordinately appealing. She'd efficiently set about securing fresh towels and washcloths from a cedar chest situated beneath a high, shuttered window, and after placing them on the end of the bed, she'd kindly offered to bring him something to eat so that he wouldn't have to venture from his room until morning. Breakfast, she'd explained, would be served at seven sharp in the kitchen off the main room. Her dine-in suggestion had sounded like a dandy arrangement to him. He'd readily accepted her offer, and then hungrily consumed the creamy clam chowder, sesame bread sticks and spiced tea she'd delivered to his bedroom door before falling into bed and experiencing one of the soundest sleeps of his life.

The sun had yet to break upon the Massachusetts coastline when he awoke with a start. The room was still cloaked in darkness, except for a faint shaft of light spilling through the bedroom door. Groggy and unfocused, Jacob at first did not pay any attention to the light. He stretched and yawned contentedly, more preoccupied with a slow-dawning realization that was beginning to take shape in his dull brain. Inching up on the pillow he inspected the undisturbed bed cover, confirming for himself the incredible fact that he'd hardly moved a fraction during the night. Amazingly he hadn't tossed, turned, moaned, groaned, woken up, checked the clock, traipsed into the bathroom for a 3:00 a.m. pit stop. For once he had actually slept straight through until morning and he felt genuinely, wonderfully rested.

As much as he hated to question a good thing, he couldn't help but wonder what had induced the uninterrupted sleep. It had been months since he'd enjoyed a full eight hours. Maybe he had needed to get away from Boston and the pressures of his job more than he thought. In just a day's time, he felt different inside. It was true! Already he sensed a change in himself, though he couldn't precisely put into words the subtle transformation taking place.

With a dismissing shrug, Jacob forsook his snug niche under the feather ticking and sat up on the edge of the bed. It was then that the stream of light filtering into the room from the hallway caught his eye. Surely he hadn't forgotten to shut the bedroom door before retiring? No, of course not, he decided, remembering that he'd closed it behind him after making a trip down the hall to use the bathroom facilities just prior to his turning in. Yes, he distinctly recollected that there was no lock by which to secure the door, so he'd merely eased it shut.

Jacob didn't expend a great deal of energy stewing over the irregularity. Being a logical person, he assumed the door's being ajar was the result of a faulty latch or perhaps an especially strong settling motion occurring within the house. Such things were indigenous to older places. It was the reason one heard creaking noises in the middle of the night.

He roused himself from off the bed, slipped on his robe and slippers and started toward the door. Midway to reaching it, the hinges groaned and the door slowly glided open. Jacob froze in his tracks, his eyes seeking out and then dropping to the unbidden intruder. There, ensconced in the doorway, was the most unusual-looking cat he had ever encountered. What was more, the animal seemed to be as intrigued with Jacob as he was with it. For a moment neither made a move; they just catalogued each other's distinguishing marks. What struck Jacob most was not that the cat was larger or silkier than the average feline, but that it was more regal—a breed apart in both pedigree and attitude from its common cousin. The white-pawed creature sat back on its haunches, studying the stranger with an imperial air.

"Well, who have we here? A privileged character, no doubt." Jacob scratched his stubbled cheek and laughed to himself at being momentarily spooked by a lady's lap cat. He squatted down, trying to coax the animal closer with a flick of his fingertips.

Mew-Sinh, poised aloofly in the doorway, ignored the overture.

"So you're a finicky sort, huh? Finicky is fine. I can respect that, so long as you do me the same courtesy and respect my privacy." Jacob eased his large frame upright.

Mew-Sinh also rose up on all fours, ever so deliberately rotating one hundred and eighty degrees and presenting its fluffy tail. With a swish and in a flash, the cat vanished from sight. Jacob stepped out into the corridor, but the only sign of the cat was a swatch of gold-tipped fur floating through the air and coming to light on the dusty rose carpet. It was as if the animal possessed some mystical ability to materialize and disappear at will, like the Cheshire cat in Lewis Carroll's classic tale. Jacob knew such a thing was utter nonsense, of course, but he could not shake the feeling that the furry visitor's interest in him was more than just idle curiosity. It was as though the cat had an unnatural fixation with him.

Jacob shook his head, mentally chastising himself for even entertaining such a ridiculous thought. "Boy! You really are functioning on the edge. Keep it up and you'll be entering the twilight zone at any moment," he mused aloud, slipping back into the room and snatching a clean towel from the foot of the bed. Looping it around his neck, he fished around in his suitcase for a fresh pair of Jockeys, then collected his shaving kit from the top of the chest of drawers and proceeded on down the hall to partake of a hot shower.

More out of a sense of uneasiness than modesty, he made doubly certain to lock the bathroom door before stripping. "A cat is a cat is a cat," he mumbled, pulling the vinyl shower curtain shut and turning on the ivory spigots full blast. "There's nothing extraordinary about this one." He tested the spray's temperature. Good and hot, just the way he liked it. He stepped into the tub and doused his head under the pulsating water. The steamy vapors cleared his head and sinuses. Yeah, all he needed was a shower, a shave and a cup of coffee in order to put the world into proper perspective. He was still tired from the long, hard drive, was all—and a little out of sync amid the unfamiliar surroundings. What other explanation could there be for a strange-looking cat to give him such a case of the willies? He lathered up, putting the silly incident from his mind.

"DAMMIT! Which is it—bay or basil leaves? I get so confused. One's for love, the other's for protection. Why, oh why, did I think I could do this?"

A teakettle whistled hysterically, the boiling contents spewing forth from beneath a rattling lid. And the woman who was normally an authority on herbs and their assorted uses was in nearly as hysterical a state, also rattling excessively.

Mew-Sinh sauntered unnoticed into the kitchen, leaped up onto the windowsill and calmly looked on as her mistress experienced an anxiety attack.

Desirée had been up and at it for hours—painstakingly applying extra touches of makeup in between preparing a hearty breakfast and trying to remember the exact measure of love potion she was to add to Mr. Malone's teacup—and the words she was to say over the mixture to empower it with the right amount of allure. Adding too much or too little, or saying too much or too little could produce the entirely wrong effect.

"It's five of seven. He's going to arrive any minute. The sausages are sticking and I think I'm going to be ill." Desirée dropped into a chair, sinking her head into her hands. "Whatever made me think I could pull this off? I should have never attempted it. What if I screw it up? What if I make some awful mistake and the whole thing backfires? Oh, my God! What if I overdo it and turn him into a raving sex maniac or something?" She squeezed her eyes shut at the appalling prospect.

Mew-Sinh yawned widely, stretching the length of the sill and soaking up the early yellow rays of sunlight.

"Now is not the time to panic." Desirée tried exerting a little self-control, but inwardly her mind and heart whirled with indecision. This was what she had so desperately wanted, wasn't it: the opportunity to know love. And now that the big moment was at hand, how was she behaving? Like some giddy schoolgirl who possessed neither the sense nor the power to take command of the situation.

She inhaled deeply through her nose and slowly exhaled through her mouth, coaching herself as she did so. "It'll be all right if you just don't choke." The pep talk seemed to produce the desired effect. She began to feel just a wee bit less frantic. She lifted her head from her hands and listened to the reassuring voice counseling her from within. *Mr. Malone isn't here by accident,* it put forth for her review. *He's come because you willed it so. As much as you might like to use the excuse of being powerless over your own destiny, it simply isn't true. Your actions will affect the outcome. You do have choices. You can either proceed as planned or spend the rest of your days wondering what might have been had you not chickened out. Which do you prefer? To feed him, then send him on his way while you hunger forever? Or to get up from this chair and take a chance by adding a smidgen of crushed violet petals to his tea?*

"A dram of crushed violet petals! That's it!" She practically vaulted from the chair to the cupboard, and rummaged through its cluttered contents for the appropriately labeled jar. Basil leaves were too strong, reserved for only the most advanced affairs. Crushed violet petals were the suitable aphrodisiac. She remembered clearly now. Mama had marked the page in the old book and underlined the words.

Venus, Cupid, Eros, Friends
Your help will serve my rightful ends.
I ask of thee one heart, not ten
Enhance my appeal to him you send.

Her fingers touched upon the all-important container as she recited the words in her mind. Clamping the tiny violet-colored tin in her hand, she leaned back against the doorjamb, shut her eyes and concentrated hard. "Venus, Cupid, Eros, Friends—"

"Good morning," Jacob greeted her a bit uncertainly, afraid that he'd intruded upon some sort of morning mantra recitation or something.

Desirée literally jumped to attention, staring at him through enormously wide eyes.

"I didn't mean to startle you."

"No, uh...I was daydreaming is all." She had never been a very good liar.

"Oh," he said, aware that she was flustered but pretending not to notice.

The small tin slipped from her sweaty hand into the pocket of the apron she wore. "Please sit down, Mr. Malone. I'll get your tea." She lowered her eyes, hurried to the stove and removed the spitting kettle from the burner.

"I'd prefer a cup of coffee if you have it."

Coffee. He prefers coffee, her mind fretted. What if the violet petals didn't mix well with coffee? What if he detected an aftertaste? She hadn't counted on the possibility of him preferring coffee to tea. *Now what!* she silently groaned. "All I have is instant," she informed him, knowing her jangled nerves were causing her to sound like some fussy old maid. Much to her dismay, he did not immediately sit down at the table, but instead came to stand at the kitchen counter directly beside her.

"Instant will be just fine."

Her plans were going amuck in a hurry. If he *had* to have coffee, why couldn't he at least be particular and drink only freshly ground? She forced a tight smile and set about retrieving the jar of instant coffee from the cupboard. If only he'd sit down! How was she supposed to slip the petals into his cup with him hovering about?

"It's not necessary for you to wait on me, Miss Warren. I'm really very accustomed to fending for myself." Spying two cup-and-saucer sets arranged on the counter, he helped himself to one and plucked the jar of coffee crystals from the crook of her arm as she passed.

This was swell, just swell. Not only was he not picky, but he was cussedly independent as well. She had to think fast. "I'm sure you are a most self-sufficient person, Mr. Malone." Strategically placing herself between him and the kettle, she confiscated the cup and saucer from his one hand and reclaimed the jar from his other. "But my waiting on you is all part of the service included in the price of your lodging. It's what *I'm* accustomed to doing," she insisted, nicely but firmly.

He thought her attitude was a little pigheaded, but he decided it wasn't an issue worth pressing. "Sure." He conceded the point with a shrug. "Whatever your fancy."

She turned her back to him, listening for the scrape of a chair across the linoleum. It came in a second or two and the tension between her shoulder blades eased slightly. Finally he was safely anchored at the table. Perhaps now she could proceed with spiking his coffee and seducing him. Stealthily, she removed the tin of violet petals from her pocket. "Did you sleep well, Mr. Malone?" The idle chitchat was merely a diversionary tactic. Engaging in small talk wasn't exactly her style, but then again, she wasn't exactly practiced in the art of bewitching a man, either. Still, she was determined to try. She'd come too far to turn back now. With a flick of her wrist, she popped the tin's lid, sprinkling two pinches of powder into the bottom of his cup.

"Actually, I had a great night's sleep," he answered, casting a casual glance around the kitchen. It was a pleasant enough room—spacious and bright with high ceiling and tall, curtainless windows that let in lots of light. Jacob especially liked the assortment of clay pots and hanging baskets containing lush green

plants and sprigs of pungent herbs. They gave off a
healthy scent and a feeling of good cheer. He was also
impressed with Miss Warren's sense of design and
color. The oblong glass table, soft green wicker chairs
with comfortable mauve print cushions and wall-to-
wall matching hutch spoke of a natural kind of ele-
gance—very subtle but striking.

Only one thing bothered him. Nothing—not the
smallest accessory in the room—was out of place. The
kitchen reminded him of the sort one saw on the covers of ladies' magazines—the ones that were invariably displayed on a rack by the checkout at the local
supermarket. Usually the cover lines read something
like, "Easy and Economic Makeovers—give your
kitchen a face-lift and your spirits a boost." The thing
that always struck him about the renovated kitchens
was the lack of everyday clutter, the absence of a lived-
in look. From where he sat, Miss Warren's kitchen had
that same quality—it was jarringly neat. No bills,
coupons, munchies, loose change or articles of clothing were strewn about as they were at his place. Even
the little geese and flower magnets attached to the side
of the refrigerator were precisely aligned. There were
no notes under them, no shopping lists or personal
reminders. He wondered suddenly how Miss Warren
spent her spare time. Realigning the magnets on the
refrigerator? Fastidiously neat rooms were kept by
people who had an aversion to spontaneity. And un-
spontaneous women bored him, he thought offhandedly.

The deed done, Desirée quickly disposed of the incriminating evidence, slipping the tin back into her apron pocket. Her heart thundered and her hands shook as she added a heaping teaspoon of coffee crystals to the crushed petals and then dissolved both ingredients in the hot water she poured from the kettle. She had to keep him distracted only a little longer. "You sound almost surprised at having gotten a good night's rest. Do your normally have trouble sleeping?" she asked, checking to be sure that no telltale grit floated on top of the liquid or ringed the edge of the cup.

"Sometimes," was his spare reply as she served him, efficiently scooting the cream pitcher and sugar bowl closer. "Thank you. I think I can handle it from here," he added. It crossed his mind that she might be inclined to tuck his napkin into his shirt collar as part of the service. Amused by the notion, he smiled.

She nodded, trying not to appear obvious while watching him put cream in his coffee and then sample it. "We have grapefruit halves, scrambled eggs, link sausages, browned potatoes and raisin toast for breakfast today."

Her recitation of the menu struck him as being unnecessarily formal and strained. He couldn't figure out if she was just a tad eccentric or totally crackers.

"If there is anything I've mentioned that you dislike, just tell me and we can make a substitution."

Unsure if Miss Warren possessed a sense of humor, Jacob sipped from his coffee cup again, swallowing the wry retort that initially popped into his head. It

took a second or two before he looked up at her with
a rather incredulous expression on his face. "I like it
all, Miss Warren," he said agreeably, "but I do have
a request."

She wiped her clammy palms on her apron and said,
"Yes, Mr. Malone?"

"Do you suppose that we could be a little less formal with each other? You seem awfully tense. Is it
me?"

She blinked dumbly. "No, uh, of course not," she
assured him. "It's just that I'm never sure how to treat
a guest. Some like to keep their distance. Some are
more social. Some like to eat alone. Some want company."

"Well, I'm the social sort, and for starters why
don't you call me Jacob and I'll call you... He left the
sentence dangling.

"Desirée," she supplied with a hint of a grin.

"Desirée," he repeated, slowly. "I don't believe I've
ever known a woman by that name. It's unusual." He
sipped again from his cup.

"Yes, well, I've been told that I am, too. So I guess
it suits me." She refrained from meeting his eyes,
turning back to the stove and dishing out a heaping
portion of food onto his plate. Mr. Malone was more
than she had bargained for—extremely direct and ex-
traordinarily good-looking. She'd expected to be a bit
uncomfortable in his presence, but he made her feel
self-conscious in a way she had not anticipated.

Jacob drained his cup. He was about to ask for a
refill when he spied the cat lounging on the window-

sill. Not much ever got to Jacob; in the middle of a heated courtroom battle he epitomized the term "calm, cool and collected." Yet, crazily, a four-legged creature was succeeding where the most cagey of Homo sapiens had failed. For some inexplicable reason, just having the furry creature within proximity addled Jacob—so much so that he missed the saucer when he set his cup down. He recovered himself and corrected his faux pas before Desirée served him his food.

"Can I get you anything else?" She stood stiffly to the side, awaiting either a dismissal or an invitation to join him.

"Not a thing." The tantalizing aroma wafting up from the plate made him momentarily forget both the cat and his manners.

Damn! She should have thrown caution to the wind and used basil leaves, she thought, annoyed. Obviously whatever pangs he was suffering at the moment had more to do with his stomach than with his heart. "Then I'll leave you to enjoy your breakfast and the morning paper," she said, making a move to leave.

Remembering the proper amenities, Jacob lowered the forkful of eggs he'd tined and gestured for her to sit down. "Please stay, Desirée."

She couldn't resist an impulse to test the violet petals' potency. "I've already eaten," she fibbed, dawdling a bit.

"Then at least have some coffee with me, won't you?"

Was he just being gracious? Or was his insistence a consequence of the herbal mickey she'd slipped him? How in the world was she supposed to know for certain? It took every ounce of composure Desirée could muster to act nonchalant. "All right. I suppose I have time for another cup of tea before opening the shop." What a ridiculous statement to make. She had all day—the rest of her life—if he needed.

Jacob gave her a quick inspection once her back was turned again. She was even more petite than he'd remembered from the night before. She probably didn't weigh a hundred pounds soaking wet, though each and every pound was nicely distributed. From his vantage point he couldn't help but notice the firm outline of her valentine-shaped fanny beneath her snug-fitting jeans. Actually, until this instant, it hadn't really struck him what a motherlode of hair she possessed. The color was pretty, although he hadn't the faintest idea as to how to describe it. Kind of a brownish red. No, that wasn't quite it. Her hair had more of a copper tinge to it, sort of like a brand-new penny.

At the clink of a spoon against the china cup as she dunked, then discarded a tea bag, he snapped back from his silly conjecturing, averting his eyes to his plate. What in the hell was he doing searching for the perfect adjective to describe a mop of hair? He had no interest in the woman. She aligned magnets on a refrigerator for fun and recited the morning menu as a matter of rule, for heaven's sake!

He speared a sausage link with his fork, eating it in two giant gulps as she seated herself at the table.

She smiled self-consciously, for the first time actually engaging his eyes.

And suddenly Jacob was seized by the eerie sensation that he'd recently encountered those exact same startling lavender-blue eyes. But where and when? He would surely have remembered a romantic liaison. A business contact, maybe? A client, perhaps? Damn! He couldn't place the occasion he'd encountered a hauntingly similar pair of eyes.

"So, what is it that you do for a living, Mr. Malone?" Desirée asked, growing uncomfortable under his penetrating stare.

He forced himself to look away, but he could not as easily dismiss the nagging feeling of déjà vu. "I practice law in Boston. And it's Jacob, remember?"

She nodded. "That's a very old and honored profession. You must derive a great deal of satisfaction from your work."

He helped himself to a slice of raisin toast. "Not really. At least, not much anymore," was all he said. Silence loomed between them as he chewed the toast and she mulled over his response.

"Can I get you more coffee?" she offered, wanting to ply him with violet petals while filling the awkward gap.

He considered having another cup, but then decided against it. "No thanks."

So much for plying him with violet petals. She sipped her tea.

"What sort of business is it that you run down-stairs?"

Though he asked the question quite casually, it had the exact opposite effect on her. Her heart hitched in her chest. There was no sense lying. He would soon see for himself. "I sell different things out of my shop." She did not look him in the eye. "From herbs, potions and magic charms to silver bells, books of sorcery and protective candles."

"You're kidding me," he said, grinning widely and scooping up the last bite of potatoes from his plate.

"No," she said with not a trace of levity in her voice. "Sometimes my establishment is more commonly referred to as an occult shop."

Her sober tone left no doubt in Jacob's mind that she was being totally serious. He swallowed the mouthful of potatoes, wiped his lips with his napkin and leaned back in his chair. "Yours is an interesting line of work, too. I'm curious. Is there much demand for your wares?"

"More than you might think, Mr. Malone." She lifted her chin just a fraction, in accordance with her reversion to the more formal address.

He was a master at reading body language. That she was sensitive about the shop was obvious. What was unclear was why. "Do you derive a great deal of satisfaction from what you do?" He threw her own question back to her.

"Not really. At least, not so much anymore." She knew she had played the word game well, parroting his earlier reply. And just as slickly, she changed the subject. "Have you come to Marblehead on business or pleasure?"

"Strictly for pleasure." A grudging grin of respect broke on his swarthy face.

On that point, their aims were in total accord, she thought. "Then you've come to the right place, Jacob. Marblehead has much to offer in the way of pleasurable alternatives. There's plenty to see and do, and yet everything moves at a slower pace. Sometimes I think we Marbleheaders adhere to the same tempo as the sailors who like it here so much. We just sort of glide through our days."

"It sounds inviting." Her gaze met his over the edge of the cup as she sipped her tea. Once again, he became absorbed in trying to figure out where he had encountered those almond-shaped lavender pools. It was driving him nuts!

"Then you will be staying for a while?" She hoped the answer was yes. She was convinced that his upcoming reply depended upon the violet petals doing their bit. The way he kept looking into her eyes heartened her wildly vacillating spirits. Was it truly possible to bind the heart of a stranger with a pinch of petals and some rhyme? What if her mother had been right and the power of the old ways was for real? What if he was truly becoming enamored with her? The prospect both thrilled and terrified Desirée. At the mere thought of the intimate adventures that might lay ahead, she choked on the last swallow of tea.

"Are you okay?" He came to her assistance with a couple of solid pats on her back.

"Fine," she wheezed, wishing she had the power to wriggle her nose and disappear in a poof. She had wanted to take his breath away with her smoldering poise. Instead it was she who seemed the more likely candidate for artificial respiration.

All the hubbub roused Mew-Sinh from her catnap. In a lithe motion, she sprang from the windowsill to a vacant wicker chair in order to more closely investigate the situation. At the animal's agitated meowing, Desirée reached over and hoisted the mammoth cat from its perch onto her lap. "No need to be alarmed. Mr. Malone means us no harm," she crooned in the tone that animal lovers who live alone take on when talking to their cherished pets. The cat rubbed the side of its slate-colored face against her bosom, then turned its attention fully upon the stranger.

It was then that it suddenly hit Jacob where he'd encountered those eyes. "It's the cat...that damn cat!" he blurted.

"Excuse me?" Desirée pulled Mew-Sinh closer.

Realizing that he probably looked as if he was about to pounce on her precious pet, he laughed out loud and relaxed back in his chair. "I'm sorry. It's just that I've been sitting here the whole time we've been sharing breakfast, racking my brains trying to figure out where it was that I'd encountered eyes like yours before. They're a very unusual shade of blue...not a color one runs into every day. It was driving me crazy. When I got a second, close-up look at your cat, it dawned on me where and when I'd confronted those unusual eyes. It was this morning, in my room, when your cat paid me an unexpected visit. I've never seen a cat like him. What breed is it?"

Desirée hid her disappointment. He hadn't been gazing intently into her eyes because he was smitten; he'd merely been intent upon figuring out where and when he'd made similar eye contact. So much for the power of petals and rhyme. "He is a she and she is a Birman," she enlightened him.

"She's a beautiful animal. Quick, too," he hastened to add. "Not what you would call overly friendly, though."

"Mew-Sinh's a snoop. I hope she didn't disturb you."

"No, I wasn't bothered in the least," he lied.

"There is a fascinating legend surrounding the Birman. If you're interested I'll tell it to you sometime." She turned Mew-Sinh loose, then stood and walked to the cupboard, removing her apron and hanging it on a hook inside the door.

"Why not now?" He was genuinely eager to hear the lore.

"I'm afraid I haven't the time to go into it right now. I'm late opening up the shop as it is. Perhaps tonight at dinner. I serve at eight."

"I'll look forward to it." His warm smile melted her heart. And he was such a gentleman—coming to his feet at the same time as her. If only he was as interested in her as he seemed to be in Mew-Sinh. Maybe she should scratch the violet petals and try something else—something stronger. She'd study her mother's journals again, keep searching and experimenting until she found the perfect spell to cast.

"Yes, well, I'm afraid I really must go." She turned to leave, then whirled back around. "You can pick up a tour map at Abbott Hall. If you should need any further assistance I'll be downstairs."

"Selling magic herbs." He shot her a wink.

"Some believe in their power, Mr. Malone."

"Some folks believe in Santa Claus and the tooth fairy, too. But not me. And it's Jacob," he reminded her.

She favored him with a timid smile, then made a quick exit from the kitchen.

He stood rooted for a second, dragging a hand through his hair and ruminating about his peculiar landlady. Maybe it was true about owners and their pets sharing characteristics. Not only did Mew-Sinh and her mistress have like eyes, but their temperaments were similar, as well. Miss Warren, like her cat, had an aloof air about her, but even more, she seemed to project an aura of mystery. Yeah, the pair of them were a bit odd, he concluded. But what the hell! When you got right down to it, most everybody was a little strange in one way or another.

He snitched the last slice of toast, deciding to forget about the eccentric Miss Warren and take a leisurely stroll about town.

CHAPTER FOUR

ONLY MEW-SINH remained behind in the kitchen. Usually the cat lolled away the mornings by brunching, browsing, and bird-watching until noon. Today, contrarily, Mew-Sinh was restless and prowling around the room in ceaseless circles. Instinct made her wary; she sensed a foreign presence intruding on her space.

The animal paused at its water bowl, lapping a bit, glancing around, then lapping a few drops more. At the soundless lift of a teacup from its saucer, Mew-Sinh's head jerked up. The thick collar of fur around her neck stood on end as her gaze honed in on the china object levitating in thin air. She crouched in readiness, warning off the invisible trespasser with a nasty hiss.

Alistair Mackey ignored the cat as he sniffed the cup, then took a teeny swig of the murky residue left at the bottom of it. ''The tea's got a bit o' a twang to it, all right,'' he deduced, smacking his lips and then wiping a khaki shirtsleeve across his mouth.

The cat's eyes narrowed to slits and she reared back, spitting in Alistair's direction as he replaced the cup on the saucer.

"Don't go getting your fur all in a ruffle, puss. Believe me, I'm not dancing in me boots about this holiday, neither." He shivered and cast a disgusted glance around his new surroundings.

Mew-Sinh continued her low, throaty burbling and, with bared claws, took a blind swipe or two in the general direction of Mackey.

"Hiss away, you heathen. You'll not bother me. I have some snooping of me own t'do." Mackey helped himself to a cold sausage link left in the skillet, wolfing it down and sucking the greasy remnants from his plump fingertips. When he spied the kettle, his face lit up for the first time since arriving back on Earth. "A spot of tea would surely warm me bones," he said happily. He checked the pot, only to find it was ice-cold. Whipping off his grungy bushman's hat, he whacked it against a thigh with a heavenward roll of his bloodshot eyes. "One bloody cup of tea—is that too much to ask?"

The skittish Mew-Sinh felt the whoosh of air and bolted to a far corner of the kitchen.

"Scaredy cat," Alistair gloated. The angel knew his behavior was totally unacceptable, but then so were the conditions he'd encountered on Earth thus far. He was cold and hungry and sleepy. First he'd forgotten his travel rations, which included a month's supply of energy supplements, so he was without nourishment. Then the shuttle ride from the Cosmos had been crowded, noisy and late, so he hadn't been able to catch any winks before arriving in Marblehead at dawn. And to top it all off, he hadn't thought to check the weather advisory before leaving the perpetually perfect climate of Heaven, so he hadn't packed anything warmer than a long-sleeved shirt. Because second-grade angels were in a transitional period, they did not enjoy the same immunity as first-class angels, who were far advanced of human frailties. They felt neither heat, nor cold, fatigue nor hunger, and they didn't experience discomfort or disease. Mackey, on the other hand, was freezing his tail off and could feel the sniffles coming on. He was most definitely not in a good humor. And when Mackey was in a foul humor, he tended to revert to his past bad habits, such as gloating, pouting, bragging and cursing.

The matter of his repeated lapses into unacceptable behavior had once been brought before the Angelic Tribunal. But the Fisherman had pleaded his cause, saying that some souls required more patience and guidance than others, and sometimes those were the very souls that proved to be the best shepherds to watch over the Almighty's flock. Who better to understand the ways of strays than a lamb who had once been lost himself? The Fisherman's parable worked. The Tribunal voted not to clip Mackey's wings. He was reinstated on a probationary basis. Even the puckish Mackey was impressed by the Fisherman's powers of persuasion.

At remembering the Fisherman's staunch defense of his ambiguous virtues, Mackey experienced a flicker of remorse. "All this blind faith you put in me can be a pain in the keester, Fisherman," he mumbled beneath his breath. "But charge me with looking after Malone, you did. And so I will."

Mackey began haphazardly opening cabinets and drawers, looking for some insight into Miss Warren and secretly hoping to run across a bottle of brandy or schnapps to ward off the chill. "'Course, I personally think Malone is more wolf than lamb, but I'm only a glorified messenger boy." Finding nothing incriminating or stronger than vanilla extract, Mackey turned his attention on the hissing cat once more. "You're beginning to wear on me nerves, puss. I can't have you stalking me about the whole while. The little lady might get suspicious." In true Aussie fashion, he pronounced the long A in lady as a long I—the word coming out sounds like *lidy*.

Mew-Sinh's jittery eyes followed the angel's scent as he crossed to the cupboard. "But how to make friends with a pesky puss, now there's the trick," Mackey jabbered to himself, opening the cupboard door and scanning the contents for a solution. "Ah hah!" he exclaimed with a cocky grin. "I'll wager that you're fond of salmon." He extracted a can from the cupboard, hiked a trouser leg and took out his trusty skinning knife, which he kept strapped to his calf. With a jab of the razor-sharp point into the tin, then a prying off of the lid, he soon had Mew-Sinh literally eating out of his hand.

He knew the Fisherman would be near apoplexy at discovering that he carried the skinning knife on his person. He'd been allowed to keep it as a memento of his adventures on Earth, but to an old croc poacher like Mackey, the formidable-looking knife was much more. It was a status symbol, rather like the American Express card. He never traveled without it. It was a handy item, too. Many a time it had saved his own skin while separating a croc from its. Though the Fisherman was bound to be boiling mad about this latest infraction of the rules, Mackey had more immediate concerns to deal with at the moment. Besides, maybe he'd get lucky and his superior would be too engrossed in other, more pressing, matters to notice.

Mackey stroked the cat as it gobbled the delicacy from the can. "That's a good puss. We'll be mates, eh?" The apron dangling from the hook inside the cupboard door caught his eye. Recalling that he'd seen the mistress of the house slip something into the pocket, he set the can of salmon on the floor in order to follow up on a hunch.

"What's this?" he asked of Mew-Sinh, turning the small tin he'd discovered over in his hand. Mackey popped the lid, sniffed, then licked the tip of his finger and tasted a pinch of the violet stuff. It was as unpalatable as quinine. He made a face and started spitting to rid himself of the bitter gunk. "Bloody awful, it is!"

Mew-Sinh was more interested in the yummy salmon. She nudged her nose deeper into the can, trying to devour the last morsel of pink flakes.

The angel was oblivious to the cat's contortions as she inadvertently pushed the can across the floor. "I got me a funny feeling," he muttered. "It's prickling the hair on the back of me neck, it is. Now why would the sheila be spiking Malone's tea?''

Having licked the can clean, Mew-Sinh now concentrated on licking her whiskers. She cocked her expressionless face, as though she could hear the angel's musing but had difficulty deciphering the alien tongue in which he spoke.

"A sheila is what we call a woman down under," he explained, conversing with the animal as though he thought it capable of comprehending. "Maybe the Fisherman was right in sending me for a look-see. There's something amiss around here, all right. And your mistress has a hand in it. But what's she up to?''

Mew-Sinh merely blinked.

"So, you're keeping what you know to yourself, eh? Well, be warned, you hissing heathen. I didn't gain a reputation for being one of the best trackers in the bush by luck," he bragged. "If Malone's soul is truly in danger, I'll ferret out the cause."

Her tummy so bloated that she could only gaze wistfully up at her favorite resting spot on the windowsill, Mew-Sinh gave a big yawn.

Mackey scowled at the unimpressed ingrate. "You're a worthless package o' fur. I'd have done better to eat the salmon meself." At the sound of approaching footsteps, he hurried to replace the apron and close the cupboard door. "Be a good puss," he coaxed. "Give me away 'n' I'll be forced to cut your meowing tongue out when next we meet." He side-stepped the cat and removed himself from Desirée's path as she breezed into the room.

Too late he remembered the empty can. He noticed it at exactly the same instant that she stepped on it.

"Salmon, Mew-Sinh?" She gazed bewilderedly at her prized pet.

Alistair sucked in his breath.

"How did you manage to wheedle such a treat from Mr. Malone?" She picked up Mew-Sinh, an amused expression on her face as she held the animal out at arm's length. "He spoils you, Mew-Sinh. I wish I were lucky enough to wield such power over him. You must share your secret," she entreated with a lilting laugh. At Mew-Sinh's cranky meow, Desirée set her free.

Alistair leaned back against the wall with a relieved sigh. Thank goodness Malone was having himself a walkabout and was unavailable to refute the little lady's assumption.

He swiped an apple from a nearby bowl and went to find the attic. Maybe the Fisherman would forgive him his unorthodox methods and provide a bed so that he could lay his weary body down. Perhaps he would even let there be a woolly blanket on hand. Oh, wouldn't that be loverly! Mackey thought wistfully. Then he shook himself. These things were really his due. After all, his needs weren't purely selfish. A clear head was required of him. How else could he even begin to sort out what in the devil was actually going on down here on Earth? One thing was certain—he couldn't return to Heaven until he had investigated the matter more thoroughly. No, nothing short of hovering on the verge of hypothermia would be considered sufficient enough cause to scruff the mission. *The*

Angel's Handbook of Ethics was most specific on the point—a guardian angel worth his wings always put the welfare of a charge before his own.

Mackey muffled a sneeze at the entryway to the attic. "I should have traded Malone for the rock star when McGillicuddy offered a swap. A bloody nuisance is what he is." With a touch of the microtransformer inserted in his ear, Mackey stowed away in the drafty attic.

PATSY JAMES'S MOUTH dropped open as Jacob strolled into the Mug and Muffin Shoppe.

Archie Hooper, who had been taking a breather, passing the time with Patsy, set aside his cup of hot chocolate and turned around in his chair to see who it was that had struck her dumb. He should have guessed, he thought with a grin. Ever since Patsy's husband had jumped the fence, anything male and breathing within a hundred-yard radius produced that same dopey response in her.

"Hello," Jacob greeted, doffing his knit cap and raking a hand through his rumpled hair. "I thought I'd take you up on that cup of coffee you offered last night." He stuffed the cap into a side pocket of his parka and hung it on a peg near the door.

"Uh-huh," Archie grunted, rising from his chair and walking to the counter. "How was your stayover, young man? Did you ever find a place warm enough to suit you?"

"I did, indeed." Jacob straddled a stool at the counter and sat down. "I thank you for the excellent recommendation."

Archie nodded, casting a glance Patsy's way as he set a mug of coffee in front of Jacob. She was busy taking stock of her reflection in the shop's window and futilely trying to resurrect her shellacked hair. Archie knew it wouldn't be long before she'd invent some flimsy excuse in order to make her way over.

"Did you come to Marblehead with a purpose or on a whim?" Archie rearranged a tray of chocolate croissants in a glass display case as he spoke.

"The truth is, I got turned around in the snowstorm yesterday and ended up in your town by accident." Jacob added a splash of cream to the coffee.

"Where were your originally headed?" Satisfied that the trays of buns and muffins were adequately replenished, Archie shut the sliding glass door and came to lean over the counter.

Patsy had also been checking out buns—the ones perched atop the stool. She thought them the most delectable in the shop. She strummed her fingers on the table, racking her brain as to how not to appear obvious. Darn Archie for not having the good manners to introduce her!

Archie was aware of Patsy's attempts to catch his eye. He ignored her silly monkeyshines, deciding to let her stew a while. In a few minutes she'd be having another of her periodic hot flashes.

"I hadn't any particular place in mind," Jacob answered between sips.

"You on vacation then?" Archie surmised.

"In a fashion. I decided to take some time off work and just knock about."

"Not many folks can afford such a luxury," Archie stated matter-of-factly.

"I'm fortunate enough that I can." Jacob seemed more disposed to scanning the headlines of the weekly paper at his elbow than elaborating on the subject of his financial situation.

Archie could almost see Patsy's ears perking. The stranger was becoming more and more attractive to her by the second. Next to breathing males, Patsy dearly loved money. Most of her conversations revolved around the three Big M's—males, money and marriage. She was constantly whining about how tired she was of scrimping and scraping to make ends meet, and how a man in her life would make it infinitely easier. Then she'd go on and on about how hard it was for a woman to be the sole supporter of her children, and how she deserved better than the sorry circumstances her poor deranged husband had left her in. She never failed to mention that the next time around she was going to marry for security, not love. Yessiree, if ever another man was to stand a chance with her, he would have to be covered in gold.

"I strolled around town this morning and from what I've seen so far, it's a real special place. I was especially taken with yachting facilities." Jacob fished his gold toothpick from the pocket of his flannel shirt.

Archie took note of the shirt. It was the sort with the big checks of yellow and black that was all the rage with the yuppies this season. And he wore the regulation round-necked, matching black T-shirt underneath. Only it looked different on the stranger—not showy but appropriate. "Into sailing, are ya?" Archie reached around for the coffeepot, holding it up for a yea or nay on a refill.

Jacob nodded. "In a big way."

"Well, you've come to the right spot then, young man. Sailing's a way of life 'round here." Archie deliberately overlooked Patsy's waving of a raised mug over in the corner.

"I saw the most incredible sloop moored at the Corinthian marina. She must've measured fifty feet and every inch of her was sheer perfection. I've never seen anything like it. *The Mariah*, I believe she's called." Jacob's green eyes lit up as he talked about the vessel.

"Uh-huh." Archie rubbed the back of his neck. "That'd be Nathan Pritchard's boat you speak of. It's a beauty, all right. Then again, it's no less or no more than should be expected from a pair of hands that built two America's Cup contenders." He replaced the coffeepot on the warmer and began reloading the napkin holders spaced at various intervals along the counter.

"You're serious?" Jacob swiveled on the stool, his gaze following the old man as he moved from metal napkin holder to metal napkin holder.

"Serious as a heart attack. That's how come Nathan had to retire from the ship-building business. His ticker gave out. He just keeled over while strolling the harbor one evening. It was months before he could do the simplest task. It was shortly after his brush with death that he sold the sail loft. He mostly spends his time these days sailing the bay. Uh-huh—'' Archie stuffed the last napkin holder ''—old Nathan takes *The Mariah* out daily. Even in the dead of winter he hoists sail with the other 'frostbiters.' ''

Jacob cast him a questioning look.

''That's what we call the diehards who sail on the coldest of winter days. You probably noticed a few out on the bay today.''

''I guess you could classify me as a 'frostbiter' then. Like Mr. Pritchard, I'd sail anytime, anywhere, and in any kind of weather. To be aboard a ship as fine as *The Mariah* would be the ultimate.'' Jacob gazed off wistfully.

Patsy was exasperated with Archie and all his talk of sailing. It afforded her no opportunity to butt in and gain the stranger's attention. She couldn't dally much longer. She was already five minutes late picking up the kids from hockey practice.

Archie noticed her antsy glances toward the clock on the wall but made no effort to include her in his conversation with the visitor. Finished with his task, he returned to where the stranger sat at the counter, leaned across the marbled Formica top and continued chatting. ''Nathan's a friendly sort. I'm sure he'd invite you aboard if he knew you were keen on taking a run of the bay with him. He likes to boast of the glory days when he built the contenders. Most the local folk take his accomplishments for granted, except for Ted

Hood. 'Course, he hasn't much time to sit and reminisce with Nathan, what with all his hard training and sail making. Uh-huh, I betcha old Nathan would relish an opportunity to spin his yarns for someone who'd appreciate the work that went into building *The Mariah*."

Jacob almost swallowed his gold toothpick. "Ted Hood, the *America*'s skipper, resides here in Marblehead?"

"The one and the same," Archie boasted. "He makes his home here. Like I said, sailing's a way of life in Marblehead. Been so since the very beginnings of the town."

Patsy expelled a loud sigh as she stood and flung her coat over an arm. She shot Archie a murderous look when she sauntered up to the counter to pay the check.

"Leaving so soon, Patsy? You sure you wouldn't care for something else? Another tart or a second cup of hot cocoa?"

His solicitous attitude did not fool her. She knew he knew precisely what would satisfy her and it wasn't posted on a menu. The old goat! "You're naughty to tempt me, Archie," she said sweetly. "You know how strictly I count calories." She sucked in her tummy, flashing the stranger her brightest smile—the toothy one she reserved for only three Big "M" candidates. "I subscribe to the theory that a woman can never be too thin or too rich," she twittered.

Archie turned his back on her, glad he had the excuse of having to ring up the sale on the old-time cash register. He wondered if the stranger was having as

much trouble as he was keeping a straight face. Lord,
but Patsy could be a twit at times!

Jacob reacted much more smoothly than Archie.
He'd had a lot of practice at it. In the course of his
many assignations he'd been exposed to every variety
of female—phony types included. This woman's silly
line had hardly been original, but he had the good
grace not to mention the fact. "A good maxim to live
by," he responded.

"I couldn't help overhearing that this is your first
trip to Marblehead. As the soon-to-be-installed
president of the Women's Old Town Beautification
Society, I'd like to welcome you and the missus to our
lovely town. The two of you really must take in the
historical sights. We've so many. I'd be glad to act as
a personal guide whenever you'd like. The tour is so
much more informative when conducted by someone
who can supply you with an in-depth background."

Jacob realized a backdoor approach when he heard
one. "That's kind of you, but I wouldn't want to impose."

"It's no imposition," she said, slipping on her coat
and flouncing her hair to free it from beneath the imitation fox collar.

"I'm not much of a history buff," he tactfully declined.

"Oh, well then, perhaps your wife would enjoy a
tour while you're otherwise occupied?" Patsy persisted.

Archie was highly entertained watching the pair
parry with each other. Patsy had no intention of giv-

ing up and going away without first discerning
whether or not the stranger was free game. And he did
not seem inclined to volunteer the information. Fold-
ing his arms across his chest, Archie looked expec-
tantly toward the stranger.

"It's not likely," Jacob hedged. "I'm traveling
alone."

"I see," Patsy said as she tugged on her Isotoner
gloves. "Of course there are other activities that may
be of interest to you. I could drop off a brochure by
your hotel. And should you decide to bring the missus the next trip, she'll already be familiar with some
of the more colorful aspects of the town."

Archie came to the rescue. "Aren't those your two
boys trudging up the street in their hockey uniforms,
Patsy?"

"Oh, damn! Yes, it is. They must've thought I'd
forgotten them and started walking home from practice." Her smile vanished and was instantly replaced
with two hard lines running from the outside of each
nostril to the corners of her mouth. "If I've told them
once, I've told them a hundred times to wait at the
rink," she clucked, scurrying toward the door like a
mother hen. Flinging it open, she hollered at the top
of her lungs, "Junior and Gordy! In the car! Now!
You two delinquents are in big trouble this time. Big,
big trouble," she warned.

Her shrill voice had the same effect on Jacob as the
childhood memory of chalk screeching across a
blackboard. God! He'd hated that sound.

Patsy stuck her head back inside the shop, and, like a dove, she cooed, "It was nice to have met you. Perhaps we'll run into one another again soon and I can convince you to take the tour." With another one of her toothy smiles, she dashed off to tend to her boys.

Archie and Jacob sighed in sync, then exchanged grins.

"Patsy's what you might call a bit pushy." Archie shook his head as he watched her catch the pair of feisty youngsters by the scruffs of their necks and then corral them into the back seat of the Japanese compact she drove.

"A bit," Jacob agreed. "Thanks for the assistance. It's Archie, isn't it?" He stuck out a hand.

"Uh-huh. Last name's Hooper," the old shopkeeper supplied with a clasp of his hand.

"Jacob Malone." In the habit of making quick assessments of people, Jacob decided he liked Hooper. He was good-natured and forthright—and those were two qualities he valued in a person.

"More coffee?" Archie asked, withdrawing his age-spotted hand.

Jacob declined with a shake of his head. "But you could do me another service."

"If I can." The old man cleared away Jacob's mug and spoon and wiped the counter with a dishrag.

"I'm really anxious to meet Nathan Pritchard and I'd rather not take the chance of missing him at the marina in the morning. Could you tell me where I might find him tonight?"

"Well, let's see...." Archie stroked his chin as he thought. "Being that this is Wednesday, Nathan will be over at The Barnacle eating supper. He plays chess afterward in the back with the owner. It's a standing tradition. The Barnacle is on the harbor near Fort Seawall. You can't miss it. The food's good. You can order most anything and not be disappointed."

"I appreciate the information. How much do I owe you?" Jacob eased his large frame from the stool.

Archie dried his hands on his apron. "No charge. It was worth a cup of coffee to watch you shadow dance with Patsy. Not too many folks can dodge her probing, especially when she's hell-bent on knowing something."

"In my line of work, one has to be able to dodge, weave and duck a question." Jacob collected his parka from the peg he'd hung it on and tugged on his cap.

Archie drew the wrong conclusion. "You must be involved in politics."

"You're not so far off with your guess. Some degree of politicking goes on in almost every profession, but maybe more so in mine. I'm a lawyer," he explained.

"Are you a good one?" Archie's eyes twinkled with good humor.

"It's been claimed so, Arch." He grinned broadly, then paused, his hand resting on the doorknob. "By the way, just for the record, there is no Mrs. Malone," he confided.

"I thought not. Is it because you're particular, or just not interested in the female sex?" The question held no judgment.

Jacob laughed at his candor. "I feel the same way about women as I do about sailing. I'm into them in a big way. That's the problem. I've got a wandering eye and I doubt I could ever be content being limited to just one woman."

"None will have you, huh?" Archie returned in a joking tone.

"An astute deduction on your part. Maybe you should consider giving up the muffin business and going into law." Zipping up his parka, he braced himself for the blast of nippy evening air before stepping out onto the sidewalk. "Thanks for the coffee and the chat. Night, Arch," he bid him, pulling shut the door.

"Night, Jacob." The shopkeeper followed him, flipping the small white sign dangling in the glass door so that the Closed side was displayed to the street.

BY NINE-THIRTY that night, Desirée had given up on the prospect of her star boarder showing up to keep their eight o'clock dinner date. She cleared the dishes from the table and stored the food away in neatly stacked containers in the refrigerator. Disappointed was hardly an apt description of the way she felt. Plain damn depressed would be closer to the truth. She made her way to her bedroom, slumped into a wooden rocking chair by the window, leaned back and stared forlornly into the inky night.

"*At this rate I'll be collecting Social Security checks before Mr. Malone takes any notice of me,*" she grumbled to herself. "*Maybe I should just abandon this crazy scheme and spare myself the humiliation of knowing that I can't even stir a man's blood when I infuse it with magic potions.*"

She wallowed in self-pity for a moment, wondering why it was that since she'd been a kid nothing had worked out the way she'd wanted. But then she envisioned Malone's handsome face and something deep inside her stirred. He was everything she had ever pictured in a lover: tall, dark, intelligent and charming. She couldn't deny that she wanted him more than she'd ever wanted anything in her life. She wanted a chance to spend time in his company—in his arms...in his bed. If only once in her life, she wanted to experience the mysterious thing called intimacy. All that she knew of it came from what she'd observed when watching couples in the park, what she'd read in books, or from what Mama had alluded to when she had spoken of past loves in her life and a state she called desire.

As a child, Desirée had wanted a real family with a father who lived with them and a mother who baked cookies instead of mixing elixirs. But Mama had said that couldn't be. She'd explained that they were different. Though the explanation hardly satisfied Desirée's need to understand or her yen for normalcy, her mother had neither elaborated, nor conformed to her daughter's ideal.

As a teenager, Desirée had wanted to blend in with her peers. Sometimes she'd even dared dream of being popular at school. But that dream had never materialized, either. She was unsure and shy and therefore always ended up apart from, rather than in with, the crowd. Again, Mama had explained her separateness as her merely being different—a late bloomer.

As a young woman, the stigma attached to her family had caused Desirée to withdraw even more from social contacts. Her shyness and sensitivity were misconstrued. The young men in town thought her uppity or odd and kept their distance. Eventually she, too, was labeled a witch, and her name was added to the perpetual whispers about the Warren women. Once the rumor was started, her fate was sealed. Desirée knew she'd find no romantic beau among the Marblehead natives. She was taboo. It would take an outsider's kiss to release her from the stigma and to fulfill her womanly needs.

Jacob Malone was the one she had yearned for and dreamed of for so many long and lonely nights. She'd be damned if she was going to let him check out of his room and her life, as if he were just another boarder. The account between them could not be settled with a "Just sign on the appropriate line of the charge slip, and thanks for your patronage."

With renewed hope and energy, Desirée sprang from the chair, going out into the hall and down the stairs to the shop below. Sensing an urgency about her mistress, Mew-Sinh scampered over to her to see what all the flurry was about. The feline jumped up onto the glass counter to gain a better vantage point. As Desirée dashed around, collecting scraps of cloth, scissors and thread from assorted drawers, and removing certain glass jars from the rows of shelves that ran the width and breadth of an entire wall, Mew-Sinh caught the scent of the trespasser on the stairs. She crooked her head, staring at the vacant spot.

The invisible Alistair, sitting semireclined on the steps, tipped his hat to the puss.

"Stronger measures, that's what we need to take, Mew-Sinh. I think it's necessary that we hurry the process along. We can't have Mr. Malone leaving us before we've accomplished our purpose." Desirée checked the jars' labels, naming out loud the contents of each to be sure she'd gathered everything necessary. "Acacia flowers, myrtle, rose petals, jasmine and lavender. All here," she said. "All right, let's be doubly sure and make two charms—one to go under my pillow and one to go under Mr. Malone's."

She cut two squares of the rose silk cloth, then two tiny red-felt hearts. "So far, so good," she muttered. "Now for the next phase." She flew around, assembling the other accessories—a candle, a dish of salt, a cup of water, two copper pennies, mortar and pestle and incense.

Alistair watched dumbfounded from the steps, totally in the dark as to what the little lady was concocting out of the scraps of cloth and various other sundries she'd assembled.

Next she fetched the old leather volume from a corner table, plopping it onto the counter with a heavy thud and wildly flipping through the pages until she located the passage she was searching for.

"Okay, I think we're ready." She took a deep breath, struck a match and lit the candle, then bent the flame of the candle to the incense. Soon the shop began to fill with the smell of frankincense.

Mew-Sinh's nostrils twitched.

So did Mackey's.

Desirée then took the mortar and pestle in hand and ground together the herbs and flowers, closing her eyes and concentrating as she did so.

The angel had no way of knowing that it was Malone's face she was visualizing behind closed lids. But after having been the invited guest at a few secret Aborigine ceremonies, he recognized a ritualistic rite when he was in the midst of one. Intrigued, he sat up straighter and paid close attention to the sheila's every move.

She opened her eyes and sprinkled half of the dry mixture into each square of rose silk. Next she added a red-felt heart and copper penny to each. And then she brought the four corners of each bundle together, twisted them and tied them up with single knots of blue thread. She blew on each bundle to charge them with air, passed them through the candle's flame, charging them with fire, and then she sprinkled a few drops of water on each, charging both with water. Then she dipped them into the bowl of salt, charging them with earth. Holding the bundles in the palms of her hands, she breathed on each one once more, and

recited from the leather volume as she tied six more
knots in each string of thread.

Ishtar, Isis, hear my cry
Without true love, my soul shall die
Aphrodite, come to me
And bring the one I ache to see.
Freya, Cupid, Eros, hear
This call I send you loud and clear.
Thor and Agni, Mighty Zeus,
My heart is clear on whom I choose.
My love's a man that's good and bold,
I charge you, mighty Gods of old
Make him dream of none but me,
And as my will so mote it be.

She stood quietly, her slim fingers closing around
the bundles and charging them with energy as she shut
her eyes and conjured up Jacob's image again.

Mackey's exposure to the Aborigines, with their
supposed telekinetic capability, had taught him not to
dismiss the power of the mind over matter. In this
case, the matter was Malone. So that was her aim, eh?
he mused. To will the scoundrel to fall in love with her.
He wasn't sure which of the two of them needed his
protection the more—his charge or the sheila. Where
romance was concerned, Mackey's instincts told him
that it was Miss Warren who was the lamb—a lamb
who could very well find herself at the mercy of a
wolf.

Desirée put the love charms in her sweater pocket, stored away all the paraphernalia, rechecked to be sure the shop door was bolted, then turned to cross the room to the stairs.

Alistair scooted out of her way, tipping his hat to Mew-Sinh once more as the cat bounded up the steps after her mistress. Desirée flicked off the light switch and Alistair settled back on the steps to brood in the dark.

What to do? he wondered. What to do? He braced an elbow on a knee and rested his chin in his palm. "How come I never get the easy assignments?" he complained. "Why me, Lord?"

The only reply was the growl of his empty tummy.

CHAPTER FIVE

A MOON, A LAGOON, mimosa and mist—this was the stuff of Jacob's dream.

The lagoon lay nestled amid high lacy ferns, and the water mirrored the pale pink cast of the flowering mimosa trees that abounded everywhere. Strangely the mist did not have the humid quality he would have expected to encounter deep in the midst of an island paradise. Rather it was dense and smoky and reminded him more of dry ice vapors. Yet the gentle breeze on his skin and the lush foliage all around him indicated a sultry climate.

Where the hell was he? He had no bearings by which to judge, only a sense of a tropical rain forest. Bright-colored birds and uniquely marked butterflies flitted hither and yon in the moonlight. The intoxicating smell of wild gardenias engulfed him. There was a definite Indonesian flavor to the place, a Bali-like beauty. And yet...

His gaze drifted out over the lagoon. On the glassy surface of the water glided rare black swans, strikingly graceful against a shimmery silvery-pink backdrop. Their mating cries were the only sounds that broke the silence. And on the bisque-colored sands of

the sloping bank, a host of peacocks stood sentinel—
their bluish-green and golden tails fanned out to provide a beautifully congruous scalloped edge around
the perimeter of the lagoon. It was a breathtaking
sight.

But it was another observation—one he made when
he lifted his eyes skyward and focused on the iridescent object dominating the infinite blackness—that
sent a shock wave surging through Jacob. A line from
The Wizard of Oz came into his head: *I don't think
we're in Kansas anymore, Toto.*

This was no ordinary moon he gazed upon. He
forced his eyes to the ground, shook his head, rubbed
his sockets with the balls of his palms and then took a
second look. No, he had not imagined the phenome-
non. This moon was not spherical, like the moon to
which he was accustomed, but consisted of two cres-
cents facing opposite directions and joined at the point
of their fullest parts, forming a peculiar H design. Nor
was the moon its usual opal color. It wasn't even
green. It was blue. Not a true blue—more of a lavender-blue. It was the damndest thing he'd ever seen.
Sure, he was familiar with the old saying, "Once in a
blue moon," but that was metaphoric. The blue moon
above him was for real.

How had he come to this place? Though he had a
vague feeling of having traveled through time and di-
mension, he had no recollection of the journey. This
was crazy—like something straight out of a science-
fiction novel! Was he hallucinating, maybe?

It was then that Jacob noticed the hazy form of another person across the lagoon. He strained his eyes, trying to bring the blurry figure into focus. Through the mist he could make out the silhouette of a woman—an incredibly shapely woman. She came to stand upon a smooth flat boulder at the water's edge. Her elevated position placed her slightly above the swirling mist. Illuminated as she was in the moonlight, Jacob could easily distinguish that she wore only a scant swimsuit and a circlet of wildflowers around her head and right ankle. The suit was a one-piece number, ultra-French cut, and made of a metallic material that glinted pewter and copper and gold with each minuscule movement of her dynamite body in the moonlight. Her hair was thick, wild and reached her waist. It, too, glinted pewter and copper and gold as she lifted the luxurious mass of kinky curls off her neck, arched her bare back and stretched languidly.

Jacob instantly fell in lust with the lagoon maid. With as little noise as possible, he moved nearer to the vision and crouched down in the ferns. Her back was turned toward him and she seemed to be unaware of his presence. From his closer vantage point, he could appreciate even more fully the hourglass symmetry of her feminine form. She was exquisite—the unattainable ideal from which erotic dreams were drawn. Primarily a legs-and-tush man, he judged hers to be among the very best he'd been privileged to admire. Every sleek inch of her, every muscle was incredibly toned. And her skin—his eyes lingered on her semiexposed buttocks, then slowly traveled down her lean,

hard limbs to her dainty feet—was the color and texture of fine ivory. He just knew if he were to run his
hand along a creamy thigh, it would feel the same as
if he'd knelt in a velvety bed of gardenia petals....

The notion was a tempting one, but he quickly ta-
bled the impulse. If the lagoon maid was a mirage, he
didn't want to verify the fact just yet. He was enjoying the fantasy much too much to end it prematurely.
And if she was not a figment of his imagination, he
certainly did not want to risk frightening her off. Real
or imagined, she was beyond a doubt the most exciting thing that had happened to him in years.

He continued to watch in fascination as the lagoon
maid prepared to dive into the water. She completed
the feat as gracefully as the black swans would have.
There was only a faint echo of a splash as she sub-
merged herself. Enchanted, he settled in the ferns,
linking his arms around his knees and taking in the
view with an appreciative smile. She was streamlined
and agile, poetry in motion, barely creating a ripple as
she backstroked through the pale pink waters. He
marveled at her tireless energy as she and the swans
performed an aquatic ballet together. Then to his delight and utter amazement, his secret wish became a
reality as she emerged from the lagoon and lifted herself back onto the boulder once more. The metallic
swimsuit was gone! She was totally and gorgeously
nude. He hadn't taken his eyes from her the whole
time she'd been swimming and she hadn't disappeared from the surface of the water after her initial
submersion, yet she was devoid of a suit, as though it

had just evaporated from her delectable body on the strength of a wish.

Impossible! he thought, blinking to make sure that his mind was not playing a cruel trick on him. It wasn't. She was still perched on the boulder, one leg sexily bent, her arms behind her, her head thrown back and her face lifted toward the moon, as if she were basking in its beams. What an exotic picture she presented—profiled on the rock and gilded in lavender moonlight, beads of water glistening like hundreds of tiny crystals on her high, small breasts and taut torso.

His mouth suddenly felt dry and he went limp inside at the sight of her. One strategic area of his anatomy, however, reacted in quite the opposite way to the visual stimuli. He felt ridiculously juvenile. He hadn't engaged in any form of voyeurism since the age of fifteen when he and a chum had come up with a grand plan of sneaking into the girls' locker room with the demented intentions of taking a few candid shots with a Polaroid. Their primary aim had been to sell the really revealing ones to the highest bidder after school. Now, as then, his arousal blurred his judgment. At fifteen, he'd been mesmerized by his first glimpse of the feminine form in the raw and had forgotten to load the film. His brain had turned to mush and his hormones had gone berserk. Nearly twenty years later, he had reverted back to the same incited condition. What was more, his intentions were not any more noble and only a little less mercenary.

Again it was as if his silent wishes were known to the lagoon maid, for suddenly she raised her head and turned his way, crooking a finger in an invitation for him to come join her on the rock.

Holy cow! Now he knew he had to be hallucinating. This couldn't really be happening to him. Like an idiot, he looked over his shoulder to see if she was signaling someone else. There was nothing but jungle, mimosa and mist behind him. Awkwardly he rose, pointing to himself to make certain it was him she was beckoning.

The lagoon maid nodded and he passed between the peacock guards like the mist through the branches of the mimosa trees. Then he waded out to the boulder and hoisted himself atop it.

The lagoon maid sat on bended knees, her head shyly bowed and her features hidden by her cascading hair. With the gentlest of touches, she turned his eyes away, forcing him to look out over the silvery pink lagoon as she situated herself behind his back, reached around and began to expertly massage his temples.

She had great hands. He was putty in them. A deep sigh escaped him at the pleasurable pressure of her fingertips as they worked through his scalp, and he brought his head back to lean against her shoulder. He could feel the electric brush of her nipples against his back. It was a fantastic sensation, but nothing in comparison to the feathery wisp of her breath along his neck as she ran her palms across his shoulders and down his biceps in firm, slow strokes. Again and again, her hands flowed over his flesh. He closed his eyes, feeling the tension leave his body, except for the part of him that craved her touch to the point of distraction.

Unable to restrain himself any longer, he reached up behind him and cupped the back of her head, drawing her down over his shoulder and forging her lush lips to his. Her kiss was as he had expected the mist to be—warm, moist and clinging. He wanted it to never end. But the lagoon maid evaded his further advances—maneuvering from his clutches and sliding off the rock into the water.

"Come." It was not a command, but an entreaty that she murmured.

He scrambled to his feet, threw off his sandals and practically jumped out of his clothes. His heart pounding like a jackhammer, he followed her into the water, wondering what in the hell was in store for him next. He soon found out as she plunged under the water, then slowly, evocatively, grazed her body the length of his as she resurfaced. The fluid friction of her flesh against his was excruciatingly divine. At last he would have a good look at the lovely water nymph, he thought, cinching his arms around her small waist. At that inopportune moment the blue moon disappeared behind a cloud, leaving them to navigate in pitch-dark.

Jacob's disappointment at being unable to distinguish her features was fleeting. The darkness seemed to make the maid bolder. She entwined her arms around his neck, raising herself up out of the water and pressing her mouth to his. This time her kiss was uninhibited and promising. He tightened his grip on her, wanting to savor the honey recesses beyond her ripe lips but unable to stop himself from devouring her once he'd tasted her sweetness.

She moaned and writhed against him, bringing a knee up and running it along his inner thigh. Up and down. Again and again. Sensuously. Wantonly.

His blood raced. His senses reeled. Every nerve in his body tingled. All traces of gentlemanly restraint left him as he wound his fingers in her wet hair, tilted back her head and parted her lips with a feverish thrust of his tongue. He was desperate to have her. Now. This instant. To hell with foreplay. To hell with all the right words and moves he had acquired by virtue of many women and many years of trial and error. This wasn't the same. *She* wasn't the same as all the others. No, she was different—totally and wonderfully different. And so would he be different—changed after making love to the lagoon maid. He knew it as surely as he could feel her surrendering shudder. He reached beneath the water, cupping her firm buttocks in his big hands. She instinctively wrapped her legs around him. He eased back and sank deeper into the water. What occurred next was a matter of combustible chemistry and water dynamics. And when it was over, he knew immediately that he was not the same man he had been before his arrival at the lagoon.

The blue moon began to emerge from behind the mass of clouds. With a press of a cheek to his, the lagoon maid wriggled from his embrace and swam off toward the bank.

"Wait. Don't go," he pleaded, striking out after her.

"I must," she called back, ceasing swimming and beginning to wade to shore. Iridescent threads of pewter, copper, and gold once more sparkled in the moonlight. Magically the swimsuit had reappeared on her body.

At the edge of the bank, he caught up to her. He became aware of a soggy weightiness around his waist and hips as he stepped onto the spongy sands. When he looked down, he was bewildered to find that he, too, was dressed again. But he didn't have time to contemplate the bizarre happening, for the lagoon maid was on the verge of disappearing, and the damn mist was congealing all around them. He couldn't see her face clearly. "Please, tell me who you are," he entreated with a staying clasp of her arm. "When will you return?"

"You already know me, Jacob," was her soft reply. "But I do not think you're ready to accept me."

Riddles. She was talking in riddles when she was about to desert him. He tried to wave the mist away, but it hung like a gauze curtain between them. "But how do I know you? I've yet to see your face. You have to tell me a name and where I can find you again," he demanded.

"Be patient, Jacob," she said soothingly, reaching out and brushing the back of her hand along his cheekbone. "For the present, I must remain what I am and you cannot follow where I go."

"Why not?" he persisted, capturing her by the shoulders and trying to forestall what she had predicted.

"Because your temporary awakening cannot be postponed and your full awakening is not yet at hand."

Her vague answers were making him crazy. "I don't understand," he groaned. "You mentioned remaining what you are. Precisely what is that?"

"At the moment, I'm only a dream."

"No, that's impossible," he argued. "I made love to you a few minutes ago. I didn't dream it. I did it. I can still touch you, smell you, even taste you. You're real," he insisted. "You've got to be."

"I'm real inasmuch as I am what you unconsciously desire." She retreated a step or two from him and, as far as he could tell, unclasped an object and removed it from about her throat. A necklace, he presumed. He thought it odd that he had not noticed the piece of jewelry before now. Wordlessly she took his hand and turned it palm up.

"Sometimes you can know a face but be blind to what exists in the heart. A remembrance of our time together." She dropped the necklace into his palm and enfolded his fingers over the gift. Then, with a gossamer brush of her lips across his, she bid him farewell before fading into the mist.

"To whose heart do you refer? Mine or another's?" He ran into the mist after her, but she had vanished from view. Only the haunting fragrance of wild gardenias remained. "Both," was the dreamy reply that whispered through the mimosa trees.

"Don't desert me," he cried out. "Come back. Please, come back."

Only stillness answered him. He opened his fingers and held the necklace up to the light. There dangling from his fingertips was a sterling silver replica of the blue moon above him—a charm molded in the same peculiar H design. The charm pendulated on the chain. To and fro. To and fro. He just stood there—hypnotized by the charm's seductive sway. *Once in a blue moon,* kept repeating in his brain. *Once in a blue moon . . . once in a blue moon.*

Jacob woke himself with his fretful mumbling. He lurched upright in the bed. The moon and lagoon, mimosa and mist was no more. It had all been just a dream, after all.

He cast a wary eye around the bedroom, taking stock of his surroundings. Though everything looked copacetic, he was still a bit shaken by the vividness of his dream. It had seemed so real. He could still smell gardenias, and his body felt as if he'd actually made wild, passionate love for hours to a water nymph.

He smiled as he reflected on the crazy fantasy. "Only in your wildest dreams, Malone," he muttered, falling back onto the pillow with a sigh. It was then that he noticed the narrow shaft of light falling across the foot of the bed. Cautiously he raised himself once more, then looked toward the partly open door. A pair of glowing eyes stared back at him from out of the darkness. It took a befuddled second or two and a faint meow for him to identify the nocturnal creature as the pesky house cat.

"I shut the damn door. I know I did." With a flip of his hand, he tried to shoo Mew-Sinh from the room.

The cat did not budge until Jacob cursed and threw back the covers. The instant his toes touched the floor, she bolted out the door and out of sight.

Jacob flopped back into bed, drawing the covers to his neck with a shiver. "Blue moons and crazy cats. What's next?" he grunted, wadding the pillow beneath his head and rearranging the rumpled covers. He shut his eyes and tried to go back to sleep. When he finally drifted off, it was a restless sleep he experienced, for he was unconsciously searching for the lost lagoon maid and seeking the meaning of the blue moon charm.

DESIRÉE WAS SITTING at the kitchen table, reading the morning paper, when he made a late appearance.

He now had two apologies to make to her—one for missing dinner the night before and one for showing up late for breakfast.

"Good morning, Jacob." There was not a trace of reproach in her tone. In fact, she seemed in an especially good mood. "There's freshly squeezed orange juice in the pitcher on the counter and freshly perked coffee on the stove."

She wasn't making a fuss about serving him today. In fact, she didn't seem much inclined to fix him anything to eat. Maybe she wasn't in as good a humor as he'd originally thought. "Thanks. I'll help myself," he tested.

She merely smiled while continuing to read the paper.

He decided to make his amends straightaway. "I'm sorry about missing dinner last night. I should have given you advance notice of my plans to eat out but it was an impromptu thing and..."

Eat out. She missed the rest of his apologetic explanation while puzzling over the mystery of the late-night raid waged on the refrigerator. Upon waking and stumbling into the kitchen at dawn for her customary ingestion of vitamin C, she'd been shocked to discover a helter-skelter mess instead of the tidy arrangement she'd left in the refrigerator the night before. Every neatly stacked container in which she'd stored leftovers had been plundered. The wrong lids had been put on the wrong bowls and only bits and scraps of the meal she'd prepared remained. She'd presumed that Jacob had come home hungry and had scoured the kitchen in search of a midnight snack. The amount of food he'd consumed had amazed her. But now to find out that he'd previously eaten! Good grief! The man had the appetite of Conan the Barbarian.

"...the time just flew by. Nathan Pritchard is one heck of a storyteller, isn't he?"

She looked up to find Jacob seated across from her at the table. Obviously he had no idea that she hadn't been listening. "Nathan Pritchard?" she repeated dumbly. "Oh, yes, he certainly is." She tried to cover her inattentiveness.

He wondered why she kept looking at him so oddly. Had he forgotten to remove the piece of toilet paper he'd applied to the nick on his chin? He checked to be sure that such was not the embarrassing case. It wasn't. "It appears as if I've missed breakfast also." Wanting to shift the emphasis from himself, he glanced to the empty stove.

Now it was her turn to be embarrassed. She hadn't thought he'd be anxious for breakfast after putting away all that he had only a few hours ago. "I, uh, wasn't sure you'd want any breakfast this morning," she stammered. "Of course, I'll fix you whatever you'd like. It won't take a minute. Please, forgive my presumptuousness. Perhaps you'd care to read the paper." She hoped her fumbling wasn't too obvious.

Something was wrong. He could plainly see that she was genuinely distressed. He placed a calming hand on hers, causing an instant flush to appear on her face. "It's no big deal, Desirée. I'm just trying to make conversation, is all. To tell you the truth, I seldom eat breakfast. A stale biscuit will do nicely." He tried to coax a smile from her.

"I think I can do better than that." His touch unsettled her even more. She was afraid she might start hyperventilating or doing something equally stupid at any moment. While in the act of extricating her hand from beneath his, she knocked a section of newspaper onto the floor, sending the sports pages scattering. *God!* she thought. He was probably an avid Celtics fan and those were the only pages in which he had any interest. "Now, look what I've done!" she fretted, getting out of her chair and stooping to gather the strewn mess.

"Let me," he offered, also leaving his seat, squatting on bended knees and starting to assist her.

She stretched for a page just out of fingertip range, bending over as she did so.

He reached for the same page at the same time.

It was then that the crisscrossed bodice of her sweater parted and the necklace that she kept safely tucked out of sight swung free. An intriguing charm pendulated on a thin silver chain. To and fro. To and fro.

Jacob froze inside. His eyes moved from the swinging object, and locked with hers. "What is that?" he asked, his voice and expression suddenly brittle.

She thought he referred to the page she'd just retrieved. "The part with the NBA standings, I believe," she answered, a bit startled by his intensity.

"Not that," he corrected her. "This!" With a lightning-quick reflex, his fingers clamped around the charm.

"It's nothing. An old charm." His hold on the chain caused the clasp to bite into the back of her neck. She hadn't meant for him to see the necklace. She did not want to have to explain its significance.

"But what does it symbolize?" He was not about to drop the subject or yield to her subtle tugging.

"It has to do with Wicca, Mr. Malone," was all she said, finally managing to extricate the necklace from his clasp. She quickly snatched up the score page and stood. "Would you prefer waffles or French toast?"

Her posture and tone were dismissive, and she made a commotion out of gathering the cooking utensils.

It took Jacob a moment to collect himself. He sat back down in his chair, swallowed a swig of coffee, and decided to pursue the matter of the charm in spite of her obvious reluctance to discuss it. "French toast would be good," he said, slanting her a sizing look as she tucked the necklace back into the bodice of her sweater. "Why do you keep the charm hidden?"

His persistence put her on edge. She was working herself into a state, and she told herself to calm down as she beat an egg-and-milk mixture extra-vigorously. "It's a habit. Wicca, and anything that pertains to it, is controversial, Mr. Malone—especially in Marblehead," was her truthful reply.

"Because it has to do with the occult?" he pressed.

"Because people mistakenly believe so." She slammed a cast-iron skillet on a burner, added butter and turned on the element.

He treaded carefully. It was apparent to him that the subject was a sensitive one. "I assure you that I harbor no prejudices, Desirée. My interest in the significance of the charm is purely personal and inspired by a healthy curiosity, not any sick sort of bias."

She met his steady green eyes and read the sincerity therein. "Then I suppose there would be no harm in revealing the charm's meaning to you." She dipped slices of bread into the egg mixture and placed them on the sizzling pan as she spoke. "In the Wicca tradition, the moon is revered. It is the heavenly projection of the Goddess herself. There are very interesting interpretations of the meanings of its various phases.''

She kept her eyes downcast, periodically checking the bread slices.

Jacob replenished his coffee cup, saying nothing, but doing a lot of analyzing of her guarded manner. For a woman who made her living selling occult to the public, she was terribly uptight when it came to talking privately about it.

She flipped the bread slices and sprinkled some cinnamon on top of them. ''The charm symbolizes the waxing and waning cycles of the moon. The waxing aspect represents the Goddess as a maiden. In this phase, she is wild and untamed—a virgin unpenetrated and belonging to no one but herself. The moon in its waxing cycle represents the power of beginning, of growth and generation. This is the time of ideas and plans before they are tempered by reality; the time of the blank page upon which life will be written.''

He was slightly taken back by the confident way in which she conveyed the information. It was if she assumed a stronger personality when she spoke of ancient mysteries. ''And what does the waning phase represent?'' he prompted, truly intrigued by the mythical connotations surrounding the charm.

She removed the golden slices of French toast from the skillet and arranged them on a plate. Then, grabbing a bottle of maple syrup, she placed it on the table along with his plate and sat down across from him to finish recounting the charm's meaning.

"The moon in its waning aspect is the Goddess as the Old Crone. She is all wise. She knows the power of ending—that all things must end to fulfill their beginnings. She knows that it is a part of life to sometimes lose. The waning moon is the culmination of all the knowledge and power preceding it in a cycle. It is the sum of the whole—all that is seen and unseen, and all that went before and will come after it."

He considered the deep philosophical implications while dribbling syrup over the French toast.

"Have I satisfied your curiosity about the charm?" she asked, making direct eye contact with him.

"Partially," he replied, suddenly feeling himself being sucked into a whirlpool of lavender-blue. Visions of the lagoon maid flickered in and out of his head. Before he realized what was happening, he began to envision Miss Warren without a stitch on. The mental images kept transposing themselves one upon the other: the lagoon maid and then Miss Warren, wild and waist-long copper hair, Miss Warren and then the lagoon maid—high, small breasts and a firm, round fanny.

"Mr. Malone?"

He could hear his name being called through a long, spiraling tunnel but he wasn't inclined to respond. He was trapped between the waxing and waning moon, the seen and the unseen, a dream and reality.

"What is it? What's wrong? Please, Mr. Malone, you're frightening me." Desirée reached over and gave his shoulder a hard shake.

He snapped to his senses. "I'm sorry." Seldom rattled, he was at a loss as to what to say or do. "I guess I'm not as hungry as I thought. I really think I could use some air. Will you excuse me?" Unable to explain his perverted musings, he wanted to run, not walk, out of the room.

"Of course," was her baffled reply.

He halted at the doorway, turning back toward her with a glazed sort of look. Something inside him could not let it be. His rational self discounted the insane notion that there existed any similarity between his erotic fantasy woman and his landlady, but he felt a crazy compulsion to try to figure out why his subconscious would engage in such a ridiculous transference.

"Would you consider having dinner with me tonight, Desirée?" he blurted. "We could go anywhere you'd like. Just name your favorite restaurant and I'll handle the reservations." The invitation was totally impromptu, and startled him as much as it did her.

"I, uh, well, yes," she agreed with a shy smile.

"I need the name of a restaurant," he reminded her.

"Giancarlo's," she supplied.

"About eight?"

"Fine," she agreed.

His odd manner and abrupt invitation surprised her. By the time she'd recovered sufficiently enough to question his motives, he was no longer available for comment.

Had he invited her to dine with him because he desired the pleasure of her company, she wondered, or

because he wanted another opportunity to grill her?
She pulled out the charm nestled at the V of her
sweater, clasping it tightly in her trembling hand. "I
must be very careful," she whispered to no one in
particular. "Jacob is an extremely sensitive man. I
have to remember that, for the present, it's only the
power of suggestion that binds him to me. I must not
mistake his curiosity about Wicca as fascination with
me. No, I must be on my guard and not let him delve
too deeply into my affiliation with the Old Ways. He's
much too smart not to suspect the magic at work between us."

In her mind, she knew that exercising patience and
prudence was her safest recourse. But deep in her soul
she yearned to act impulsively. It was so hard to be
sensible when her heart wanted nothing more than to
be spontaneous and reckless. She stood and whirled,
letting go with a whoop of glee. Desirée Warren was
actually going to have her first honest-to-goodness
date with a man. She was positively giddy with excitement.

IN THE DRAFTY ATTIC, Alistair Mackey rolled over
onto his swollen stomach and let loose with an indelicate belch. The old rollaway's rusty springs creaked
beneath his bloated weight. He'd said his prayers, and
had included a thankful mention of the little lady's
tasty leftovers. He'd thought some rest would be good
for the digestion—just a short nap....

Malone had gone off to sail with the old man, Nathan. Alistair hadn't seen the sense in his tagging

along. Malone would be safer than he was out at sea;
tough old croc poacher that he was, he'd suffer from
motion sickness in a bath tub. Besides, his cold had
gotten worse. He'd thought it better for him to catch
a little snooze while Malone was away from the house
and the tempting Miss Warren. After all, even the
most dedicated of guardian angels had to take time out
to recharge their batteries.

He yawned and then turned his face into the pillow
to muffle an ear-popping sneeze. "I wonder if it's
possible to die twice?" he sniffed, pressing a hand to
his brow. "I knew it. I've taken a bloody fever. This
is just ducky. Now I'm going to have to raid the med-
icine chest as well." Feeling heartily sorry for himself,
Alistair Mackey stuck out his lips in a pout and closed
his red-rimmed eyes. In a matter of minutes, he was
dreaming of a heavenly warm bed in his heavenly
warm home light years away from Marblehead. Fortunately his angelic snoring could not be detected by
human ears.

CHAPTER SIX

JACOB WAS acutely aware of the attention they drew
from the other patrons as they entered Giancarlo's
Ristorante. The looks leveled in their direction were
much like those he got from the slack-jawed, gawking
groupies who invariably congregated outside a courtroom whenever he represented an especially controversial or famous client. Instinctively his arm moved
to encircle Desirée's back. Other than stiffening a bit,
she made no move to negate his attempt to insulate her
against the frosty reception.

"We've reservations for two under the name Malone," he informed the hostess.

The woman checked her book, confirming the
same, then led the way to a linen-draped table in the
center of the room. Once Jacob had pulled out Desirée's chair and seated himself, the hostess offered him
the wine list with a pinched smile. "Thank you," he
said, sensing but not understanding the woman's almost tangible animosity.

Her black eyes darted to Desirée as she slipped the
wool cloak from her shoulders and arranged it over
the back of the chair. Jacob thought he detected a
wariness in the woman's fleeting glance but if so, she

quickly masked it behind hooded lids, nodding curtly before withdrawing.

He flipped open the wine list and skimmed its contents. "Have you a favorite vintage or year?"

His casual demeanor contrasted strikingly with his impeccable attire. He cut a dashing figure in his obviously custom-tailored gray suit, white-on-white dress shirt, onyx-and-gold cuff links and burgundy silk tie. Desirée had to make a concerted effort to keep from ogling his perfect person. Suddenly she felt dowdy by comparison. The simple sheath she had chosen to wear was all wrong. She had originally thought the jade silk material, mandarin collar and high side slits flattering to her curves and coloring. Now, sitting in the shadow of his sophistication, she felt like a geisha girl reject. Jacob exuded class. Moreover, he was not conscious of the effect he had on people, which made his charm even more potent; it caused those around him to be acutely aware of the sore lack of it within themselves.

He captured her attention with a wave of the wine list.

"I'm sorry." She cast him a tentative smile. "What was it you asked?" The peripheral shuffling of chairs and people all around them saved her from having to explain her distraction.

Jacob viewed the commotion with detached objectivity. It was obvious to him that one by one, many of the people seated at tables close to theirs were making a switch to tables farther away. And they weren't going to a hell of a lot of trouble to hide their mass exodus.

Those who hadn't traded tables were making sure to keep their heads averted and their backs turned. And Jacob knew he wasn't imagining it; the room was fairly abuzz with shuffling and whispering. But why? he wondered. Was it something about him that they found offensive? Or was Desirée the sole target of the cold-shoulder treatment? He set aside the wine list, calmly leaned back in his chair and fixed his gaze on his landlady. "Okay, what's going on here, Desirée?"

"I don't know what you mean." Her attempt to dodge the issue was feeble at best.

"We can sit here and pretend not to notice what's happening all around us, or we can address the point." His eyes were soft when assessing her, but his inflection indicated that he had every intention of pursuing the matter until she provided some enlightenment.

She had no choice but to be candid about the reason for her quarantinelike status within the community. Dammit! Why hadn't she considered the consequences of making a public appearance with him? She should have anticipated the speculative whispers that the sight of her on a man's arm would incite. It was as though she, like the tragic character in Hawthorne's novel, wore a scarlet letter on her chest— a big bold W that marked her as a witch. Wherever a Warren woman went, prying eyes followed. Whatever she did caused tongues to wag. And whomever she came into contact with ran the risk of being branded by association.

Taking a nervous sip from her water glass, she tried to formulate her reply so that it sounded convincingly blasé. "It isn't you who's caused all the silly commotion, Jacob. It's me. Because my mother and her mother before her were Wicca followers, there are those in Marblehead who believe me to be a witch, too. They take a dim view of anything that is in the least bit out of the ordinary. They're fearful of what they don't understand or can't influence. The 'tainted' genes and occult shop I inherited are endless sources of juicy town gossip."

Desirée made light of the situation, her lips curling into a wry smile as she told him, "My mother made a pact with the devil, don't you know? She sold her soul in order to learn dark secrets. It's said that I'm the result of that pact. So beware, Jacob. I am a shady lady, indeed."

Her gamble paid off. Her outrageous suggestion produced the desired result. He actually laughed at the idea that he was in dangerous company. For the benefit of those watching, he leaned forward in his chair, reached across the table and claimed her hand. "There have been a few femme fatales in my past and I managed to emerge unscathed from the encounters. I appreciate the warning but, quite frankly, I'm really not overly concerned." He gave her a devilish wink, then released her hand. "Can I ask you a personal question, Desirée?" The mirth faded from his eyes.

She knew full well what it was he wanted to know. Her body tensed beneath the silk sheath, but she demurred with a nod.

"Do you subscribe to the same philosophies as your mother and grandmother?"

There was a long pause. Once again he noticed an ever-so-slight lift of her chin before she replied, "Do you usually inquire as to a lady's religious persuasion prior to making a wine selection?"

He smiled. She had every right to refuse to satisfy his morbid curiosity. In truth, that was what had prompted his improper probe. He, like all the other buffoons in the room, wanted to pry into her personal life. It was a gross invasion of privacy. "Not generally and I withdraw the question," he said, picking up the wine list once more.

"Spoken like a true lawyer." Her heartbeat returned to a normal rhythm as she relaxed her guard a bit.

Their waiter approached and, to Jacob's surprise, the fellow greeted Desirée warmly in lyrical Italian. After placing their drink order, Jacob shot her a quizzical look.

"There are some in town who don't look upon me as an oddity," she offered. "Mr. Avonni is very kind to me whenever I come in here." She plucked a bread stick from the basket and nibbled at the crusty edges. "These are tasty. Try one."

He acted on her recommendation, saving his next remark until after Mr. Avonni had served the wine and placed the food menu at his elbow. "I'm sure it must have been difficult growing up with the stigma of having a witch for a mother. I mean, kids are always claiming that their mothers are certifiable witches but it's generally just a flip expression. In your case it was actually true."

She smiled and sipped the wine. It tasted strange to her—fruity and rather strong. It was also strange to have someone broach the subject of her background and not act as though they were conversing with an alien from some far and forbidden planet.

Jacob misinterpreted her silence. He'd done it again—made mention of something that was none of his affair. "If you'd prefer to talk about something else—"

"In this instance, I don't mind," she assured him, sampling the wine again. "As a matter of fact, I was just thinking that no one has ever really discussed with me the pros and cons of having been the daughter of the town witch."

"What was it like?" He whiffed the wine, then savored its ambrosia as it flowed past his discerning palate.

"Lonely," she summed up in a word. "When I was very young I didn't understand why I was being shunned. If I was lucky enough to find a new playmate, once their parents learned who my mother was they instantly manufactured polite excuses as to why Sally or Sue couldn't come out to play with me. Mostly they'd say that Sally or Sue were napping. It could be nine in the morning or six in the evening and the story was the same—'sorry, dear, Sally or Sue is taking her nap.' After a while I got weary of making trip after trip to my newfound friends' houses, only to be disappointed again and again. Given enough rejection, even a six-year-old can take a hint."

Jacob replenished her half-empty wineglass. "And they say that kids can be cruel," he mumbled more to himself than to her.

"Oh, but they can be, Jacob. By the time I was a teenager, I didn't try to make friends anymore. My schoolmates adopted the same attitudes as their parents. If anything, their bigotry was even more intense. They were constantly making snide comments about me, my mother, and my grandmother. One of the worst memories of my life is a high-school English class. We were studying Macbeth. I'm sure you recall the opening scene with the three witches huddled around the black cauldron and prophesying. What I'm sure you can't imagine is the cruelty of my classmates, who made mocking comparisons to my family. Fortunately it was my senior year and I was graduating in a month. Otherwise, I swear I would have quit school then and there." She washed down the lump in her throat with a swig of the wine. Her eyes glimmered in the candlelight as she flicked back the hair from her face. "Would you like to hear something hilarious?"

"Sure." He studied her candlelit features, thinking that she looked rather unique and fragile—like an ephemeral snowflake momentarily framed in flickering amber light.

Desirée was beginning to feel wonderfully relaxed. It didn't bother her anymore if everyone in the restaurant was eavesdropping. She propped her elbow on the table and her chin on the back of her hand, and drank in Jacob's handsome face as she took him into her confidence. "Some of those ex-classmates of mine are the very same hypocrites who come into my shop to buy magic roots and potions in the hopes of curing everything that ails them. Baldness to bunions, sexual problems to money worries, they come to me—the local witch doctor—for help. Of course, these are the same fine, upstanding folk who won't deign to give me the time of day when they pass me on the street. Ironic, isn't it?"

"I'm not so sure that Marbleheaders are any bigger hypocrites than the rest of us," Jacob returned. "At least you knew from a very young age that the potential exists within people to be calloused toward those who don't conform. Through the years I've defended clients who were completely unprepared for the consequences of nonconformity. One or two individuals I represented were former public heroes who had fallen from grace because of unpopular ideologies they'd supported. They were prepared to submit to prison terms because of their convictions, but they were totally shattered by the personal attacks waged against them in the press and by demonstrators. I think it's a much harder proposition to adapt to ostracism when it happens out of the blue and one has no prior experience by which to gauge a response."

She was truly in awe of his eloquence. She wasn't sure she agreed with all he'd said but she certainly loved the way he'd said it. "So what you're implying, in essence, is that you think I take myself too seriously." She slanted him a cool look over the rim of her wineglass as she drained it.

He would not be baited. "What I'm saying is that you take the opinion of others too seriously," he clarified. "Shady ladies aren't supposed to give a damn what people think."

God! He was clever. And handsome. And exciting. And how fortunate she was to have him for an escort. And even luckier still that he could not read her mind. For then he would know—

"I'm hungry. How about you?" He picked up the menu at his elbow and studied it.

Feeling lightheaded from the wine, she was tempted to purr, *Yes, Jacob, but only for you*. Instead she gave an indifferent shrug of her shoulders, replying, "A little."

"Since you dine here occasionally you must know which entrées are the best. What do you recommend?"

I recommend that we go home and make endless love. "Veal," she blurted, at which he raised his brows and gave her a bemused look. "I mean, if you like veal, the piccata is excellent." She hid her lascivious thoughts behind a benign smile.

"That sounds good to me." He closed the menu, signaled Mr. Avonni and apprised him of their selection. There was an awkward lull in the conversation as he fiddled with his wineglass and she twiddled with the scarab pendant she wore.

The oval object caught his eye. "I presume that your moon charm is safely tucked away." He followed up the deduction with one of his engaging winks.

She touched the space at the point her breasts divided.

He nodded and smiled. "Considering the reaction of our fellow patrons, that was probably a wise decision. I like the scarab necklace. It's becoming on you."

Having received very few compliments from members of the opposite sex, she grew uncomfortable beneath his attentive scrutiny. "Thank you," she said, looking off.

"You're welcome," he responded, finding her shyness refreshing. Most women he knew basked in the glory of eliciting compliments from men. "I know a little more about scarab stones than I did about moon charms," he went on, regaining her attention.

Her interest piqued, she examined the greenish gold stone. "I'm unfamiliar with its origins," she admitted.

"The gem takes its name and oval shape from the scarabaeid beetle. Ancient Egyptians considered them to be sacred."

"Then the stone has something in common with my Mew-Sinh," she mused aloud, letting go of the scarab pendant. It settled between her breasts.

Jacob couldn't help but notice the outline of her breasts beneath the soft silk. It was evident to him that Desirée was not wearing a bra. It was also obvious to him that she was either chilled or stimulated. He quickly discounted the latter hypothesis since scarabaeid beetles could hardly be considered stimulating—not even in the loose context of dinner chat.

He dragged his gaze back to her candlelit face, flipping on the playback tape in his brain and keying in on Desirée's last statement. She'd made reference to the scarab and her crazy cat having something in common, he recalled. Yeah, that was it. "What could the two possibly have in common?" he asked, hoping to goodness that there had not been a five-minute interval between her remark and his reply.

"The Birman breed is also considered to be sacred," she explained, seemingly unaware of his having mentally taken her bust measurement in the time between the exchange.

"Is that so?" he said, twisting a bit in his chair and trying his damndest to keep his mind on the subject and his eyes off the place where the pendant lay nestled.

"I promised to tell you the legend surrounding the Birman breed that first morning when you were so intrigued with Mew-Sinh," she reminded him.

"Yes, I recall." He reached for his wineglass, casting her an indulgent grin and prompting, "So, what is the story of Mew-Sinh's ancestry?"

She seemed pleased by the invitation to recount it. "The legend originated in Burma," she began, pausing only long enough to take an appreciative whiff of the dishes Mr. Avonni was passing beneath her nose and bestow a smile of approval upon him as he set them down. "Long before the time of Buddha, the Khmer people built beautiful temples in remote mountain retreats. One of these, the Temple of Lao-Tsun, honored the god Song-Hyo and the goddess

Tsun-Kyan-Kse. Priests and monks dedicated their lives to worshiping the goddess symbolized by a golden statue with sapphire eyes.''

He twirled some fettuccine Alfredo on his fork, listening attentively as he ingested the creamy pasta.

She continued weaving the story in between taking dainty bites. ''One hundred pure white cats lived with the priests. It was believed that after death, a priest returned to the temple as one of the white cats. These cats, therefore, were honored and beloved guests. One of the cats, Sinh, was the devoted companion of a very old priest, Mun-Ha, whose golden beard was said to have been braided by the god Song-Hyo himself.''

''So your cat is named for the one in the legend,'' he interrupted, tasting the veal piccata.

She nodded.

The thinly sliced veal just about melted in his mouth. ''Mmmm, really good,'' was his enthusiastic endorsement.

''I'm glad you're not disappointed.'' She drank from her wineglass and then continued recounting the myth. ''One night when Mun-Ha was praying before the golden goddess, Thai raiders attacked the temple and the old priest was killed. Immediately Sinh leaped upon the body of his master, faced the statue, gazed into the sapphire eyes, and silently appealed to the goddess who governed the transmutation of souls. As the priest's soul entered Sinh the white hair of the cat's body became golden like the old priest's beard and its eyes became sapphire-blue like those of the goddess. Sinh's face, tail and legs turned brown like the earth except where the feet rested on the slain priest. There they remained white, denoting purity," she embellished for his benefit.

"And that is how the Birman got its distinctive markings," he surmised.

"Yes, as legend would have it, that is the reason why its four paws are white and its fur is gold tipped," she confirmed, going on with the tale. "Sinh's transformation inspired the other priests to drive the raiders away. Seven days later, Sinh died and carried the soul of Mun-Ha into paradise. The next morning all the other white temple cats had undergone the same transformation as Sinh. Since then, the priests have fiercely guarded their golden cats, believing the transformation of Sinh to have been a divine sign that the animals do, in fact, have custody of the souls of priests. The legend ends with a maxim: woe to he who brings the end of one of these marvelous beasts," she recited. "For even if he didn't mean to, the harm doer will surely suffer the most cruel torments until the soul he has upset has been appeased."

Remembering the murderous thoughts he'd entertained about Mew-Sinh upon awakening to find himself in the company of a sneaky feline rather than a fetching female, Jacob swallowed the last of the veal in a hard gulp. "I will be careful not to cramp Mew-Sinh's style or step on his tail," he said, half in jest and half in seriousness.

"Her tail," she corrected him. "Mew-Sinh has a mild and loving nature. She would never wish you to suffer the terrible fate of the legend's warning." Being more hyper than hungry, Desirée left much of her dinner untouched. She dabbed her lips with the napkin, and then cast him a faint smile. "The dinner was very nice, Jacob. It was kind of you to ask me out for the evening."

"Surely you're not ready to end it so soon? It's early yet. Wouldn't you like to have dessert?"

She glanced around the room, noting the disapproving faces that immediately turned away at direct eye contact with her. She could not in good conscience subject Jacob to the circuslike atmosphere any longer. "I would, but I'd prefer to have it in the privacy of my own home. We could put on the kettle, and there's a cherry cheesecake in the fridge I made to go with last night's dinner. Of course, if you're not fond of cheesecake, we can stay and you could order something more to your liking," she hastened to add.

He was sensitive to her discomfort. Actually he was impressed by the poise she'd exhibited thus far in the high-pressure situation. In fact, he mused, the petite Miss Warren had more grit than the heavyweight contender he'd represented a few years back in a defamation suit. One of Jacob's most vivid recollections was of the giant fighter breaking down on the witness stand during a grueling and especially vicious cross-examination by the opposing attorney. If nothing else, the incident had taught Jacob not to equate outer appearances with inner strength. Or, at least, he liked to think it had. In any case, he certainly understood Miss Warren's wish to forego the unpleasantness of any further mingling with her neighbors. Cheesecake was not a particular favorite of his, but after all the trouble she'd undergone on his account, he would rather have eaten dirt than let her know.

"Cheesecake at your place, it is then," he seconded the suggestion. "We can leave anytime you're ready."

"Immediately would be good for me." She feared she was beginning to sound like the recluse that she was.

"It'll just be a minute," he assured her, signaling Mr. Avonni to bring the check.

Mustering a false bravura, she ignored the nudges and whispers the mere act of their imminent departure caused. Her face expressionless and her head high, she gathered her cloak from off the back of her chair and arranged it around her shoulders.

Jacob left an extra generous gratuity for Mr. Avonni, and then scrawled his distinctive signature on the appropriate line of the charge slip.

"Grazie, grazie!" Mr. Avonni thanked Jacob profusely, and offered a gentlemanly assist to Desirée. "You come again."

Jacob gave the fellow a noncommittal smile and assumed a bodyguard-like posture as he escorted his landlady from the dining room.

The hostess pretended to be engrossed in the reservation list as they passed her. Unlike Mr. Avonni, she had no intention of extending an open invitation to them.

At the restaurant door, Jacob suddenly drew up, turned and retraced his steps to the dining-room

archway where the hostess stood behind a podiumlike
structure. He dawdled over the complimentary bowl
of mints perched atop her walnut redan until she had
no choice but to acknowledge his hovering presence.
"The food and service were excellent." His praise of
Mr. Avonni was sincere; his smile, phony as hell. "So
good, in fact, we may very well decide to make this a
weekly outing."

"Oh, ah, well," she sputtered, "we're pleased that
you're pleased. Of course, we'd be delighted to have
you come again." Her blanched face looked as though
she was anything but pleased and delighted.

"Somehow I knew you would be," he needled.
"Have a good night," he bid her, proceeding into the
foyer and opening the door for Desirée.

Once they were outside on the sidewalk, Desirée
could not contain herself any longer. "You're an agi-
tator, Jacob," she giggled. "You know perfectly well
that she'll have nightmares about the restaurant becoming a favorite haunt of the town witch."

"She deserved it. The woman's more of a witch
than you ever were."

Blustery and cold as it was on the streets of Marblehead, Desirée felt warm and protected in his chiv-
alrous company. She pulled the ermine-trimmed hood
of her cloak lower over her face in the pretext of
shielding herself from the wind. Actually, she did so
because she dared not expose the telltale glow of utter
enchantment that she feared must surely be visible.

MACKEY AND MEW-SINH were ensconced in the kitchen—Mew-Sinh lapping up cream from her bowl and Mackey licking the cherry glaze from his fingers—when the slam of the downstairs shop door warned the pair of Desirée's return. Mackey hastily tried to smooth the finger furrows he had made in the cheesecake and quickly return it to the fridge before she came upstairs. Then he dashed to collect the cat's bowl, dumping the incriminating cream down the drain and hurrying to replace the empty dish on the mat. Mew-Sinh was highly miffed at having been deprived of the treat. Her whining and winding in between Alistair's legs caused him to trip and bump his noggin on one of the hanging clay pots.

The bumbling angel put a hand to the smarting lump above his brow and a red-stained finger to his lips, motioning Mew-Sinh to keep quiet. "Damn your nine souls." He grimaced and steadied the swaying pot. "When will you get it through that thick skull of yours that I can't have the little lady thinking there's gremlins lurking about? Act natural now, eh?"

With a none-too-limber hoist, he perched himself atop the counter—bracing his back against the wall and crossing his stretched-out legs at the ankles. Since Mackey could maneuver as well as Mew-Sinh in the dark, he hadn't bothered with the lights. At Desirée's flicking on of the wall switch the kitchen was suffused in bright light. But it wasn't the harsh glare that caused Alistair to blink; it was the shock of seeing Malone with the sheila.

"I'll put on the kettle," she was saying, untying her cloak and throwing it haphazardly onto the counter. It landed atop Mackey's head. He flung it off, rubbing a hand beneath his nose where the fur had tickled.

"The cheesecake is in the refrigerator. Would you mind getting it out?" She turned on the burner beneath the copper pot, came to where Alistair was seated, and reached for the tea canister. He scrambled to hug his knees to his chest, so as not to impair her reach. It was then that he felt something pop in his back. Probably his sacroiliac, he guessed.

As Desirée slid the canister across the counter, she thought of the violet petals and glanced toward the cupboard.

Mackey followed her gaze and surmised her thoughts.

Too risky, she decided, electing to brew unadulterated orange pekoe on this occasion.

Jacob retrieved the cheesecake from the refrigerator, noticing but not commenting on the deep grooves in the top and sides of it. He assumed that Miss Warren was prone to dipping into her baked goods. A person could have worse habits, he thought. For instance, he had an aunt who was prone to dipping into the sauce from time to time. "What else can I do for you?" he offered.

The wall phone extension jangled. Desirée reached around, pulling the long extension cord across the counter and propping the receiver between an ear and a shoulder. At the same time she added two spoonfuls of the tea to the simmering water.

Neither Jacob nor his guardian angel paid much attention to the call until they heard his name mentioned.

"Yes, Mr. Malone is registered here. May I ask who's calling?" She looked over at Jacob as she repeated, "Adeline Van Cleve. Just a minute, please, and I'll see if he's in."

Jacob grinned at her tactful screening of his call. He came to where she stood and removed the receiver from the crook of her shoulder. "Hi, Addie. What's up?"

Both Mackey and Desirée listened in on his conversation—Mackey bending forward and Desirée leaning ever-so-slightly backward.

"You can handle it without me, Addie," Malone was insisting. "The man is merely coming into the office to discuss our representing the case. You don't even know yet whether or not he'll want to retain us. Umm-hmm." He took the cup Desirée held out to him and mouthed a thank-you. "Yeah, Addie, I'm acquainted with the precedent Marvin Mitchelson set. Uh-huh. No, it's not every day a national talk-show host gets slapped with a palimony suit. I know. I know, Addie! I've caught his show a time or two myself. Yes, I'm sure he can be every bit as intimidating in person as he is on the tube. You just have to be more assertive than him." Jacob expelled a sigh. "Can't do it, Addie," he said flatly. "Jeez, I haven't been gone

more than a few days and I only just called you this
morning with the number and already you're—"

Jacob switched the receiver to the other ear, sighing again as he did. "Umm-hmm. Yeah, I'm sure it's
a real bitch having to deal with all the hassles by your
lonesome. No, I'm not *trying* to be sarcastic," he said
with an amused grin. "You're always under stress,
Addie. You function best that way. You'll do fine," he
encouraged her. "No, nothing you can say will change
my mind. I'm not returning to Boston for an hour's
consultation with a prospective client. Just remember
to hard-sell yourself and soft-pedal our fee." He
feigned a wounded tone. "That remark is beneath
you, Addie. *Up yours* is not a remark a proper Vassar
graduate makes." He held the phone out from his ear,
untangled the cord and passed the receiver to Desirée
to hang up.

"Did you get disconnected?" she asked innocently.

"Intentionally, I'm sure." He pictured Addie
storming around the office, slamming file drawers and
vowing to unload her no-account partner upon his return to Boston. Even long-distance, he could rile her.
The thought amused him.

"The call sounded important." Desirée tried to act
nonchalant, though she was beside herself to know
how important the lady caller was to Jacob.

Mackey had figured out the woman's identity and
already knew what role the other sheila played in Malone's life.

Desirée collected a couple of plates and forks and carried them along with her teacup to the table. She gestured for Jacob to come sit down.

"Addie is my law partner," he explained as he settled in a chair. "I'm still pretty full. Just a small piece of cheesecake for me, please."

She nodded, cutting and serving him a narrow wedge. "Oh, I see," she said, heartened to hear that the woman on the phone was not a serious rival for his affection.

"Well, actually, she's more than just a partner," he elaborated, sipping the tea and setting it aside. He preferred coffee to tea. If he had to drink the bland stuff, he liked it better over ice.

"Oh," she repeated herself, her heart sinking at the unexpected complication. Her emotions were peaking and dipping like a roller coaster.

"We go back a long way, Addie and I. She's really a very special person." He rambled on about Addie as an excuse to delay having to eat the cheesecake.

Desirée did not reveal the deep effect his words were having on her. "I'm sure she must be," was all she replied.

Alistair could see and hear what Jacob could not—the sag of her small shoulders and the disappointment in her voice. The little lady was shaken by the misconceptions he was presenting.

"Addie is probably the smartest woman I've ever known. You wouldn't believe some of the legal angles she comes up with. I'm shrewd but she's brilliant. There's a difference between the two, but most people

don't recognize it," he went on, spreading the cheesecake around the plate with his fork so it appeared as
though a part of the dessert had been eaten. "I think
well on my feet because I read people easier than I do
legal texts. Addie, on the other hand, is much better
at the small print than she is at analyzing jurors and
witnesses."

"Is she pretty?" The question spilled from her before she could stop herself. A part of her wished to re-
tract it; a part of her had to know.

Since he thought of Addie more in the vein of a
partner than a female, he didn't have an immediate or
firm reply. He mulled it over as he stood and carried
his plate and cup to the sink. "Ask a dozen different
men their definition of pretty and you'll get as many
opinions. Yeah, I suppose if I were to classify Addie
on my own personal standards, I'd have to say she was
pretty. Not stunning, like some women, but striking in
an understated sort of way."

She had to ask! So far they'd established that his
partner was both brilliant and striking looking. What
would be revealed next? Wonder Woman probably
had a saintly disposition, too!

"Addie may look like an angel but she can be a
royal pain sometimes." Jacob addressed Desirée's
unspoken thought. "I can almost assure you that right
about now she's throwing a grand-scale temper fit and
hoping some vile fate will befall me." He found the
prospect funny.

Desirée didn't. "Oh, surely not."

"I might be exaggerating a little," he admitted. "She's hot, though."

"What did you do to make her so angry?"

"It's what I didn't do. She wanted me to come back to Boston and be on hand for a meeting with a prospective client."

"It doesn't seem such an unreasonable request. You are partners, after all." Desirée was not rationalizing Addie's position as much as she was trying to discover the reason behind his refusal to return.

Jacob provided some insight, but not nearly as much as she would have liked. "Addie only thinks she needs assistance. I have confidence in her ability to handle the situation, even if she doesn't. I came to Marblehead because I needed time to myself, time to sort out my thoughts. I don't know if I'm only temporarily or permanently burned out, but at the moment, the only aspect of my profession toward which I feel any allegiance is my partner. But not even she is going to lure me back to Boston or private practice until I'm absolutely positive it's what I want."

Desirée wondered if he had deliberately chosen not to address the personal side of his relationship with Miss Van Cleve. Was she or was she not a rival to be reckoned with? "And what if you should decide that law *has* lost its meaning for you?" she pressed.

His face grew sober. "I don't know," he answered simply. "Maybe I'll commission Nathan Pritchard to build me a customized sailboat and set out on a sea odyssey." The notion really did hold a certain appeal for him.

Her soft laugh jolted him back to his senses.

"I guess everyone experiences flights into fantasy now and then." He shrugged and checked the time.

Oh, yes, my dear Jacob. If only you knew. "Yes, I suspect it's quite common." she answered him.

"It's getting late. I think I'll turn in," he said more to himself than to her.

She stood and approached him, extending her hand. "Thank you again for a very pleasant evening."

He was amazed at how delicate her hand felt within his own. Her fragility was even more pronounced when measured against his strength. Her touch felt nice. "The pleasure was all mine." The accuracy of the cliché struck him. It had been one of the most enjoyable evenings he'd spent in a very long time.

She gazed directly into his eyes and for a second or two—in the space of a heartbeat—he felt a tug on his subconscious, felt the graze of the moon maiden's flesh against his.

Then he realized the sensation was due merely to the landlady slipping her hand from his.

"Sleep well, Jacob," she bid him.

He nodded vaguely, and, with an easy stride, left her for his dreams.

Only after he was out of hearing range did she expel the sigh she'd been smothering the long night. When Mew-Sinh rubbed against her leg, she reached down and lifted the big cat into her arms. "Oh, Mew-Sinh," she cooed, cuddling the furry pet under her chin, "I'm not sure whether we're creating heaven or havoc with our tampering. He is everything I've ever wished for, but…'' Her words trailed off as she gazed wistfully beyond the kitchen window at the winter moon. ''It is written that it is wrong to bind another's heart against its will. Is Jacob meant for me or for another? I only wished to influence, not to interfere with, his destiny. Is this Addie person more important to him than he admits to himself or others?'' she wondered aloud.

Mew-Sinh purred and lovingly nuzzled her mistress's neck.

''The starlight vision we mortals seek, is it true or false, Mew-Sinh?'' Desirée murmured sleepily. ''Perhaps it is nothing more than the distorted reflection of our own selfish desires.'' With that, she dismissed the moon and turned off the light. Then she, too, retired to her bedroom for the night.

Only Alistair Mackey was left to contemplate the bits and pieces of the puzzle. Though he perhaps had a broader view of what was occurring between the little lady and his charge than they did, even he, with all of his vast worldly experience and keen instinct could not figure out how to deal with the intricacies of the situation. He needed the Fisherman's wise counsel.

He swung his legs from off the counter and carefully eased himself to the floor. His back was killing him. His head hurt. He had the sniffles and the fever. And he was miserably homesick for Heaven.

Mackey made ready to catch the next cosmos-bound shuttle. It was time to make his initial report to the Fisherman. Oh, how bloody divine it would be to feel the blessed warmth of home again.

CHAPTER SEVEN

ONLY AFTER CATCHING up on his sleep, having a good sweat in the solar sauna and doing a stint in the crystal clear Stream of Consciousness, did Mackey get around to making his preliminary report to the Fisherman.

As the guardian angel second-grade related the facts and offered his personal view of the earthly situation, his superior sat quietly listening.

"I'm convinced the little lady means Malone no harm," Alistair concluded. "She has a good heart."

"That may be, Alistair, but there is the matter of her methods." The Fisherman tapped a forefinger against his temple, as was his custom when he was engaged in deep thought.

"She only dabbles a bit." Alistair tried to make Desirée's offense sound insignificant.

"It is the act itself, not the degree to which she practices it, that is the problem."

The reluctant angel shifted his weight, giving an exaggerated wince as he rubbed his lower back. "If it's all the same to you, could I sit down while we continue our talk? Me back isn't quite right yet." He made his voice sound a touch strained for dramatic effect.

"Of course." The Fisherman waved aside protocol, gesturing for his subordinate to take a chair.

"Ahhh, that's much better. Where were we now?" Alistair feigned forgetfulness.

The Fisherman was not fooled. "We were discussing the dubious actions of your charge's landlady, I believe."

A timely sneeze allowed Mackey to stall a little longer. Unthinkingly he used the tail of his tunic to stay the spread of germs. "I wouldn't exactly phrase it the same way," he said, sniffing. "Miss Warren's a bit eccentric, is all." Again he tried to downplay the seriousness of her unacceptable behavior.

The Fisherman offered Alistair the tissue box with an indulgent smile. "You've obviously grown very fond of this woman during your short stay on Earth."

Mackey plucked a few tissues from the box and haphazardly swiped at the spittle stain on his tunic. "The lady puts me in mind of me sweet Flo." This time, he sighed wistfully, for sentimental effect. "'Course, I don't think Miss Warren's prone to blowin' the froth off a cup like me Flo was apt t'do on occasion," he added by way of an aside. "She's mild natured—a characteristic uncommon of red-haired sheilas. Me one and only had a temperament to match her flame hair—a regular spitfire, she was." Mackey got momentarily sidetracked by the memories of his earthy wife. "We was good together, me and Flo. 'Course we had our spats. Usually they was over me spending so much time in the Outback. Couldn't stand to be without me, she couldn't. That's probably the reason for her remarrying so soon after me passin'. Out of her mind with grief, she must've been.''

The Fisherman was accustomed to hearing such rationalizations. Alistair had not been an ideal husband, nor Flo a devoted wife. They had not been good together. He had wandered too often and she indulged too much. But the Fisherman did not correct him. Mackey would come to accept the true facts in good time. It was part of the heavenly process.

"Tell me more of Miss Warren." He gently guided the conversation back around to the soul that concerned him most at present.

Alistair forgot Flo and concentrated on fudging his report. He wanted it to sound more favorable than damaging to the little lady. "She's a shy thing but that's only because she's unsure of herself. That's the reason for her dabbling in the Craft, don't you see?''

"Not really, but perhaps it will become clear as you share your insightful impressions with me," the Fisherman prompted.

"Ahhh, right. Well, here goes. I don't think the sheila is confident in her own charms, so she borrows some from the witchcraft manual. She thinks that by chanting the right words, spiking his drink with the right powder, and putting scraps of silk tied in thread beneath his pillow, he'll fall under a spell and in love with her. It's nonsense and almost sad, because she trusts the magic to do what she doesn't trust herself to.''

"An interesting observation," the Fisherman interjected.

Mackey forged ahead with his plea on Miss Warren's behalf. "Witchcraft isn't necessarily a bad thing, Your Eminence. It's based on the belief that all creatures are interdependent and therefore mutually responsible to one another. An act that harms anyone harms everyone." He'd done a little borrowing himself and was now quoting from the late-night reading material he'd lifted from Miss Warren's private library.

The Fisherman was truly impressed. "You've apparently been researching the subject."

"A trick I learned from me years in the Outback. The more a hunter learns about his quarry, the better he can track him. And, in me time down under, I was the best tracker around," he bragged.

The Fisherman wondered if Mackey would ever learn the lesson of humility. "So is it your educated opinion that there is no danger in the practice of witchcraft?" he tested.

"I don't think it's my place to judge the right or wrong of it. I'll leave that to a higher mate. As for the danger, well, I suppose any belief can be dangerous in excess. Look at the Crusades, for instance. Or the Inquisition. Or—"

"You make your point, Alistair," the Fisherman conceded, much surprised by his underling's philosophical spouting. It was evident to him that the junior angel was taking his duties more seriously these days. Finally he seemed to be grasping the importance of not forming hasty opinions and/or acting upon them impulsively. Obviously Mackey's latest assignment had been a catalyst for spiritual growth. The Fisherman was greatly heartened by the promising change he witnessed in Alistair.

"To tell you the truth, Your Eminence, I'm not sure whether Miss Warren goes through the ceremonial motions because she's a devoted follower or because she's a hopeless romantic."

"The latest computer readings on your charge still indicate that he is undergoing a personal conflict of major proportion, the cause of which is unclear to us. If it is not the woman who is the source of his inner turmoil, what, then, could be the cause?"

Mackey wanted to leave himself margin for error. There always existed the remote possibility that his instincts were off. He didn't think it likely, but he wanted to cover his angelic butt in any case. "I'm not entirely discounting the bewitching tricks the little lady is using on him. She could be playing with his psyche. I seen such as that during me time in the Outback. The Aborigines was big on mind power. They could send messages through the bush with nary a drumbeat being heard." Mackey enjoyed having the advantage over his superior for once. His brushes with supernatural phenomena on Earth lent a certain credibility to his evaluation. "It's me bush experience that makes me think there's more at work inside Malone than flower petals and suggestion."

The Fisherman had difficulty following his subordinate's logic. "Are you saying, then, that he's not being influenced?"

"I'm saying if he is being coerced, it's his own discontent that's making him open to suggestion."

After eons of hearing about the same kind of mortal distress, the Fisherman was all too familiar with the symptom Mackey described. "Another lost soul searching for meaning in his life," he concluded, sighing deeply.

"Me humble opinion exactly. Sometimes it gets to be a blood—" he caught himself in the nick of time "—a blasted nuisance keeping tabs on all these lost lambs of yours, Fisherman. Maybe there's something to the rhyme about leaving 'em alone and letting 'em come home, a' wagging their wayward tails behind 'em." Alistair thought the notion clever. It only took a look from the Fisherman for him to realize that his superior did not.

"Upon what do you base your *humble* opinion?" The Fisherman would not stray from the topic of Jacob Malone's distress.

Mackey decided to tell all. "Well, he's brooding about his life's work, for one thing. He takes no satisfaction from it anymore. Just the other night he was telling the little lady that he wasn't sure whether or not he wanted to pursue his trade. But I'm thinking his discontent goes a lot deeper. I believe it's his life's purpose that he's questioning. He's having a hard time of it because what he used to think was important

HARLEQUIN DELIVERS FIRST-CLASS ROMANCE— DIRECT TO YOUR DOOR

Mail the Heart sticker on the postpaid order card today and you'll receive:

—4 new Harlequin Superromance® novels—FREE
—a lovely bracelet watch—FREE
—and a surprise mystery bonus—FREE

But that's not all. You'll also get:

Money-Saving Home Delivery

When you subscribe to Harlequin Reader Service, the excitement, romance and faraway adventures of these novels can be yours for previewing in the convenience of your own home at less than cover prices. Every month we'll deliver 4 new books right to your door. If you decide to keep them, they'll be yours for only $2.74* each. That's 21¢ less than the cover price plus only 49¢ postage and handling for the entire shipment! There is no obligation to buy—you can cancel Reader Service privileges at any time by writing "cancel" on your statement or returning a shipment of books to us at our expense.

Special Extras—FREE

Because our home subscribers are our most valued readers, we'll also be sending you additional free gifts from time to time in our monthly book shipments, as a token of our appreciation.

OPEN YOUR MAILBOX TO A WORLD OF LOVE AND ROMANCE EACH MONTH. JUST COMPLETE, DETACH AND MAIL YOUR FREE OFFER CARD TODAY!

*Terms and prices subject to change without notice.

You'll love your elegant bracelet watch— this classic LCD quartz watch is a perfect expression of your style and good taste—and it's yours free as an added thanks for giving our Reader Service a try!

Remember! To receive your free books, bracelet watch and mystery gift, return the postpaid card below. But don't delay!

DETACH AND MAIL CARD TODAY.

If offer card has been removed, write to: Harlequin Reader Service,
P.O. Box 609, Fort Erie, Ontario L2A 5X3

**Business
Reply Mail**

No Postage Stamp
Necessary if Mailed
in Canada

Postage will be paid by

Harlequin Reader Service
P.O. Box 609
Fort Erie, Ontario
L2A 9Z9

Canada Post
Postes Canada
125

MAIL THE POSTPAID CARD TODAY!

don't seem so anymore and he keeps confusing smart choices with easy ones."

"Then it is your responsibility to help him make the right choices. You must guide him toward the path that will eventually lead him here," was the firm instruction.

"That's easier said than done, Your Eminence. Malone's a tough case. He's cynical. He's greedy. And he's full of himself."

"Since these are some of the very same traits that you yourself exhibited on Earth, I can only defer to your expert judgment, and trust in your resourcefulness. Often it is by virtue of our own mortal failings that we receive the insight and strength to help our fellow man." The Fisherman smiled warmly. "Your task may be difficult, but as you so wisely stated, the easy ways do not necessarily challenge us or bring about satisfaction. Trust in that keen instinct of yours, Alistair," he counseled. "It will show you the way to deliver Malone out from the dark of disillusionment and into the light."

Mackey knew he'd been handed his traveling papers once more. He stood and bowed his head respectfully. "I'll do me best." He refrained from adding his personal view, which was that the "witch" the Fisherman seemed so concerned about might prove to be Jacob Malone's salvation. Mackey was sure she was a *good* influence, not a bad one. But saying so would undoubtedly be pushing his luck.

"That's all we ask of you." The Fisherman placed a hand on the guardian angel's bent head. "Bless you and your mission. And never forget, Alistair, to also trust in the higher power who gave you the gift of intuition.''

Mackey acknowledged the blessing with a meek nod of his head and then started to withdraw.

"Be sure to remember your travel rations this trip," the Fisherman reminded.

"Yes, Your Eminence."

"And have the Supply Master issue you warmer apparel for the return journey."

"I'll do that, Your Eminence." Mackey was almost to the double doors.

"Oh, and Alistair," the Fisherman called after him.

The subordinate turned to face his superior.

"Stop bullying the lady's cat. Such behavior is unbecoming of a future first-class angel."

"I'll behave meself. I promise, I will. The puss and me, we'll be mates. G'day, Your Eminence."

The Fisherman smiled to himself and shook his head as Mackey donned his scruffy bushman's hat and waltzed out the door.

CHAPTER EIGHT

WHILE MACKEY WAS on holiday in Heaven, it was life as usual in Marblehead. Desirée sold her wares by day and dabbled in witchcraft at night; Jacob divided his time between recreation and reflection.

The days came and passed uneventfully, and Jacob was surprised to discover that he very much liked the easy pace of the quaint New England borough. He had thought he would miss the culture of Boston and the adrenaline rush of big cases for big bucks. But oddly enough, he wasn't all that anxious to get back to Boston or his practice. He rather liked the rustic solitude of Marblehead. And he loved his time on the sea with the salt spray in his face, the gushing water against the bow and the flapping of sails against the wind. Out there it was only him, the ship, the wind, the water, the horizon and the force that governed it all. Out there, Jacob felt closer to the omnipotent force than at any other time.

Jacob had also begun to notice and appreciate the subtle attributes of his somewhat unorthodox landlady. It gradually came to his attention that she, like the town, possessed a certain quiet charm. She did not impose herself upon a person; she just naturally grew on one after a while. She was well-read, quick-witted, gentle mannered and kind-hearted. What was more, in recent days he'd started to think of her as being more attractive than he'd originally thought. Again she did not possess the kind of beauty that immediately struck a man. Rather she exuded an innate sensuality that seeped into the male consciousness on a subliminal level. Once seated in the mind, the suggestion of passion lingering just below the surface became not only intriguing, but indelible.

These random thoughts sifted in and out of his head as he, for lack of anything better to do one lazy Saturday afternoon, browsed in her shop. He'd been wanting to explore the curious realm over which she reigned from nine to seven, six days a week. It seemed to him that Desirée was in her element when she went below to peddle her magic to the tourists. When she assumed the role of proprietress, a noticeable transformation took place. Among her jars of herbs, bottles of elixirs and assortment of amulets, Desirée took on an air of mystery and mastery. The lady most definitely knew her craft.

"Are you appropriately shocked?" she finally asked him.

"No, but I'm getting the distinct impression that you expect me to be," he replied, strolling over to a table tucked into a far corner of the store and running his fingertips over a thick leather volume resting on top of it.

Her smile was strained. "Force of habit, I suppose."

"What's this?" He opened the old book and began flipping through the yellowed pages.

She brushed off its importance with a shrug. "My mother collected many books on the Craft. I merely display that particular old volume in the shop because it looks authentic and adds a nice touch for the tourists," she fibbed.

"It does look authentic, all right," he agreed, his eyes narrowing as they scanned the florid script. His Latin was rusty but he could make out a word here and there—enough to intrigue him. "This is interesting reading material. It appears as though some sort of ancient myth has been written down." He read aloud from the book. "In this word...no, that's wrong." He backed up. "In this world," he corrected himself, "the Goddess is seen in the moon, in the light that shines in the darkness."

"The rain bringer, mover of tides, Mistress of mysteries," she recited from memory, at which he turned to cast her an appraising look. "I know it by heart," she said in response to his unspoken question. "Other children heard nursery rhymes at bedtime. I was told the myths."

"Latin was never my best subject. Please, go on." He pulled out a stool from behind the counter, perched himself on it and sat eagerly, awaiting a full recitation.

"A customer could come in," she said hesitantly.

"No problem. I'm flexible," he insisted.

She knew from his expression that he was determined to have his way. Grinning, she gave in. "And as the moon waxes and wanes, and walks three nights of its cycle in darkness, so, it is said, the Goddess once spent three nights with the Lord of Shadows in the Kingdom of Death.'' She picked up a feather duster from off the counter, and busied herself with flicking it over the nearby shelves as she continued recounting the myth.

''For in love she ever sought her other Self, and once, in the winter of the year, when He had disappeared from the green earth, She followed Him and came at last to the gates beyond which the living do not go.

''The Guardian of the Gate, the Lord of Shadows, challenged her, and She stripped Herself of her clothing and jewels, for nothing may be brought into that land.''

Jacob was enchanted by the melodious manner her voice acquired when telling the myth.

'' 'Do not return to the living world, but stay here with me, and have peace and rest and comfort,' the Lord of Shadows implored her.

''But she answered, 'Why do you cause all things I love and delight in to wither away?'

'' 'Lady,' he said, 'It is the fate of all that lives to die. Everything passes. All fades away. I bring comfort and consolation to those who pass the gates, that they may grow young again.' ''

Desirée could not keep her eyes from drifting in Jacob's direction as she repeated the poignant passage, '' 'But you are my heart's desire. Return not, but stay here with Me.' ''

Jacob felt a queer stirring deep within him, but then she looked away and the inexplicable flicker was extinguished.

"And She remained with him three days and three nights, and at the end of the third night She took up his crown, and it became a circlet that She placed around her neck, saying, 'Here is the circle of rebirth. Through you all passes out of life, but through Me all may be born again. Everything passes, everything changes. Even death is not eternal. Mine is the mystery of the womb, that is the cauldron of rebirth.'"

Desirée abandoned her busywork, once more engaging Jacob's eyes as she whispered the words, "'Enter into Me and know Me, Lord of Shadows, and You will be free of all fear. You will know true love.'"

And once more Jacob felt a strange tingle within, only this time he half consciously recognized the stimulus that had triggered the reaction. His landlady could weave a spell with her soft looks and voice, could make a myth come to life and make a man wish to trade places with the Lord of Shadows.

"In love, He entered into Her, and so was reborn into life. Yet is He still known as Lord of Shadows, Guardian of the Gates, the giver of peace and rest. But She is the Moon Goddess, the Queen of all the Wise, Lady of beauty and strength, power and compassion, honor and humility, mirth and reverence. All acts of love and pleasure are Her rituals. From Her all things proceed and to Her they return again. In Her are the mysteries, the cycle of life. In Her is the fulfillment of all love."

For a suspended moment neither one could break away from the magnetic energy generating between them. Had it not been for the obtrusive tinkle of the shop's bell, they might have remained in the trance-like state interminably. It was Desirée who first blinked and regained her senses. She turned toward the customer, finding a tiny old woman with a crinkled face and cloudy eyes standing midway between the door and the counter and looking around uncertainly.

"May I help you?" she gently prodded.

"Oh, I don't know. I'm not sure. Perhaps I shouldn't have come." The old woman presented a very frail and anxious figure as she stood muttering to herself and wringing her hands.

Desirée wondered if the poor old soul was senile. "Maybe I can be of assistance if you'll tell me what it is you are in need of," she coaxed.

"Money, child," the woman clucked, venturing nearer. "I am in desperate need of funds," she confided, plopping her tapestry bag on the counter.

Desirée and Jacob exchanged leery glances. The old woman's appearance was as baffling as her vague mutterings. She was dressed in a coat that had obviously been cut from fine quality wool but which had grown threadbare with time. Her gray curls were tucked under a babushka. She had no boots, but her black ankle-high shoes were polished, though it was plainly evident they had long ago outserved their usefulness. She was either a meticulously neat bag lady or a genteel old soul whose resources were not what they had once been.

Desirée treated her with kind respect. "In what way can I be of service to you?"

The old woman seemed more intent on scanning the roots and amulets displayed in the glass case than explaining her dire straits. "Oh, I don't know which is the right one to choose. I've never resorted to such as this before. It was on my neighbor's recommendation that I came to see you. Normally I wouldn't heed her advice. She's not the most reliable sort. She believes in the stars and claims to have actually traveled through time once or twice."

Desirée instantly knew to whom the old woman referred. Only one of her customers professed to have been a Romanov countess during the Russian Revolution. "Oh, yes, Miss Anna frequently visits my shop," she remarked.

The old woman nodded. "Anna swears by your magic herbs and roots. Oh, only this once, I do hope she's right. I must come up with fifty more dollars by Monday or else . . ." Her voice quivered and her hand trembled.

Desirée's heart went out to the old woman. She patted her gnarled hand as she said soothingly, "You mustn't upset yourself so. It's possible that I have within my shop the means by which you can secure the necessary money. But first, let me provide you with a chair and a nice cup of hot tea, and afterward we'll discuss your problem in detail." She looked to Jacob for assistance. As she helped the old woman off with her coat, he gallantly offered his stool, then went upstairs to fix the tea.

By the time he returned, brandishing a tray with three steaming mugs of tea balanced on it, the old woman seemed a bit more composed.

Desirée telegraphed her thanks and made a point to include him in the conversation. "Mrs. Doblinkov was just telling me of her dilemma. It seems that because she's short fifty dollars on her rent, her landlord is threatening to evict her from the building she's lived in for the past forty years."

"I've tried everything to come up with it, short of asking my family or friends, that is. I will not be a charity case. Never in my life have I asked for a handout and I won't take up the unseemly habit at this late date. It would be too humiliating."

Jacob had to admire the old woman's spunk. "I can understand," he sympathized.

"I would have had the full sum if it hadn't been for an unexpected medical expense. I've searched every old handbag and every ginger jar and teapot in the hopes of finding money I've forgotten about or misplaced. But so far, nothing." Her shoulders sagged and she expelled a resigned sigh. "I have never been in arrears on my rent. Never!" she stated emphatically. "You would think the young man would trust me after all my years of timely payment. Mr. Hoffman would have," she said with conviction.

"So you've had a change of landlords lately?" Jacob surmised.

The old woman nodded brusquely and sipped her tea. "Mr. Hoffman died a few months ago and his wife sold the building to a lawyer from Gloucester. He can't be bothered to fix the back porch step but he shows up promptly the first of each month to collect the rent.''

"Lawyers are a lazy, heartless breed," he commiserated, winking at Desirée.

"Don't I know it," the old woman agreed. "I have no idea where I can go, except maybe to the streets, if he puts me out of my home." At the mention of having to abandon her apartment, she teared up.

"We'll see what we can do to prevent that from happening," Desirée assured her. "I think I have something that will work the right magic for you," she mused aloud, setting aside her mug and going behind the counter to bring forth the miracle fix.

Jacob did not believe that she would actually take advantage of a desperate old woman's naivete. He tried to rationalize her motives, but the best he could do was halfway convince himself that she herself partially believed in the power of the wares she sold. His expression grew stony as he watched her remove a toothy-looking root from the glass case and offer it as a remedy.

"This should do it," was her enthusiastic endorsement. "For the price of a dollar, the magic money root is said to bring the petitioner the sum asked for. But you must not be greedy," she cautioned. "Only ask for what you truly need or it may not work."

The old woman fished into her tapestry handbag for her change purse and eagerly handed over the correct amount in silver coins, never suspecting Desirée had drastically reduced the root's price. "Are you absolutely sure of its power?" She sought reassurance.

It was all Jacob could do to hold his tongue. The angle from which he was observing the scene enabled him to see what the old woman could not: Desirée's removal of a number of bills from the register as she dropped in the woman's change. He saw her roll the bills and keep them hidden in the palm of her hand as she bagged the root and handed it over to the elderly customer with precise instructions. "Remember to wrap the root in a new one-dollar bill and place it under your pillow tonight. And then search very carefully through everything once more to be sure you did not overlook anything."

"Oh, yes, dear. I'll do exactly as you say," the old woman promised, her dull eyes not catching what Jacob's sharp ones had. Desirée had slickly slipped the essential sum into the old woman's coat pocket as she'd helped her on with it.

"Thank you so much, dear."

"Don't worry, Mrs. Doblinkov. Everything is going to be all right." Desirée opened the shop door. "Oh, and you should also be sure to check the linings of your wraps," she added, pretending it was merely an afterthought. "I once had a customer tell me she found lost money that way."

The old woman nodded, touching Desirée's cheek as she passed. Seeing her clutch the small bag containing the precious root to her bosom as she made her way up the street caused Jacob to consider ferreting out the identity of his parasitical peer and beating the crap out of him.

"You had me worried there for a bit," he informed his landlady as she closed the door to the shop.

"Why is that?" was her offhand reply.

"I thought for a moment you were going to leave her with a wrongful impression."

"What wrongful impression were you thinking of?" She walked around the shop as she spoke, straightening this and stacking that.

He smiled at her coy reply. "The notion that a worthless root can magically produce money."

"Are you so certain it's impossible?" She braced her hands against a table, leaning back and slanting him an inquiring look.

"Uh-huh, I am. I saw you slip the money into her pocket," he said smugly.

Her lips pulled into a slow smile. "You're such a cynic, Jacob. Don't be so quick to discount the possibility of magic. Inexplicable things do happen occasionally. Call it good or bad luck or merely strange coincidence, if you will, but each of us experiences extraordinary occurrences at given moments throughout our lives. Whether we recognize them as such is another matter."

"If you're so convinced of that, then why did you feel the need to sneak the money into Mrs. Doblinkov's pocket?" He had her there! Jacob assumed a similar posture, resting his elbows on the counter, leaning back and awaiting her retraction.

"Merely a precautionary measure." She smoothly countered his point.

"Oh, really," he scoffed. "Don't you think Mrs. Doblinkov is going to believe it curiously coincidental, not to mention terribly convenient, that she'll reach into her pocket and pull out the tidy sum of fifty dollars shortly after you helped her on with her coat?"

"No," she answered simply.

"No!" he said mockingly. "Come on, Desirée. Even a half-senile old woman could figure it out. There's nothing magical about it."

"Perhaps not. Then again, if Mrs. Doblinkov does as I instructed her, she may very well come into a larger windfall than the fifty dollars I dropped into the lining of her coat through an opportune hole in the pocket." At his startled expression, she elaborated. "I wondered how I would ever be able to supply her the rent money without her knowing. I knew her pride wouldn't let her accept the gift. Fortunately a way was provided for me to tend to her need without offending her. A small hole in a pocket *magically* solved the problem."

Some of the best legal minds in the country had not accomplished what she'd just done—outstrategized him. But more than anything, it was her unselfishness that gained her his utmost respect. He straightened his large frame and spoke with a newly acquired regard. "You're a good person, Desirée."

"Considering the fact that I'm the daughter of a witch," she retorted, embarrassed by the compliment he'd paid her.

"By any standard," he qualified. Suddenly he found himself more cognizant of the beauty beneath the womanly packaging, which was a real first for him. He wasn't comfortable with looking deep into a person's soul. In fact, he'd made a practice of avoiding the disturbing process, especially in regard to himself. Life was much simpler when conducted on a superficial level. Taking things seriously implied commitment, and to him the mere word implied a condition incongruent to independent thinking or action. Now, suddenly, he was struck with a rankling sense of having missed out on profound moments with special people because he'd glossed over the importance of connecting with others.

Desirée could sense a tension building in him, and though the physical space separating them remained unchanged, she felt him moving closer to her.

They both started at the jangling of the shop's bell.

"Hello, Jacob," a familiar soprano voice called.

He swung around to discover his partner poised in the doorway. "Addie," he uttered dumbly.

She smiled uneasily. "What a look. Anyone would think I'd returned from the dead."

He grinned and came to where she stood, giving her a quick peck on the cheek. "I'm just surprised by the impromptu visit, is all." Draping an arm about the padded shoulders of her suede jacket, he teased, "I'm sure you didn't just happen to be in the neighborhood and decide to drop in on the spur of the moment."

Desirée watched as the very elegant, very blond woman glanced around hesitantly as Jacob led her further into the interior of the shop.

"So," said Jacob, "to what do I owe the honor of your presence in Marblehead?"

"As a matter of fact, I *was* in the general vicinity and thought it would be a nice gesture to pop in and say hello."

His grin widened as he gestured toward the stool Mrs. Doblinkov had occupied earlier. "You lie so poorly, I don't know why you even bother. We can discuss the real reason for your being here in a bit."

Addie was about to object when she noted for the first time the presence of another. She engaged Desirée's eyes and immediately felt an inexplicable wariness.

Following the train of Addie's gaze, Jacob rushed to amend his tactlessness. "My landlady, Desirée Warren," he said by way of introduction. "And this is—"

"I know," Desirée acknowledged her rival with a stiff smile. "Your partner, Adeline Van Cleve."

"It's nice to meet you," was Addie's perfunctory greeting.

Desirée wanted to reply, *Jacob is right. You don't lie well.* "Jacob has said many good things about you," she said instead. The comment was followed by an awkward pause.

Jacob was at a loss to explain the discordant vibes traversing between the two women. "I suppose you've noticed that Desirée doesn't run your typical souvenir shop," he said to Addie in a chatty tone, trying to bridge the silent gap.

Desirée could feel Addie's mounting shock and disapproval as she methodically surveyed the shop's interior.

"Yes, it's most unusual," she remarked finally, working hard at keeping her expression placid.

"I cater to a very select clientele," Desirée informed her in that tone Jacob had come to recognize as defensive.

"That's obvious," Addie commented with a condescension Jacob knew well but generally chose to overlook. Addie only behaved snootily when something or someone struck a nerve.

Desirée pretended not to notice the other woman's tight lips and arched brows. "Please, feel free to browse. If some piece catches your fancy, I'd be happy to sell it to you at a reduced price." She pulled a large ledger from beneath the counter, exempting herself from any further conversation with an exaggerated sigh and a transparent excuse. "I'm afraid I must balance the accounts. You'll pardon me while I tend to business."

"Of course," was Addie's overly gracious reply as she turned her attention back to Jacob. "I'm sure Miss Warren could concentrate better with us out of the way. Why don't you give me the grand tour?" she proposed.

"If you'd like," he agreed, but not without reservation. He could read his partner like a book. There was a purpose to her presence in Marblehead and she wanted time in order to broach it. "My jacket's upstairs. Amuse yourself for a minute while I go get it."

Addie was not at all thrilled at the prospect of being left alone, even for a minute, with the peculiar proprietress. She cast a nervous look in the woman's direction and was relieved to note that she seemed absorbed in her accounts and no more inclined to make small talk than she. So Addie meandered around the shop, taking inventory of the bizarre trappings as she did so. The place gave her the willies. She couldn't imagine why Jacob would choose to stay in such a spook house.

"Ready to go?"

She jerked around at the sound of Jacob's voice. Nodding, she turned to Desirée, her eyes and tone properly neutral. "I'm afraid I found nothing of interest to me. Perhaps I will at some other time."

Desirée knew better. "As I said, Miss Van Cleve, I cater to a very special clientele," she reiterated. "I hope you enjoy the tour of our town. And do drop in again whenever the mood moves you." The invitation she extended was merely a formality. She no more wanted to deal with Addie than Addie wished to tarry or trade at The Magic Herb Hut.

"Yes, well, perhaps we will come into contact again in the future." Such would not be the case if Addie had any choice in the matter.

"Perhaps," Desirée parroted, not bothering to sound very enthused about the prospect.

Addie linked her arm through Jacob's. "Let's make the first stop on the tour someplace private where we can get a hot toddy and talk. So much has been going on in your absence. There's a lot we need to discuss.'' She managed to usurp his attention before the two of them had even cleared the doorway.

Once they had crossed the street, Desirée gave full vent to the spectrum of emotions welling inside of her. She shoved the ledger into a drawer and then slammed it shut with an exaggerated heave. Frustration, jealousy and uncertainty ate away at her confidence and distorted her perceptions until Addie became disproportionately imposing in her mind. She fumed over the woman's striking looks and elegant dress, she mentally mimicked her precise and uppity speech patterns, and aimed a dirty look at her rival's back as she sashayed up the hill and around the corner.

Propping her elbows on the counter and putting her chin in her hands, Desirée voiced the question uppermost on her mind. "Where is it that you belong, Jacob Malone?" She gazed blankly into space and murmured, "With her in Boston or here with me?"

She blinked and directed a look beyond the window once more, half hoping Jacob would reappear *alone* and thereby supply the crucial answer. But there was no sign of him on the shoveled walk—not one small indication of where his destiny ultimately lay.

She straightened. Her gaze panned the vast array of herbs, potions and charms at her ready disposal and she pondered her options. Should she leave Jacob's future to chance—let fate run its natural course?

Unaware of what she was doing, she passed her left hand over the collection of stones on the top shelf of the display case until it came to rest above a pearly moonstone. She reached in to remove it, and pressed it into her palm, admiring the stone's smooth symmetry. Though she'd made a random selection, she felt a powerful connection with Jacob through the moonstone. She did not utter any fervent plea, did not work any magic. Not then. Maybe never again, she mused. It was hard to resist the impulse when she cared so deeply for Jacob, but for the moment she merely held on to the bit of stone, as if it were a little bit of hope.

Then the bell tinkled, announcing another customer, and she was forced to slip the moonstone into a pocket and tend shop.

CHAPTER NINE

"So, you see what I'm up against on this one, Jacob," Addie concluded after reciting the facts over a hot toddy at a local watering hole. "We're not talking a palimony suit. Except for a very discreet accountant who made out a check each month payable to a private mental institution in the Virgin Islands, no one knew our client had a catatonic wife he never bothered to divorce and continued to subsidize for over twenty years. When the information finally came to light, it totally changed the complexion of the case. To my knowledge this is a first. The mistress is suing for a modest million on the grounds that our client broke a verbal contract with her." Glumly, she added "Personally, after meeting the injured party, I think she has a chance of pulling it off. She's wholesome looking, sincere and presents a damn good case against him. She's got documented proof of their long-standing liaison and a host of credible witnesses to back up her claim that the king of the late night airwaves is not all wit and warmth. She contends that he continually promised marriage but neglected to mention the wee little detail of his already having a wife."

"Yeah, well, a wife in the closet is a somewhat compromising development," Jacob said wryly. "You can't key in on his humble television persona and attempt to pass him off as an exploited patsy once it becomes public knowledge that Mr. Wit and Warmth isn't exactly kosher. The press is going to have a heyday with this one. You might want to consider having your hair highlighted. Those tabloid candids are the worst. You don't want to look drab." He had tried to lighten her dismal mood.

"That's a terrific suggestion. I'm hip deep in quicksand and you're throwing out jokes instead of a rope." Addie didn't crack a smile.

"Okay. I'll quit with the wisecracks and give you my gut feeling, for what it's worth." Jacob assumed a serious tone. "I think your smartest recourse is to go to trial quickly. It's in the other side's best interest to delay, not ours. The bad press works to their advantage and they'll want to capitalize on it as much as possible. The less time the sensational stories have to take effect, the better our client's chances. A defense will be touchy but not impossible.

"Play down his omissions and play up the mistress's opportunism. Use the batty wife as a plus, not a negative. Beat the opposition to the punch. You be the one to bring it out into the open. Put it in your opening statement. Parade the experts through. Present testimony attesting to the wife's incompetency and his sense of responsibility. Show that, in essence, she was only a shell of a woman. Point out that marriage implies a viable mate, consistent companionship and occasional copulation—none of which our client has experienced in past years. Was he, therefore, truly married? Technically, yes; realistically, no. Was he committing adultery? Technically yes; realistically no." Jacob's voice rose as he hit the point home. "Did he, therefore, deceive the plaintiff? Technically, yes; realistically, no." He lowered his voice again. "And so on and so on until you convince everyone in the courtroom that he was a man trapped between love and loyalty, lust and honor, desire and divorce—a man whose very actions prove that he takes his commitments seriously and does not make promises lightly." He paused.

"And then you start discrediting the mistress by painting an unflattering picture of her. The usual stuff—she's insensitive, capitalizing, fickle. It'll get nasty. These sorts of cases always do. I know how much you like to stay lily white, but if you want to win you're going to have to be prepared to get in the trenches and get as dirty as the rest of 'em," he advised her.

Addie set aside her glass and gave him a long, hard look. "Technically, yes; realistically, no, is a good angle, but I didn't drive all the way up here for a crash course in witness smearing or a pep talk, Jake. You know I can't handle the courtroom theatrics. That's your specialty. I want you to come back to Boston within a day or two and take over the case."

"Not this time, Addie," he said.

"And just what the hell does that mean?" She raised her tone and a brow.

"It means that I'm still disenchanted with the law. I won't be returning until I'm ready or unless I'm positively certain I want to resume my practice," he explained.

Addie was having none of it. "Oh, wonderful! What am I supposed to tell the client? 'Sorry, sir, I realize that when you retained Malone and Van Cleve you believed you would be the recipient of the joint expertise implied by the small print in the Yellow Pages ad. Unfortunately, however, you'll only be receiving half a defense in return for full fee. You see, Mr. Malone is away on a personal quest. He cannot be summoned to Boston since he is presently incommunicado high atop the cliffs of Marblehead and engaged in deep meditation he hopes will reveal the meaning of life.' "

"Nicely put, Addie," he said, grinning. "You've a flair for dramatics, after all."

She only got hotter under her lace collar. "Is nothing I'm saying getting through to you? I went along with your taking off with no advance notice and in the midst of pending litigation. Even though I thought this sudden need of yours for space was a bit quirky, I didn't offer much objection."

That wasn't precisely the way Jacob remembered her reacting to his leaving, but he thought it more prudent not to correct the misconception.

"I gave you a few weeks to find yourself or whatever it was you were supposed to be doing. I didn't even mind that you didn't get in touch for days on end."

He concluded that she most definitely had minded or else she wouldn't have mentioned it.

"But it's gone on long enough, Jake. Like it or not, you do have obligations back in Boston that you can't turn your back on whenever you please. It's totally unrealistic to think that you can just sluff off a court appearance by merely stating you're not ready to do legal battle. What's come over you? The Jake Malone of old would never have even entertained the idea of reneging on such an important case."

"Things change, Addie. Maybe I'm not the same person you went into partnership with several years back." He'd let her absorb the full impact of his statement as he ordered another round of drinks.

"Of course you are." She refused to accept the possibility that their partnership might dissolve. "You're just suffering from a mild mid-life crisis or something. It happens to everyone. I've been reading up on it. It passes, Jacob. Good grief, we're talking your life's work! A person doesn't simply decide one day to stop being who he or she is. You're a lawyer—a good one. So start acting like one again." Her tone was scolding.

"Don't pressure me, Addie. I won't be any good to you back in a courtroom if I'm not sure it's where I belong."

She took a swig of her drink, then stated, "We're a good team, Jacob. Look at all we've achieved together."

"Maybe that's part of the problem, Addie. Maybe we've relied too heavily on each other and neither of us is sure of our separate abilities or aware of our individual aspirations any longer. I know one thing for certain. In this particular instance, the client's interests are better served by you, with all of your self-doubt and stage fright, than would they be by my halfhearted efforts.''

"You honestly believe that?" Her disbelief was evident. It registered on her face and in her voice.

"At the moment, yes," was his candid answer.

"You're scaring me, Jake. I mean *really* scaring me," she emphasized. "I hate hearing you talk this way. You sound so vague about the future. Admittedly I have a selfish interest in wanting you to return to Boston and the firm.'' She dragged a lock of blond hair from her eyes and tucked it behind an ear. "Damn! We're on a roll. It took a few years, but finally Malone and Van Cleve get top billing whenever they play the courthouse.''

They both grinned, then lapsed into sober silence for a moment as they simultaneously sipped their drinks.

"Don't screw it up, Jake," she cautioned him when she took the glass from her lips. "You have everything going for you. I'm sure this dissatisfaction with the law is only a temporary thing. You're overanalyzing your life.''

"Maybe," he conceded. "But do you want to know something funny, Addie?"

"What?" she asked.

"I don't miss it.''

"What don't you miss? Boston, the law, the fat income, fast cars and women...me?" The last she added almost timidly.

"You I occasionally do miss," he admitted. "As far as the law goes, I guess you could say that I'm neutral. Sometimes I miss it. Sometimes I don't. But crazy as it sounds, I really don't give a damn about the rest of the frills."

"You're happy living in a tourist trap of a fishing village?" Addie slanted him a skeptical look.

"I like it here."

"That's it!" she exploded, throwing up her hands in utter exasperation. "Now I'm convinced you've flipped out. Nobody in their right mind would actually like being holed up in that spooky place with that peculiar woman."

"Desirée is a nice person. She's just a bit introverted and hard to get to know at first." It surprised him how quickly he'd jumped to Desirée's defense. Sure, he thought her interesting—attractive, even, in a quiet sort of way—but it wasn't as if he carried a torch for her. She definitely wasn't his type.

Was she?

"The woman's strange, Jake. She's into the occult, for heaven's sake. She's even got an odd look about her. Haven't you noticed her eyes? They're eerie. They follow you even when she's not looking at you."

"The woman isn't a voodoo priestess, Addie. She sells harmless herbs and magic trinkets. She's just trying to make a living the same as everybody else.

Granted, she's a little unusual, but I find her refreshing."

"I suppose you'd find the little ladies from *Arsenic and Old Lace* refreshing," she said with a roll of her eyes. "You've been involved with some off-the-wall types before, Jake, but this one's a pip."

"I'm not involved with her," he argued. "She's my landlady, that's all. We share meals and conversation, nothing more."

"I'm sure she's just a wealth of information. Well traveled, well versed . . ." she needled.

"Cattiness doesn't become you, Addie. Desirée may not be worldly but she doesn't lack the social graces or suffer from any intellectual deficiency. In fact, her uncommon background is precisely the reason why she is especially knowledgeable on certain subjects."

"Don't tell me, let me guess. Her ancestors beamed down from another galaxy and she's really an extraterrestrial in disguise," was Addie's flip reply.

"Cute, Addie. Real cute." Tired of his partner's razzing, he signaled for the check.

Addie grew sullen and said nothing more until they were about to part company at her car. As Jacob opened the door for her, she turned to him, wordlessly slipping an arm around his neck and pressing a cheek to his. "I don't know why I gave you such a hard time about everything. It's just that I have this unsettling feeling where you're concerned, Jacob. I can't explain it exactly. It's just something I sense. It's like you're losing touch with the familiar and retreating further and further from contact with those of us who dwell in the real world outside of this sleepy little town."

"I'm fine, Addie," he reassured her. "And so will you be once you quit manufacturing problems to worry about." He tweaked her upturned nose playfully. "I promise not to make any drastic changes in either my professional or personal life without first consulting you."

"Liar. I know better. You'll do as you damn well please and inform me after the fact." She cast him an indulgent smile and slid behind the wheel.

"Not so," he corrected her. "Not when the decision I arrive at has a bearing on your future as well. I hope you know that I would never leave you in the lurch."

"You're referring to our business arrangement, I assume."

"Well, yeah. What else?" he said with a baffled look.

"I was just wondering about Addie and Jake's future." When he still didn't catch her drift, she grew more specific. "If there is no more Malone and Van Cleve—no more partnership—what happens to us?"

"Need you ask?" He was truly stunned by the question.

"I think so. I want to be clear on where I stand with you, Jake."

He rested a hand on the door and the other on her shoulder, leaning slightly in the car. "We may not always be partners, but we'll always be friends, Addie. Surely you know how special you are to me."

"In what way am I special, Jake?" she pressed.

It was then that he began to understand what she was really getting at. Her eyes were staring straight ahead and her shoulders were squared. He realized she was braced for whatever reply he might give. He wanted to kick himself for not realizing sooner. Squatting down beside her, he said what was necessary, but as tenderly as possible. "I care for you a great deal, Addie. I always have and I always will. I'd do anything for you. You're like a sister to me."

She merely nodded and then turned the key in the ignition. "I won't pretend that I'm not disappointed. I thought maybe there was a chance that eventually you might see me in a different light. I suppose it was silly of me to presume that just because we were such a good match professionally, the same would hold true romantically."

"It wasn't silly. I'm flattered to have even been considered a serious contender for your affection, but I'm not for you, Addie. You haven't had enough exposure to the opposite sex to realize that I'm not 'serious' material. In the not-too-distant future, I'm sure you'll be enormously relieved that you didn't mistake regard for love."

"Well, now that I've made a total ass of myself, I think it's time to make a discreet exit and drive slowly off into the sunset." They both knew her bravura was phony but necessary.

He stood, shooting her a customary wink. "Keep me posted on the case."

"Thanks for the helpful suggestions. I'll think I will push for an early trial date." As she reached for the door handle, she added, "And as for highlighting my hair, check out next month's rag sheets. It'll be hard to tell me from Cybill Shepherd."

"See you in the funny papers," he kidded her.

"Definitely not in your dreams," she retorted, slamming shut the door and waving before pulling out from the curb. He watched the sleek sports car until it turned off for Boston.

Jacob wasn't able to dismiss the interchange between him and his partner, though he knew he'd made the right decision in refusing to return to Boston and take over the case for Addie. Giving in to her wouldn't have served either of their best interests. It would have been too damn difficult for him and too damn easy for her.

Back in his room he thrashed around in his bed, wrestled with the covers and pounded the pillow. After a bit more squirming and wriggling, he finally struck a comfortable pose, closed his eyes and tried to clear his mind.

It was impossible. Certain phrases kept repeating in his head. *You're just suffering from a mild mid-life crisis or something. It happens to everyone. It passes, Jacob.*

He felt hot. He slung a leg on top of the patchwork quilt. *Good grief, we're talking your life's work! A person doesn't simply decide one day to stop being who he or she is. You're a lawyer—a good one. So start acting like one again.*

He rolled over onto his side and tried to blank his thoughts. *You're happy living in a tourist trap of a fishing village?... Now I'm convinced you've flipped out. Nobody in their right mind would actually like being holed up in that spooky place with that peculiar woman.*

He rearranged his head on the pillow, muttering, "Give it a rest, Addie."

Her voice echoed in his head. *She's strange, Jacob. Haven't you noticed her eyes? They're eerie. They follow you even when she's not looking at you.*

Jacob eased onto his back. His own eyes were still shut. Against the blackness, a pair of lavender-blue orbs suddenly appeared. They followed him as he flipped onto his side and scrunched the pillow into a ball. His eyelids fluttered open and he lay staring at the illuminated clock and listening to its monotonous ticking. The hall clock chimed again. Twice. The whole damn house was alive with clocks. Time was ticking away. Minutes of his life were slowly passing.

Again Addie's words churned in his brain. *It took a few years but finally Malone and Van Cleve get top billing whenever they play the courthouse.... Don't screw it up, Jake.... You're overanalyzing your life.*

He rolled over onto his stomach and jerked the pillow over his head, trying to block out the sound of Addie's voice and the clocks. *You've been involved with some off-the-wall types before, Jake, but this one's a pip.*

"I'm not involved with her," came the muffled mutter from under the pillow.

I was just wondering about Addie and Jake's future.... I want to be clear on where I stand with you, Jake.... You're losing touch with the familiar....retreating further and further from contact with those of us who dwell in the real world outside of this sleepy little town.

Addie's and his own words became jumbled. *I need you back in Boston.... I like it here.... You can't just turn your back on your obligations.... I don't miss it. The woman's strange.... She sells harmless herbs and magic trinkets.... See you in the funny papers.... Definitely not in your dreams....*

He finally lay still, finally turned it off, finally drifted into a deep sleep.

HE STROLLED IN an open meadow. The sun was hot overhead, but he was cooled by a balmy breeze blowing across the treeless grassland. Wildflowers of every variety and color bloomed as far as the eye could see. There was a feeling of endlessness, as if one could walk for miles and miles in any direction and still the wildflowers would stretch forward in splashes of vivid color to the point on the horizon where the meadow and sky merged.

In the shimmering distance, he saw what looked to be the outline of a woman. She wore a white sundress and a wide-brimmed hat. The sundress's sash and the hat's pastel ribbons fluttered in the breeze as she walked toward him. The woman carried herself gracefully. She virtually glided through the maze of wildflowers. He couldn't take his eyes off her, and as she came closer his breath came faster.

She paused a few yards from him and waited, her cotton sundress ruffling in the breeze. He wasn't sure what was expected of him. He squinted in the bright sunlight, trying to make out the lady's partially shadowed features. Only her chin and mouth were revealed. Her chin was delicately shaped and her lips were full and as rich in color as the scarlet poppies.

"It's wonderful to see you again, Jacob," she greeted him in a hauntingly familiar voice.

He felt a queer flutter in the pit of his stomach. Should he know this woman? She behaved as if he should. There was something about her voice that sent an excited current coursing through him from his brain to his groin. "I'm sorry. I can't place you. Where and when did we meet previously?" he asked, moving a bit closer to her.

She laughed softly. "We shared an enchanted evening together once, you and I. I gave you a gift to remember me by."

He froze where he stood. Was he sleepwalking again? He glanced around, then up at the sky. Everything looked to be natural and normal—the proper color, shape and consistency. Still he had an uneasy feeling that wherever he was at the moment, it was far from an ordinary place. He looked back at the woman. Her smile triggered a fond memory.

"You can't be her," he whispered. "She was only a figment of my imagination—a dream. Unless . . ."

His eyes were drawn to the sky above her. It had turned a magnificent shade of mauve. Flakes as white as her dress and as delicate as lace began to drift down from the heavens. It was snowing. In the middle of a hot summer day, in the midst of a field of wild-flowers, it was snowing. Holy cow, it was happening again!

"Unless this, too, is a dream." She completed his unspoken thought. "Don't worry, my darling. You'll awaken soon and everything will be commonplace. Forgive me for arranging it so that we might be together another time."

"You can do that? Control my subconscious and summon yourself into my dreams?"

"Only if you are receptive," she explained.

"But why do you bother? I mean, what's the use? Hell, none of it's real. The mauve sky. The snow. The meadow and wildflowers. You and me. We're just part of a crazy dream."

"Haven't you missed me, Jacob? Haven't you thought about making love to me again?"

She had him there. He'd thought of her, all right. He'd relived the dream of their lovemaking about a hundred times.

The snow fell harder, clinging like fine sugarcoating to the pampas grass and flower petals and adding to the surrealism of the moment. "Now and then," he admitted.

"I know differently. I know your unconscious desires," she gently said.

"Well, then, you know a whole hell of a lot more than I do." He tilted his head to the side, trying to steal a peek beneath the floppy brim and get a look at her face.

"You want to confront your desire. You're eager to know her face and learn her name," she put forth.

His heart pounded in anticipation. "Yes," he answered her.

"What is revealed to you may be hard for you to accept," she cautioned him.

"I'll risk it," was his cocky reply.

Slowly she lifted her hand to the floppy hat. "My name," she said in a prelude to the unveiling, "is spelled the same as desire—" in an excruciatingly slow motion, she removed the hat from her head "—only with two e's."

"Desirée," he gasped.

She stepped nearer—to within inches of him. "I once told you, my love, that you can know a face and still not know what is in a heart."

He was in shock. Struck dumb. What kind of Freudian nonsense was this? he wondered. She'd been absolutely right. The notion of her being the object of his unconscious desire was unacceptable—preposterous. It was beyond belief that the lagoon maid of his dreams and the shy proprietress of Marblehead could be one and the same. Good grief! That meant that he was having erotic dreams about his landlady!

"It's true, Jacob. You are." She addressed his unvoiced conclusion.

"Oh, boy," was all he could manage to utter.

She reached out a hand and gently traced his jaw-line with her fingertips. "I want you, Jacob."

The sound of her husky voice stirred images of their previous interlude. Her hands moved to his shirt, and she deftly unbuttoned it. Spreading the two front panels wide apart, she grazed her lips from his midriff, along and across his chest, up to the throbbing pulse beating at his neck. Her touch was like no other. He couldn't deny that she aroused him. Her arms slid around his neck and she stood on tiptoe, her head slightly thrown back, her eyes closed, her lips parted and waiting. He didn't have the strength of will to resist the natural meld of their bodies and the magnetic fusion of their lips.

"I would never hurt you, my love," she murmured against his mouth. He clasped her tighter, groaning as she weaved her fingers through his hair and rotated her hips against him.

"I only want to make you happy... give you pleasure," was her breathy promise as their linked forms gradually sank to the bed of wildflowers.

Reason didn't exist for him any longer. There was only Desirée and desire; desire and Desirée. The two were inseparable, indistinguishable. He ran his hand under her dress and along a smooth thigh. A mere dream could not feel as incredibly soft, as wonderfully responsive as she did. A dream didn't shudder with passion or smell of French perfume.

"Desirée," he heard himself whispering as she boldly touched him, expertly stroked him. Gradually, his vision grew hazy and the sound of his own heartbeat became a roar in his ears. Unwittingly, it seemed, he'd crossed some invisible boundary and tumbled headlong into a bottomless abyss of abandonment. He was no longer fully lucid—no longer in complete possession of his mind, body and soul.

What followed was a blur of impressions: each of them stripping the other down to the buff; wild kisses amid wildflowers; his bare back and buttocks nestled in wet grass; Desirée above him framed against a mauve sky. . . .

Snowflakes were everywhere—in the air and in her hair, on the ground and on her lashes. Desirée was moving rhythmically. He felt feverish friction and pleasure unlike anything he'd ever known. His muscles flexed and coiled. His hands on Desirée's firm hips, he eased her up, then guided her down. Her body arched; he groaned. He soared and a hot explosion went off inside his head—and another inside of Desirée. Waves of release washed over him as she wilted on top of him. Her fragrant hair spilled across his face and her heart thudded against his chest. He felt the gentle press of her lips at his throat. She was daintiness embraced in brawn. And he was utterly content.

But the most jolting, most lasting impression of all was a whisper. "I love you, Jacob. I swear it by all that is holy and by the power of three times three."

JACOB JERKED AWAKE. His heart beat like a jackhammer and beads of perspiration glistened on his forehead. He sat up on the edge of the bed, listening to the hall clock strike five o'clock and waiting for the shakes to subside.

Mew-Sinh blinked in the darkness and swished her tail.

Edgy and on guard, Jacob cocked his eyes in the cat's direction. "What the hell?" he boomed. "Scat! Go on! Get lost!" He shooed the cat away with a sweep of an arm.

Mew-Sinh hauled tail, shooting like a bullet out the door—the same door that Jacob was positively certain he had shut before retiring. He dragged himself up off the bed, shoved the door closed, then rested his back against it. "Okay, Malone—" he raked a hand through his rumpled hair "—don't make more of it than you should. It's probably just coincidence. So you dream about your landlady. It's no big deal. So the cat's got some kind of morbid fixation about you. It's no major thing." It wasn't working. He was bothered and bewildered and no amount of talking to himself was going to eliminate his jitters.

Jacob straightened and stumbled around the room, conducting a haphazard search for his robe. It was a cinch he wasn't going to be able to get back to sleep. Besides, he wanted to be sure to be on hand for breakfast this morning. He had a few questions to put to his landlady, and if she didn't come up with some damn good answers, he intended to check out of his whacky lodgings posthaste.

"YOU'RE VERY QUIET this morning," Desirée commented, passing the plate of fresh pastries to him. "These are sinfully good. Try the—"

"What does the phrase 'By the power of three times three' mean to you?" He deliberately interrupted her, hoping to catch her off guard and maybe get a knee-jerk response.

Her reaction was perfectly appropriate. She merely acted mildly surprised. "Wherever did you hear such an expression?" She continued holding out the plate—steadily so.

He helped himself to a raspberry-and-cheese Danish and licked the filling from his fingers. "In my dreams," he replied offhandedly, still watching her for any telltale sign that might indicate whether she had any foreknowledge of his out-of-body experiences.

"Are you feeling all right?" she inquired, casting him a concerned look over the edge of her teacup.

"I feel fine. Why? Is there some reason I shouldn't?" He took a swig of his juice.

"None that I know of." She shrugged. "You say that the phrase was somehow incorporated in a dream?" She returned to the subject without giving him the slightest hint that she was anything but merely curious.

"Mmm," he confirmed, swallowing a bite of Danish, which could have been made of cardboard for all he knew or cared. "I had a weird dream last night and in it someone spoke those words to me. It sounded very much like the archaic language in that old book downstairs. I thought maybe you might know what it meant." He studied her when she got up to replenish her tea. She seemed thoughtful, but nothing else.

"Actually the expression does have to do with the Craft." Her voice was as evenly measured as the liquid she poured into the china cup. "It's a strong belief among those of the Wicca way—"

"You mean among witches." He purposely made her uncomfortable, thinking that if he didn't tiptoe around things, she might be more direct, also.

"Yes," she went on, seemingly unperturbed by his bluntness. "They—witches and wizards—believe that everything is interconnected. Every action, every movement changes the universe. One must not alter a thing—not one pebble or grain of sand, until it is known what good and evil will follow the act." She sat back down at the table, taking a second to sip her tea before continuing.

"You're talking physics, Desirée. I only wanted to know about a simple phrase," he said, a little testily.

"One has to do with the other. Witches knew long ago what physicists only recently recognized. All things are comprised of energy. The world is in balance, in equilibrium. And those with the power to summon and direct energy can also alter the balance of the world. It is most perilous, that power. It must follow knowledge and serve need. There must be discipline to magic. There is a saying that aptly describes the care witches take when channeling energy. *To light a candle is to cast a shadow.* It is a warning to exercise judgment and caution whenever energy is projected."

"Very interesting, but what, precisely, has all that to do with my original question?" He wasn't about to let her sidetrack him. He wanted to know how the three times three quote fit into his dream. Moreover, he wanted to know how Desirée herself fit into the whole crazy scheme of things.

"I'm trying to explain," she said with just a hint of annoyance.

"I'm sorry. Please, go on."

"The old ways are steeped in superstition. Even I don't fully understand it all. I only know what my grandmother and mother believed. They were convinced that whenever energy was projected from one source to another—be it positive or negative energy—it caused the source from which the energy flowed to also become vulnerable. In other words, in order for a connection to be made, a witch must identify with the other person. They become each other. The source of energy—the witch—is apt to be more strongly affected than the object of her intent. Three times so."

"You mean if a witch whammies someone, it can backfire on her three times over?"

She looked amused. "Witches hex or curse. They never whammy. The phrase is most commonly used when binding a spell.

By all the power
Of three times three,
This spell bound round
shall be.
To cause no harm,

Nor return on me.
As I do will,
So mote it be!"

It was all he could do not to stare.

"That's how it generally goes," she said uneasily, growing uncomfortable under his penetrating gaze. "Perhaps if you told me more about your dream and the context in which the words were spoken, I could tell you more...."

He was tempted—sorely tempted. The thought occurred to him that maybe, just maybe, Desirée possessed more than just a scant familiarity with the Craft. Maybe she'd acquired a *working* knowledge at her mother's knee. Maybe she knew every detail of his dream because she had generated it, identified with it, made herself the object of his unconscious desire. Maybe she only feigned ignorance because she was afraid to acknowledge her ties to the old ways.

Maybe she was a witch and actively practicing in Marblehead!

"Jacob?" She could see that he was lost in reflection. Did he suspect? Had she said or done something to reveal herself? Oh, God! What would she say if he confronted her? What excuse could she offer? *You see, Jacob, I was so very lonesome and wanted a lover. The book was handy, the notion so tempting. I've never done anything like this before. I know I was crazy to attempt it. I had no idea the magic was real. Believe me, I was as shocked as you that it actually worked. Please don't be upset with me. Please don't leave me.*

I promise not to ever dabble again. I swear it by the power of three times three.

They exchanged a long, searching look.

"I'm sorry. I was preoccupied with that three times three thing," he finally said, noticing for the first time how pale she'd grown.

She prayed she wouldn't faint. "It was only a dream, Jacob. You mustn't let it upset you so."

"Yeah, well, some things aren't easily dismissed, Desirée." He flung aside his napkin and stood. "By the way, is there some special reason that Mew-Sinh keeps seeking out my room at night?"

"She's a creature of habit. The bed you occupy is her favorite napping spot."

"I find it strange that she always manages to get into my room when I distinctly remember closing the bedroom door before retiring."

"Probably a faulty latch. I'll have someone take a look at it later today."

"I'd appreciate it."

"I'm happy to do it."

Jacob nodded. Then she did. It was a standoff. Both of them sensed the other's wariness, but neither one was willing to talk about the strained climate that had suddenly developed between them. Once again, they exchanged sizing looks.

Jacob was the one to break eye contact first. He didn't even attempt to bridge the awkward silence. He merely turned and strode out of the room.

Desirée went limp at his departure. Collapsing into a chair, she put her head between her knees to ward off the black dizziness that descended upon her. Mew-Sinh forsook her hiding place beneath the sink and came to sit beneath the chair. The cat quirked its head and gazed quizzically at her upside-down mistress.

"We're in big trouble, Mew-Sinh," Desirée muttered, feeling the blood rush to her head.

Mew-Sinh's way of reacting to the grim news was to take a playful swipe at her mistress's dangling ringlets.

The dizzy spell eventually passed. Desirée wished with all her heart that the same would happen to Jacob's suspicions. But she knew better. As he had told her, some things could not easily be dismissed. Jacob was wary of her. It was in his eyes.

"What have I done," she whispered to Mew-Sinh. But the cat only stared.

CHAPTER TEN

"LOOK!" Patsy James jerked the mug from her lips so suddenly that coffee streamed down the front of her ruffled blouse.

"At what?" Marilyn Estes saw nothing to warrant such excitement.

"At them," Patsy pointed to Jacob and Desirée across the street. "They're leaving together again." She blindly swiped at the stain on her blouse with a napkin. "That's twice this week." Her bosom jiggled and her bracelets jangled as she flicked the napkin to and fro over the cream-colored material until it fairly crackled with static electricity. "Now what do you suppose is going on?" Her snippy tone indicated that she'd already drawn her own nasty conclusions.

Marilyn, a spanking new member of the Women's Old Town Beautification Society, was wishing she had not accepted the newly installed president's invitation to celebrate her inauguration at the Mug and Muffin Shoppe. "So they're taking a walk together. I hardly think there's anything depraved about that." The newcomer was really getting weary of Patsy's endless haranguing of Desirée Warren.

"Ha!" Patsy snorted. "I'll just bet you there's more to it than just an innocent stroll in the park, my dear. There's no telling what kind of degenerate things have been going on behind closed doors. The woman's a—"

"More coffee, ladies?" Archie Hooper butted in.

Marilyn almost sighed aloud with relief. Mr. Hooper's presence was a godsend. It always tickled her how the old gent could slip in the zingers on Patsy without her even being aware. "Please, join us. I always welcome your company."

"Uh-huh, I figure so." he said, shooting her a wink as he warmed up her coffee.

Patsy, on the other hand, was not nearly so receptive to his presence or his offer of a refill. She placed a hand over her cup and declined with a cool, "I'm fine, thank you."

He set the glass pot on a nearby table and plopped himself in a chair. "I see you've got the splotches again, Patsy. You had your blood pressure checked lately?"

Her skin grew even more mottled at the remark. "As a matter of fact, I saw Doc Greely just last week and my blood pressure is fine, just fine, thank you," she snapped.

He turned to Marilyn Estes and shrugged his shoulders. "I guess we can safely assume that she's fine, just fine."

Marilyn just loved his dry humor.

"If that's your subtle way of insinuating that I'm in a tizzy of some sort—"

"I never meant to imply tizziness of any sort," he was quick to inject. "I only said that you're looking a little flushed today. Now that I think on it, I suppose it's understandable if you're engine's running hot. It's probably the stress of holding high office."

Marilyn choked midswallow. Quickly she snatched her own napkin from off her lap and covered her mouth before coffee sprayed everywhere.

Patsy seemed somewhat appeased. The fact that her attention was divided worked to Archie's benefit. She was having difficulty spying on the competition while sparring with him.

"I am not, as you so crudely put it, running hot," she retorted, her eyes shifting toward the window again.

"I didn't think the circus was due to hit town for another month or so," he remarked, causing both Marilyn and Patsy to cast him puzzled looks.

"What *are* you talking about?" Patsy's impatience with him was fast approaching a red-alert level.

"The way you keep looking out the window every two seconds, I thought maybe there was a parade coming down the street or something," he said in a needling tone.

Patsy's nostrils flared. Immediately she switched her focus, immersing herself in arranging the empty cream containers in a neat little row. "I was merely noticing the way the Warren woman was cozying up to her new boarder. Somebody should warn the man off. I'm sure he has no idea of the trouble he's courting." She looked down her nose at the row of ruffles fanned across her bulbous breasts and then gave them—the ruffles—a prissy flounce.

"Patsy thinks there's something going on between the two of them," Marilyn offered.

"That so." A mischievous glint lit the shopkeeper's eyes.

"I know that smirky tone, Archie Hooper. Don't think I don't. You think I'm paranoid where Desirée Warren is concerned. You know what? You're right. I am. I'd walk a mile around her. And if you or anybody else in this town had any sense, you'd do the same."

"You are a tad touchy about her," Archie agreed, tilting back his chair and studying her through the lower half of his bifocals.

"You're damn right I am," she said huffily. "How does the saying go—like mother; like daughter? Bad blood is passed on, you know."

Archie shook his head.

Patsy ignored him and addressed herself to Marilyn Estes. "She's cast a spell over that unsuspecting man. Mark my words. It's history repeating itself. That's the way they do it—the way they keep the line alive. They lure a man into their clutches by renting him a room, probably at some ridiculously low rate. Then they lure him into their bed by using witchcraft, probably potions and such. I shiver to think what happens to the poor fella after the deed is done and the bad seed is sown. The others just disappeared. They were probably hacked to pieces and buried in the cellar."

Marilyn's eyes grew round at the thought.

"For crying out loud, Patsy!" Archie almost fell backward in his chair. "I never heard such crapola. These outlandish fabrications of yours have got to stop." He managed to set the chair down on all four legs and shoot her a stern look.

"Nobody knows for sure what happened to the other men who stayed over in that house. They could have met some foul fate," she contended stubbornly.

"The men were transients. They drifted in and out of town and nobody took any special notice of 'em. Has the thought ever occurred to you that maybe Chelsey and her mother had a personal life? Who's to say, except the Warren women themselves, which men among us were their lovers and the fathers of their children?" he put forth.

"Are you suggesting that maybe someone in this town fathered Desirée?" She hooted. "I hardly think so. The men of Marblehead knew Chelsey for the black widow that she was. No man in his right mind would have had anything to do with her. No, it would've had to have been one of those migrants types that came and went during the peak fishing seasons. Those Warren witches probably drugged them with hallucinogenic herbs, and then seduced them, and then—"

"You're not listening to anything but your own petty paranoia." He'd had it with her wild conjecturing. "Bitterness is one thing, Patsy. Viciousness is another."

She was aghast at his outburst. "Well, I certainly don't intend to sit here and be maligned because I happen to be concerned about the well-being of my neighbors and this town. You may think the Warren woman is a pillar of the community. I think she's an evil influence and a menace to us all." Once again, her bosom jiggled and her bracelets jangled as she grabbed her purse and stood. "The trouble with you, Archie Hooper, is that you've no sense of Christian duty or civic pride. Well, I do." Her nose was high in the air. "What's more, I intend to do something about that, that, that—" her eyelids fluttered and her chin quivered; she was more mottled than a dalmation and nearly in the same state of frenzy as a pit bull smelling blood "—that witch," she finally spit out.

"I'd think twice if I were you before I started a stink, Patsy," Archie warned.

She tucked her purse beneath her arm and stuck out her chin. "There are ways to deal with undesirables— legal ways," she said smugly, pivoting and walking to the door. She flung it open and strutted out, making it almost to the street before turning around and marching back in. "And for your information, Archibald Hooper, the legal ways I speak of are far more formidable than the Old Ways you're always jabbering about." She stormed out again, leaving Archie and Marilyn momentarily stupefied.

"What brought all that on?" Marilyn wondered aloud.

"Jealousy," was the old shopkeeper's pensive reply.

The newcomer said nothing, afraid any inquisitiveness would be misconstrued as meddling.

Becoming aware of her silence, Archie cast her a lame smile. "Patsy tends to fly off the handle easily," he commented.

She returned his smile and agreed with a nod.

"She's been carrying a grudge against Chelsey Warren for nye onto sixteen years now," he reminded her.

Again she nodded.

"It's not true, you know. Chelsey wasn't responsible for Patsy's husband running off. It was obvious to anyone with eyes that Chelsey had no interest in the man. And she didn't hex him, like Patsy claims. Patsy just never could face the truth. It was easier for her to blame somebody else for the breakup of her marriage. She just couldn't admit Steven's and her own shortcomings. Still can't. She always was a prideful woman."

"But why did she cast the Warren woman in the role of villainess?" Marilyn found herself quizzing him in spite of herself.

"I suppose because Chelsey was a natural choice. She had the misfortune of being both a very pretty and extremely passionate woman. By passionate, I mean intense, but some folks around here thought her just plain extreme. Patsy, for one. She had it in for Chelsey from the start. Maybe she sensed Steven's infatuation with her. Chelsey was something in her day. Smoldering is the word that comes to mind when I think of her," he reminisced.

Marilyn could detect a bit of infatuation in Archie, too.

"I guess it was inevitable that Patsy would convince herself that Chelsey was the source of all her trouble. Steven hadn't been gone from Marblehead a day when Patsy started telling everyone that Chelsey caused his defection. She started circulating horror stories about the goings-on at Chelsey's place—grisly tales of black magic and orgies. I think she told the stories so often that she began to believe them herself. So did more than a few others. Because of Patsy's unfounded accusations, it became very difficult for Chelsey to practice her trade and religion in this town."

"Considering all the ill will fostered against her, I wonder why Chelsey stayed on in Marblehead?" Marilyn could not resist delving a little deeper into the plight of Chelsey Warren.

"Chelsey was a witch, and witches are accustomed to being the object of curiosity and ugly talk. Chelsey was also a woman of strong character and belief. She refused to cave in to the pressure by fleeing town, or compromise her beliefs by pretending to be something other than what she was. She was of Wicca mind, as was her mother before her. And there was nothing anyone could have said or done to change her mind. The Old Ways were her ways and she practiced them until the day she died."

"But what about Patsy's claim that the Warren women can hold a man spellbound?" Marilyn asked.

The gleam reappeared in the old man's eyes. He took his time answering. A smile spread across his face as he looked toward the red-frame two-story on the corner. "Maybe only in that one respect does Patsy come close to the truth," he told her. "The Warren women do seem to have quite an effect on men."

"Why is it that I get the impression you're speaking from personal experience?" The observation popped out of Marilyn's mouth before she could check herself.

"Me?" He seemed genuinely stunned at the suggestion—but also a bit flattered. "No, I'm an admirer of Chelsey's, but nothing more."

"I hadn't meant to pry. It's just that when you speak of her, it's with such fond familiarity." Marilyn felt obliged to try to explain her presumptuous blunder.

"Uh-huh, I was fond of Chelsey." His expression became somber suddenly. "Sometimes I'm ashamed of myself for not speaking up in her behalf more than I did, especially when people would run her down in my presence. She had some dark days in this town— days when she received nary a smile or a passing 'howdy-do.' I never shunned her, though. I always tipped my hat and passed the time of day with her whenever we met up. In all honesty, I have to admit that I was a bit smitten with her as a young man. I think she knew. She never failed to say something nice—like how she liked my new bow tie or how distinguished looking she thought a moustache made a man look. She didn't ever linger long, more for my sake than hers, I'm sure. She didn't want me tainted by association with her. And I, like a damn fool, respected the polite distance she kept.''

''You mustn't be too hard on yourself, Mr. Hooper,'' Marilyn said kindly. ''Times were different then. People were leery of anything or anyone having to do with the supernatural. But attitudes have changed since then. The New Age has dawned and now it's chic to be into the metaphysical.''

He smiled sadly. ''When you've lived as long as I have, Ms Estes, you'll come to realize that people don't change all that much. In some respects they evolve, but the more primitive instincts stay virtually intact. Don't kid yourself. Superstitiousness and a strong survival streak run through us all. But that wasn't what was at the core of Chelsey's ostracism in this town.'' Leaning back in his chair again, he continued. ''In the beginning, Marbleheaders were generally neutral about her presence here. As long as she minded her business and didn't disrupt the flow of things, they mostly overlooked her Old Ways. I suppose they figured she didn't do any harm, and it might even be of some use, in certain extenuating instances, to have ready access to a local witch. So they neither accepted nor rejected Chelsey. They simply coexisted with her. At least, until Patsy came along and started stirring things up.'' Sourly, he said, ''It wasn't Christian or civic concern that prompted her persecution of Chelsey. No, far from it.'' He stood, and grimaced as he rolled a shoulder. ''If I sit too long in one spot, arthritis sets in," he complained. "It's hell to get old, Ms Estes."

She started to offer the pat cliché of one only being as old as one felt, then realized it would not have been comforting to him. Deciding it was safer to revert back to nonverbal communication, she merely nodded again.

Archie reached into his apron pocket and withdrew a small plastic bottle. "Bufferin," he explained in a word, popping the lid, then putting two tablets in his mouth and swallowing them dry.

Marilyn couldn't stand it any longer. If there was one thing that bothered her about the old shopkeeper, it was the habit he had of fueling his customers' interest with a pointed remark and then delaying addressing the point for long intervals. "Then why did Patsy do it?" she prodded.

"Do what?" He'd lost his train of thought.

"Make Chelsey's life miserable," she cued him.

"For the reason I mentioned earlier. It's what's at the root of her vendetta against the Warren women."

Marilyn was having trouble following. "I'm sorry. I must not have been paying attention. What was it you said earlier?"

"Jealousy, Ms Estes. That's what's firing up Patsy. It was the reason she went after Chelsey and it's the reason she'll go after Desirée."

"I understand why she might have been jealous of Chelsey. Wives tend to turn into green-eyed monsters when they think their husbands are attracted to another woman. But why is jealousy a factor with Desirée?'' By now, Marilyn had completely done away with her concern about overstepping her newcomer's boundaries. She wanted to know Mr. Hooper's opinion of what was really behind Patsy's nonstop denunciation of the shy proprietress across the street.

''It's because of the stranger,'' was his nonplussed reply.

''Who?''

''The boarder—Mr. Malone. Patsy has designs of her own concerning him.''

Archie acted too sure of his facts not to be believed. ''Oh, dear,'' was all Marilyn could say when the full implication of what Archie had revealed suddenly hit.

''Uh-huh, it's a bad situation,'' he concurred. ''I wish I was wrong but I know better. The reason I know is because it was here, in my shop, that Patsy first set eyes on Mr. Malone and instantly started mooning all over herself. I never saw anyone go through more contortions to get noticed. And since then, she's made it her business to find out all about him. I think Patsy missed her calling. She ought to be working for the CIA.''

''Now I understand why she was so agitated at seeing him with Desirée.'' Everything was becoming clearer to Marilyn.

''You should have seen her when she found out where he was staying. She turned into one solid splotch and I was afraid she was going to have a stroke right here in my shop.''

''Oh, dear.'' Marilyn sighed.

"Uh-huh, it's a bad situation," Archie concurred. "She's been following him all around town for weeks. She knows his daily routine better than he does. He comes in here most every day after sailing with Nathan Pritchard. Usually it's around ten-thirty. I could set my clock by Patsy's arrival. Ten-forty on the dot. She's making a nuisance of herself. And she's about as subtle as a sledgehammer—gushing and giggling like some schoolgirl. It's embarrassing Mr. Malone. 'Course, he's too much of a gentleman to say so. I've tried making hints to her, but she's oblivious to 'em. She just keeps coming in and carrying on with the stranger."

"Oh, dear," Marilyn said again.

"Uh-huh, it's a bad situation," Mr. Hooper concurred once more.

"Maybe not. We're assuming a lot. We don't know that the stranger plans to stay on in town. In all likelihood, he'll be gone soon."

"From our chats together, I get the impression that the young fella isn't in any big hurry to leave," Archie rebutted. "He likes it here, he says."

"Oh, dear," Marilyn said once again, worriedly.

"Uh-huh, it's a bad situation," Archie concurred.

"Maybe not. I mean, Patsy's jealousy could be unfounded. Mr. Malone and Desirée may mean nothing to each other. Their relationship could be perfectly platonic. And if Desirée poses no threat to Patsy's romantic ambitions, then Patsy would have no reason to do whatever it is she's plotting." Marilyn kept throwing out hopeful suppositions.

"Except that Mr. Malone does talk frequently and very favorably about his landlady. I gather from what he says that she's one of the primary reasons he likes it here." Archie kept throwing a wet blanket on Marilyn's optimism.

"Maybe Mr. Malone will lose appeal for Patsy," she said, determined to make him believe all would end happily. "Sometimes these things fizzle out quickly. Someone else could come along and—"

"It's kind of unlikely, Ms Estes," he pointed out. "Mr. Malone is the first man to have come along in fifteen years and shake Patsy's peaches. I think she's got her heart set on having him take up where Steven left off. And she isn't about to let another Warren woman steal away what's hers."

"Oh, dear," Marilyn despaired.

"Uh-huh. It's a bad situation," Archie concurred.

CHAPTER ELEVEN

AN EARLY SPRING and unseasonably warm temperatures blew into Marblehead on March winds. Even the old-timers remarked that they could not recall such a sudden thaw. The pleasant weather prompted a rescheduling of the Marblehead Arts and Culture Committee's annual spring concert.

Everyone in town looked forward to the festive event at which the finest musicians for miles around assembled at Clark's Landing at the foot of State Street and filled the balmy breezes with the sound of Brahms. People would sit on the grassy knoll and gaze out over the bay to see the sunlight dance and glimmer, the sailboats glide and pitch, and the gulls soar and swoop in sync with the classical movements. Listening to the instruments mingle with the metallic ring of the halyards, the crisp flapping of the colorful sails, and the dulcet lapping of the Atlantic waters was almost a spiritual experience.

Desirée was as anxious as everyone else to close up shop and get to the Landing on the designated mid-March afternoon. Maybe even more so, for Jacob was accompanying her to the concert. She'd been up since dawn, flitting around the house, making ready for the

Saturday outing. It had taken her hours to select the right outfit, do and redo her hair and makeup, and pack and repack the wicker basket with a lavish assortment of mouth-watering delicacies. Desirée was almost beside herself with anticipation. It was all she could do to keep her mind on business. Luckily there were only a few scattered customers to tend to throughout the morning. The hours dragged by. In the end, her excitement got the better of her and she decided to close up shop thirty minutes early.

After flipping the sign on the door, she went to the bottom of the steps and hollered up to Jacob. "If we want to get a good spot, we need to leave in a few minutes."

"I'll be down shortly," he hollered back.

"Oh, and Jacob..."

"Yeah?"

"Bring the wicker basket from off the kitchen counter, will you?" she requested.

"I'll try to remember, Desirée," he shouted back down the steps. It was the third time in the last hour that she'd reminded him.

That minor detail attended to, she returned to the counter and set about tallying the morning's receipts. Her sales had been scant, so there was only a small amount of cash. She stuffed the day's take into a small cloth sack and deposited it into a lockbox she kept hidden beneath the counter.

She glanced to the stairs and checked her wristwatch. People would be beginning to gather soon at the landing. What in the world was taking him so long?

At the urgent rapping on the shop's door, she started. A young man was peering in at her through the glass. There was no escaping the summons.

"Dammit! Can't he read?" she muttered to herself, crossing to the door and pointing to the sign that informed the persistent young man in big, bold letters that she was closed.

"Please, ma'am. It's an emergency," he pleaded through the door.

She turned the bolt and let him in.

"Thanks," he gasped, stepping inside. "I ran all the way here, hoping to catch you before you closed."

The boy looked to be in his late teens and was definitely in a state of panic. His eyes glowed as if he had a fever, and he was sweating profusely.

"You say that it's an emergency of some sort?" she prompted.

"I need a magic fix. The strongest you got. My whole life depends on it," he blurted.

"Goodness, it sounds serious. What sort of trouble plagues you?"

"Aunt Annie said you could help." He ran his fingers through his spiked hair and began to pace. "She said you'd know what to do. I'm going out of my gourd. Look at my hands." He held them out for her inspection. "I can't steady 'em."

Desirée could deduce little from his incoherent ramblings. "In order for me to know what to recommend to you, you must first tell me your complaint. Please, just calm down and tell me what's wrong."

"What's wrong is that I'm about to blow the best thing that's happened in my life," he exploded. "Finally I get a chance to be with Stacie. A one-on-one scene—just me and her. Finally she agrees to go to the concert with me. And I can't get it together. I mean, look at me—I'm freaking out! She's gonna think I'm a geek." The glum appraisal was followed by a miserable groan.

Jacob had started to make his descent to the shop below, but upon overhearing the animated exchange between Desirée and her customer, he decided it was not a good time to barge in. Having once been young and unsure of himself, he was acutely aware of how shattering it could be for the lad to know a total stranger had been privy to his sensitive admissions. Yet Jacob didn't dare risk a retreat; the old steps creaked. He had no choice but to set down the wicker basket on one step and settle himself on another, waiting for a more appropriate moment to either advance or retreat.

Desirée, too, knew what a traumatizing predicament the boy faced. She proceeded with great care. "Before I suggest anything specific, I must first know exactly what it is you wish to accomplish. These matters of the heart are very delicate. I wouldn't want to make a mistake."

The lad turned crimson. "I dunno," he mumbled. "I suppose I want her to think I'm a hunk—to be hot for me." Afraid Desirée would misinterpret his meaning, he quickly added, "But I'm not looking to score. I mean, I've thought about making it with her, sure," he admitted. "But it's more serious with me. Heavy-duty, you know?" He searched her face to see if she understood what he was trying to communicate.

"I'm sure you've only the most noble intentions."

"Yeah, well, mostly." He grinned sheepishly.

Attracted by the smell of fried chicken, Mew-Sinh came bounding down the steps and sniffed at the wicker basket.

Alistair had also come to light on the stairs. He was bored with watching Saturday cartoons, especially since his favorites—*Alf* and *The Muppets*—were over. Struck with a sudden and severe case of cabin fever, he'd thought maybe he'd tag along to the concert. Upon finding Jacob perched on the stairs, he plunked his invisible self two steps above his charge and one step above the wicker basket. Like Mew-Sinh, he was drawn to the tantalizing aroma. His mouth watered and he watched with an envious eye as Mew-Sinh pawed at the checkered cloth covering the crispy chicken.

"What is your name, son?" Desirée asked.

"Wesley," he answered. "But everybody calls me Wes."

"Well, Wes—" she assumed a motherly tone as she made her way behind the counter. "—I will try to assist you, but there are some things you need to be aware of first. Love spells are extremely potent—potent and unpredictable. Love seeks its own fulfillment. It cannot be forced. If you try to bind a heart against its will, the act will surely cause you grief."

"It doesn't have to be anything totally rad," Wesley said, reconsidering.

"So, you think a milder and more general love spell would best serve your needs?" she gently guided him.

"Yeah, I suppose," was his uncertain reply.

Mew-Sinh succeeded at working loose the checkered cloth. She thrust her nose into the wicker basket and nimbly lifted out a piece of chicken. Mackey made a lunge for her as she charged past, the prized drumstick clamped between her teeth.

Too late Jacob realized Mew-Sinh's thievery. The great chicken caper was a matter of history and so was Mew-Sinh.

Jacob made the mistake of leaving the basket where it sat, and merely tossing, rather than tucking the checkered cloth back over the chicken. Mackey, recognizing an opportunity when he saw one, inched himself down a step, then scooted closer to the basket. Soundlessly he slid a hand under the cloth and heisted yet another piece of chicken. He quickly stuffed it inside his khaki shirt and cautiously retreated to his former step.

"A love potion or oil would be too much," Desirée deliberated aloud. "A talisman might do. Yes, it would do nicely, especially if it were somehow connected with Stacie. Do you happen to know the girl's sign?"

"You mean like that astrology stuff my aunt is always rappin' about?"

"Miss Annie knows her zodiac." Desirée mildly admonished the boy for not showing proper respect.

"Yeah, she's a trip," he said with all due affection. "I don't know Stacie's sign but I know her birthday. You can figure it out from that, can't you?"

"Most certainly," she assured him.

"August 24th," he informed her straightaway.

"That would make her sun sign Cancer," she concluded, glancing down into the glass case. "And her lucky and protective stones would be opals, pearls, emeralds, or moonstones. Her mineral would be silver. And her color would be pearl or rose." She checked her available stock of stones. Everything but a moonstone was on hand.

Moonstone...moonstone... Of course! That accounted for the strong connection she felt with Jacob whenever she rubbed her own moonstone. Instantly her hand dipped into her blazer pocket, and with her fingertips, she stroked the moonstone.

"A rock is gonna make me irresistible to Stacie?" The young man slanted her a skeptical look.

"A stone," she corrected him. "Energy flows from stones. Certain ones hold particular power for those born under a certain sign. If you hold that power in your hand and either visualize or touch the person who is connected with that power, you are also connected. The stone is a conductor of energy," she explained.

"Oh, I get it. It's kind of like 'May the force be with you.'" At her blank expression, he tried to jog her memory. "You know. Luke Skywalker...Darth Vader."

"Oh, yes," she answered vaguely.

"Okay. That'll probably work. How much are one of those rocks?"

"Stones," she corrected him again. "Well, I'm afraid of those I have on hand, the cheapest would be the opal. It's twenty-two, fifty, plus tax."

His hand froze on his back pocket. He looked devastated. "That's a little more than I got on me."

"I see," she said.

Jacob's butt was getting numb sitting on the step. He wished he could think of a way to slip the kid the cash he needed.

Mackey wondered what Miss Warren would do. How she responded to the poor bloke's dilemma would tell a lot about her character.

"I may have something a little less expensive. Let me check." She bent below the counter, removing the moonstone from the pocket of her blazer. Her fingers closed around it. Could she do it—make such a personal sacrifice for the sake of a young man's romantic notions and his future self-assurance? For a fleeting second, she resisted the idea. After all, the moonstone was her only connection to Jacob. But then, her more noble instincts won out. She stood, and held out the translucent talisman to the teenager. "A moonstone is every bit as powerful, and much cheaper."

"How much cheaper?" he asked, pulling out his wallet and taking inventory of his funds.

Desirée spied a five-dollar bill. "Five dollars plus tax," she quoted.

"Great! That I can handle. Don't bother to wrap it. I'm gonna stick it in my pocket right away."

One last time her fingers cupped the moonstone.

"What's the tax?" he asked.

"Seventy-five cents," she responded, sick at the thought of parting with the moonstone, at giving up her powerful connection with Jacob. She'd been good. She'd refrained from any major dabbling. She'd only held on to the bit of stone...a bit of hope. But no more.

"Five-seventy-five. Here ya go." He counted out the exact change and placed it on the counter. "Can I have my lucky rock now?"

She blinked, then slowly uncurled her fingers.

The young man claimed his purchase. "I'll let you know if it does me any good. Thanks." With a cavalier grin, he strolled out the door.

Desirée did not notice Jacob until he swung the picnic basket onto the counter.

"How much of a beating did you take?"

"Pardon?"

"I know you gave the kid a break on the stone. It was really a nice thing you did. It's all bunk, of course, but as long as the kid believes it...." He left the thought unfinished. "How does the expression go? Nary a faint heart won a fair lady. Something like that." He flashed her a dazzling smile. "Are you ready for a bit of chicken and culture, Miss Warren?" He swooped up the picnic basket in an exaggerated gesture and flung open the shop door.

At his clowning, a grudging smile broke out on her face. "Yes, indeed, Mr. Malone," she agreed, coming out from behind the counter and walking over to the door.

After securing it, he offered his free arm to her.

"Very gallant, but not smart, Jacob. People will automatically assume you've fallen under my dark influence." She cast a nervous glance around.

"Maybe I have, Desirée," was his startling reply. But then he winked at her and she had no idea whether or not to take him seriously.

Linking her arm through his, she donned a confident expression. Together they joined the flow of folk headed toward the Landing.

THEY SAT ON a blanket, nibbling Brie, munching grapes and listening to Brahms. They'd managed to find a high spot on the grassy knoll. The view of the bay was breathtaking; the music, transporting.

"I've really enjoyed today, Desirée. I can't remember when I've felt more at peace." His green eyes were dreamy.

"I'm glad, Jacob. It's been wonderful for me, too." She smiled softly at him, then looked out over the bay. "When I was small, barely six or seven, I used to skip school and come up here. Mother and Nanna used to threaten me with spankings, but I came all the same."

"Was this your daydreaming spot?"

"Uh-huh. I'd sit up here for hours, just thinking and watching the boats come and go. I always dreamed of traveling to faraway places and doing exceptional things."

"What did you want to be when you grew up?" He leaned back on his elbows, cocking his head in amusement.

"Oh, it varied with my mood. Mostly, I just wanted to be rich and famous. Doesn't every kid?" she joked.

"Yeah, that's what we shoot for." His tone held just a hint of cynicism.

"I used to tell myself that I'd leave Marblehead just as soon as I was big, and seek my fortune across the sea. I truly imagined myself accomplishing some great feat and becoming the toast of Europe. As I grew older, I expanded on the fantasy so that it included a wonderfully passionate but terribly tragic love affair. A real-life prince would fall madly in love with me but, alas, his royal duties would claim his loyalties in the end. I, of course, eventually married a wealthy and prominent man and had two residences—a flat in Paris and a château in the French countryside; two darling children—a boy and a girl; and two pets—a lovable old basset hound and a cuddly cat."

"How perfect for you," he quipped, highly entertained by her fantasizing.

"Yes, well, as you can plainly see, things didn't exactly work out the way I'd planned. *C'est la vie*." She shrugged.

Jacob laughed out loud. "I like your attitude. It's a good one to take. I wish I could be as philosophical about my own unfulfilled dreams."

"What do you dream of?" she foolishly asked.

He directed a long, hard look at her. "You don't want to know," he finally answered, looking away and once again becoming intent upon gazing out over the bay.

"I'm interested in everything about you," she said softly.

The music muffled her words. He did not respond.

She sighed and popped another grape in her mouth. "Sometimes I wish I had left Marblehead," she mulled aloud. "Gone somewhere else and started anew. It's been so lonesome for me here."

His eyes returned to her. "I'm sure," was all he said.

"Do you realize, Jacob, that you are my very first real friend? I don't know how I'll stand it when you're gone." The revelation just tumbled from her. She was utterly mortified that she had voiced her secret. She hung her head, unable to look at him.

He moved closer to her, slipping his large hand over her small one and lacing his fingers with hers. "I'm not going anywhere for a while, Desirée. I've grown very fond of my temporary lodgings and my enchanting landlady."

Her head jerked up and she stared deeply into his eyes.

A jolt hit him—like white lightning passing through his body. Then a feeling—a feeling more intense and more compelling than he had ever before experienced in his life—gripped him. "I'm strongly attracted to you, Desirée. I don't know when it happened or how it happened, but I am," he confessed. "I'm saying this badly. Actually nothing about my life is making much sense lately." He shook his head. "I'm sure I resisted the attraction for a long time. I've never met anyone like you. And, quite frankly, I'm not at all sure I'm good enough for you. I would certainly understand if you had reservations about getting involved with someone as mixed up as me. No woman in her right mind would."

As she had waited so long to hear one word of encouragement from him, it struck her as incredibly ironic that he would even think she might reject him. "Oh, Jacob—" a hysterical giggle welled in her throat "—I should think just the opposite is true—no woman in her right mind could ever refuse you anything."

"I'm no prince, Desirée." He reached up, sliding a hand in her hair and gently cupping the back of her neck. Her breath caught in her throat as he guided her mouth to his. "But I am a loyal cuss," he murmured against her lips.

She melted into his kiss. The strains of Brahms grew fainter and fainter. Jacob's arms enfolded her. He was what she had prayed for, what she had in all probability damned her soul for. She loved him. Oh, how she loved him.

IT WAS LATE. The house was still, except for the usual creaks and groans of old New England timber. Every-

one had been in bed for hours. But not Mackey. He'd
been too keyed up to sleep. The kiss he'd witnessed at
the Landing had him in a dither. Instinct told him that
all the various factors were coming into play and soon
his charge's turning point would be at hand. A tem-
pest was brewing. That much he knew for certain.
Passions were running high. The air fairly crackled
with static energy. He could feel it all around him, and
Mackey always paid attention to his built-in radar. If
the hair on the back of his neck prickled, trouble lay
dead ahead.

Having just finished sudsing out his socks and
skivvies, he was tiptoeing his way back down the hall
when he heard the soft sound of approaching slippers. He quickly jumped behind a potted ficus tree and
waited to get a look-see at whoever else was prowling
around.

Through the leaves he saw Miss Warren come to
Malone's door, but then pause short of entering. She
turned away, as if to leave, hesitated, then did a one-
eighty, clasped the knob and eased open the door.

She snapped her fingers. Mew-Sinh emerged from
the interior of the darkened room and came to sit at
her mistress's feet. The little lady pointed down the
hall and the cat instantly obeyed her silent command.
Then she flicked back her unbound hair, drew a deep
breath and proceeded to soundlessly steal inside Malone's room.

Mackey waited for a minute or two until he thought
the coast was clear. No sooner had he stepped from

behind the ficus when Mew-Sinh, now keen to his scent, came for a look-see of her own.

"I'm here, you nosy puss," he hissed. "Quit your sniffing about."

Mew-Sinh sat back on her haunches and perked up her ears.

Mackey pushed his bushman's hat back on his head and scratched his stubbled cheek. "We should give 'em their privacy, eh?"

Mew-Sinh meowed.

Mackey's hand snaked out and muzzled the cat. "Shush before you wake up the whole bloody house." He took his hand away, motioning for Mew-Sinh to follow him down the hall. "We'll have us a midnight snack," he whispered. "Be a good puss and I'll treat you to cold chicken."

Lucky bloke! Mackey thought to himself as he sneaked past Malone's door.

THE ROOM WAS pitch-black. Familiar with the surroundings, Desirée navigated her way to the edge of Jacob's bed. The mattress creaked as he shifted his weight, freezing her in her tracks. But then, the sounds of his even breathing resumed and she dared to go on. Quietly she shed her slippers, then slipped her nightgown with its thin spaghetti straps from her shoulders and let it fall in a satin heap at her feet. Lifting the covers gently, she slid between the sheets and lay there for a moment, unsure of how to proceed. She had never made love to a man before. How did one begin? she wondered.

Jacob solved the problem for her. He turned over in his sleep and flung an arm across her stomach. She inched closer to him, barely rustling the covers as she did so. His arm encircled her and, mistaking her for the feather pillow, he towed her in to the curve of his body and snuggled up to her.

He slept nude, a fact which did not surprise her all that much. Sometimes when she stripped the sheets on his bed, she would daydream about him. In the raw was how she always imagined him when smoothing out and tucking in the fresh linens upon which he would later lay.

She molded herself against his warmth, amazed by how natural it felt to have his flesh pressed against hers. She couldn't resist exploring him a little. With a gossamer touch she let her hand roam down his muscled back, over his smooth buttock and along his taut thigh. She wasn't timid or embarrassed. His manly anatomy did not repulse or intimidate her; it intrigued and excited her. Jacob was so much larger and harder than she was. He smelled nice, too—a little like her pungent herbs. His distinctive cologne even permeated the bed covers. Having grown up in a household of women, Desirée had had little exposure to the masculine mystique. She was filled with wonder and almost kittenish curiosity.

Jacob sighed deeply and nestled his cheek in her hair. She turned to face him, impishly tracing the deep cleft in his chin with a fingertip. "Jacob." She spoke his name in a hushed tone.

"Mmmmm." His grip on her loosened.

She raised herself up a bit and began feathering kisses along his neck to the sensitive area behind his ear. "Are you awake?"

"Mmmmm." He rolled over onto his back.

She smiled and bent her mouth to his, kissing him tenderly at first, then ardently.

His eyes flew open and his body lurched.

"Don't be frightened. It's just me," she murmured.

"Me, who?" he uttered groggily.

"Desirée, silly," she giggled.

"Mmmm." He sighed. It was happening again; he was having another erotic dream about Desirée.

She smoothed a hand along his cheek while threading a silky leg between his brawny ones. "I want to make love, Jacob."

Oh, boy! This one was a lulu. No mimosa and no mist. No snow in the meadow. Just Desirée's voice and touch coming out of inky space.

She kissed him once more.

He groaned with pleasure as her bare breasts brushed across his chest. His arms wrapped around her slim back, forging her to him. "We have to quit meeting like this," he murmured in twilight consciousness, rolling over and assuming the missionary position.

Her answer was a gasp as she felt his hand glide between her legs. Sensuously, expertly, he introduced her to the mysteries of erotica.

Throughout the wee hours she learned much about the art of making love. She was an eager student. Under his masterful tutelage she came to understand the subtle nuances of the mating ritual—came to know what it was truly like to leave one's own body and temporarily merge with another's soul. And when Jacob collapsed on top of her, his body damp and limp from seeking to gratify her every desire, she cradled his head against her shoulder and smoothed his hair until he once again fell into a deep and contented sleep.

She pulled the coverlet over them and kissed his temple. For hours, she lay beside him, wide awake and overwhelmed by her thoughts and feelings. Just prior to dawn, she slipped from between the covers and got dressed again. Missing her body in the bed, he fumbled for the pillow and hugged it in her stead. Afraid he might wake up, she tarried only a moment longer to smooth the bed covers around him and admire his swarthy good looks in the pale morning light.

"Yours is the stronger magic, Jacob," she whispered. "For surely there can be no power greater than the power of love."

With those words, she retreated and left him to his dreams.

CHAPTER TWELVE

JACOB WOKE to the persistent buzzing of the alarm. He stretched out an arm and blindly groped for the snooze button. Directly, the bothersome buzzing ceased.

He draped an arm over his eyes to block out the harsh morning light, and half drifted off again. Snatches of the latest episode in an ever-continuing phantasm bleeped into his foggy brain. He had vivid flashes of making love to Desirée. *Really vivid flashes!*

Slowly he took his arm from across his eyes and peeked over at the opposite side of the bed. He was alone. It had only been another dream. But then, why did it all seem so damn real?

The snooze alarm buzzed again. He rolled over and switched it off, then plopped back against the pillow with a lazy yawn. He remembered the gist of the dream: he and Desirée had engaged in X-rated fantasia throughout the livelong night.

"You wish it were real," he muttered scoffingly, flinging back the coverlet and preparing to alight from the bed. It was then that a glimmer of silver caught his attention. His stomach did a flip-flop as his fingers tentatively stretched toward the thin chain sticking out from underneath the pillow.

He knew what he suspected was true even before confirming it. The glimmering bit of silver was Desirée's necklace—the moon charm that she kept tucked from view. She *had* been in his bed last night! What other explanation could there possibly be?

He shook his head to clear it. "Okay, don't come unraveled just yet," he told himself. There had to be some rational explanation. All he had to do was think logically about it. A, he'd dreamed about making love to Desirée. B, he'd woken up alone, but had later found her necklace in his bed. C, he could conclude that she was, in fact, in his bed last night and the two of them actually did do what he'd thought he had only dreamed, or, D, she had lost her necklace when tidying up his bedroom and he was jumping to one hell of a conclusion.

He decided to examine the evidence more closely. On second inspection, he noted that the necklace's clasp was indeed broken. "A-hah!" he said aloud. "She was holding the pillow under her chin in order to slip on the clean pillowcase." He snatched up the pillow and reenacted the crime. "Somehow the catch gave way when she dropped the pillow to the bed and the necklace came with it." He tossed the pillow aside. The theory sounded reasonable. But there was another supposition to consider: that while they had been engaged in blind and mad passion, the necklace had somehow become twisted or tangled and the clasp had broken, causing the chain to slip undetected from her neck.

"Damn it! Which is it? Did we or didn't we?" His knuckles grew whiter and whiter as his fingers clamped tighter and tighter around the necklace.

At that indelicate moment, Mew-Sinh scratched at the door.

The latch, for once, held.

Stark naked and wholly confused, Jacob just sat there transfixed while Mew-Sinh kept up her infernal scratching. Dazedly he unknotted his fist, letting the chain and moon charm spill from his hand onto the nightstand. "You're losing it, Malone. No doubt about it. A day or two ago you were halfway convinced that the ditzo cat could walk through walls."

He flopped backward on the bed and stared up at the ceiling. "What do I say? Oh, by the way, Desirée, did we happen to get it on last night? Cripes! She's going to think I'm crazy!"

WHILE JACOB AGONIZED in his room above The Magic Herb Hut, Archie Hooper was having coffee and donuts in the church fellowship hall a few blocks away. He always arrived thirty minutes early for nine o'clock services so he could chat with members of the congregation and catch up on the scuttlebutt before listening to the gospel. He usually stood in the same spot near the hall door and conversed with a few old cohorts who were still spry and cognizant enough to attend Sunday services.

"Guess you heard about Amos McWhorter," Nathan Pritchard said between slurps of his coffee.

"Uh-huh." Archie shook his head sadly. "His daughter put him in Golden Acres first of the week."

Nathan nodded. "Declared him incompetent and stuck him in the home. Amos was a bit forgetful, that's all. His daughter just wanted him out of the way."

"He was more than a bit forgetful, Nathan. He wandered off regularly. Last time the troopers picked him up outside of town, he was in his doughboy uniform and slippers and kept insisting he was making his way back to the front."

"Well, he was a damn good chess player in his day."

"Uh-huh, that he was," Archie concurred. "Maybe we can visit him in the home and play a match or two with him."

"Not likely," Nathan said. "He keeps forgetting whether he picked white or black."

Archie and the others observed a moment of silence in memory of Amos, who was as good as dead since his internment at Golden Acres. Then the threesome—Nathan Pritchard, Sidney Farb and Archie—took swigs of their coffee and looked off into space. It was then that Archie spied Patsy James flitting from one cluster of folks to another with a clipboard in her hand. From the way that she was flapping her jaws and waving her hands, Archie figured she was filibustering about something. "What's Patsy doing? Taking a census or something?" he asked.

Sidney Farb on his left was the first to speak up. "She's getting signatures on a petition. Been at it since yesterday."

"What's she up in arms about now?" Archie finished off his coffee and tossed the Styrofoam cup into the trash barrel behind him.

"I don't know for sure. She talks so fast it's hard to catch everything she's saying." Sidney was getting more deaf by the day, but he refused to wear a hearing aid. "The best I understand it, she wants to bring warrant for a special town meeting."

"For what reason?" Archie's eyes followed her as she moved to the next group and pitched her petition.

"It has to do with zoning restrictions in the Old Town. She claims one of the businesses is in violation. She wants to shut 'em down. I signed it, but I don't quite understand it." Sidney polished off the glazed donut and brushed off his hands.

"You shouldn't sign anything you don't understand," Archie scolded him. "You do and you might just end up being Amos's roommate at Golden Acres. Your own daughter took a tour of the place the same time as his did. I know 'cause they stopped off at my shop afterward. So I'd watch my P's and Q's if I were you. And I'd watch what I signed in the future," he warned him.

Sidney's eyes darted to his spinster daughter, who was at that moment signing Patsy's petition.

"I read the thing," Nathan Pritchard put in. "There's a lot of fancy wording. Article this, Section that. What it boils down to is just what Sidney says.

Patsy wants a public hearing on whether or not a certain establishment's historical status is valid according to the stipulations set out in the town charter.''

"Which establishment is she claiming to be in breach of the zoning regulations?'' Archie had a pretty good idea what his friend's reply would be.

"The Magic Herb Hut.''

"Uh-huh, I thought as much.'' His eyes narrowed as he saw the clipboard going from hand to hand and people affixing their signatures to the petition. "Did you add your John Henry to it, Nathan?''

"Nope. I think it's a witch-hunt and I want no part of it,'' the old sailor declared.

"Uh-huh. That's what it is,'' Archie agreed.

"But Patsy said it was our Christian and civic duty to uphold the decent standards and bylaws of Marblehead,'' Sidney blustered.

"Oh, horse feathers!'' Archie spat. "Patsy James isn't collecting signatures for the good of anyone else but herself. Go scratch your name off that petition, Sidney, unless you don't mind acting like a doddering old fool.''

Sidney sucked in his paunch. "Who are you calling an old fool, you old fart? I got a right to my opinions, same as you,'' he bristled.

Archie immediately regretted having spoken to his longtime friend in such a demeaning way; Sidney was deaf, but he wasn't dumb. He pulled out a handkerchief from his pocket and offered to his old buddy with a contrite smile. "Well, then at least wipe the sugar from off your chin.''

Sidney accepted the handkerchief and Archie's unspoken apology. "I was going to do it anyway," he mumbled, swiping at his chin.

"Which? Scratch your name off or wipe your chin?" Archie flashed him a tickled look.

"Both," Sidney grunted. "After what you told me, I don't trust anything that daughter of mine puts her signature to. Did I get it all off?" He stuck out his chin for inspection.

"Uh-huh," Archie assured him, taking his handkerchief back.

The church bells chimed, calling the congregation to worship. The three old-timers straightened their bow ties and suspenders, and then set off to pray.

JACOB BARELY TOUCHED his breakfast. Desirée noticed but reserved comment since she did not know what to make of his brooding mood. Having had no prior experience, she didn't have an inkling as to what was proper morning-after etiquette. Perhaps these things were not discussed. Not wanting to make some gross faux pas, she decided to say nothing of what had transpired between them until he did.

Jacob gave serious thought to chickening out and leaving the table without saying one word about the dream or the necklace, but curiosity prevailed over cowardice in the end. He let his fork drop to the plate with an attention-getting clunk, shoved back his chair and prepared to make an ass of himself.

She eased her own fork down and gazed puzzledly at him.

"I need to ask you a question, Desirée. It may sound off-the-wall, but please bear with me, okay?"

She agreed with a nod.

"Have you a habit of sleepwalking?"

She looked amused. "Not since I was a child."

"Are you sure you don't still occasionally wander around at night?" He didn't know which would be worse—a yes or a no reply.

"I don't think so," was her inconclusive answer.

He expelled a deep sigh. "Okay. I give up. There's no delicate way around this," he muttered to himself.

"Around what?" His agitated state was beginning to make her nervous. It seemed to her that he was searching for an excuse to discount what had happened between them.

"You see, Desirée, I've been having these really strange dreams...." He shifted his weight in his chair and raked a hand through his hair. "And I, uh, had another one last night . . . or at least, I thought I did." He could not maintain eye contact with her as he fished into his shirt pocket and withdrew the necklace. "But then I found this in my bed. It's yours, I believe." He dropped the moon charm onto the table.

Her hand flew to her neck. She hadn't realized it was missing.

"Oh, boy! This is harder than I thought." He squared his shoulders, pushed up his sleeves, and drew a deep breath. "I'm probably crazy for thinking what I'm thinking. I'm sure it's just a coincidence but—" he shot her a helpless look "—these dreams I mentioned are pretty racy . . . and, uh, well, you're a principal player in them. Last night I dreamed you were in my room...in my bed...and this morning the feeling that you were actually there got stronger and stronger. Pretty far-out, huh?" He did not expect or pause for an answer. "Ordinarily I'd dismiss it as an eerie by-product of my overactive imagination, but then I found the necklace. I'm sure you probably just lost it when you were making up the bed or something, and what I'm about to suggest will convince you that I'm totally crackers—"

She could not let him go on any longer. "I was there, Jacob. In your room, in your bed. We made love."

"We did?" he uttered dumbly.

"We did," she confirmed.

"Oh—" he took a swig of juice "—I thought it was just an especially vivid dream," he croaked.

"You seem upset to find out that it wasn't. Was last night such an unpleasant experience for you?" She, too, was stunned—hurt by his less-than-flattering reaction.

"No! It was great," he assured her, though not very convincingly, since he was still reeling from the shock she'd just dealt him. "It's just that I'm still somewhat confused about how we came to, uh...well, you know," he fumbled, hoping she would spare him from having to be explicit.

"Make love," she supplied.

"Yeah." Her matter-of-fact comportment made him even more uncomfortable. "I'm a bit blurry on a few small facts—like when we decided to, uh...get together in my room. I know I had a couple of glasses of wine after we got back from the Landing, but it certainly wasn't enough to cause a major blackout. I really don't remember suggesting that we... ah, you know—''

"Make love." She filled in the blanks once more.

He nodded.

"You didn't. It was entirely my idea," she said simply.

"It was?" His relief was plainly evident.

"It was." She allayed his fears.

"What prompted you to do such a thing?" He could not reconcile her bold behavior with her shy nature.

"I thought it was what two people did when they were strongly attracted to each other. I've waited such a long time to experience sex. I always wondered what it would be like.''

"So you just acted on your feelings?"

"Isn't that the proper thing to do?"

He didn't know which astounded him more—her frankness or her naïveté. "Well, it's not that it's improper, exactly. It's just that these things generally progress a little more slowly."

"Why?" she asked.

"It's hard to explain." He had never felt as awkward in his entire life. "Men and women don't usually fall into bed with one another after one kiss."

"Why do they delay?" she asked quizzically.

"Because it's a more enriching experience if they've moved gradually toward each other." He had no earthly idea why he was advocating restraint since he seldom practiced it himself. Quite often he had fallen into bed with a woman after sharing little more than basic facts and a few cocktails. He could see that she was also having difficulty following his logic. "Delaying gratification arouses the senses and heightens the excitement," he further expounded.

"You seemed highly aroused last night. Did you not find the act sufficiently exciting?"

He had to grin. She sounded like Mister Spock. "Extremely so," he admitted. "But usually a man likes to assume the more aggressive role."

"Oh," she said. "Then you would have preferred to have come to my room?"

What was he to do with her? he wondered. A voice inside his head cued him. *Appreciate her, you damn fool.* His eyes grew warm as he took her hand and brought it to his lips. "You really are delightful, Desirée. I don't think I have ever met a more beguiling lady. You're straightforwardness amazes me."

"You give me too much credit, Jacob. At the risk of your becoming disenchanted with me, I must tell you something that may cause you as much distress as your dreams." She lowered her head ashamedly.

"What is it, Desirée?" He tipped her chin with a fingertip, forcing her to confront his searching eyes.

"I'm the reason that you have such crazy dreams," she confessed.

"I know. You've somehow managed to captivate my senses." His wink was as suggestive as it was playful.

"No, I mean I *cause* them," she tried to explain. "You would not have come to Marblehead or been plagued by dreams of me had it not been for my dabbling in the Craft." Imploringly, she added, "You have to believe me, Jacob, when I tell you that I've never done anything like this before. I don't know what came over me. I was so very lonely and the thought occurred to me that perhaps one of the spells in the old book could work for me. So I read and learned and one foggy night I just did it. I cast a spell. A few days later you came to my doorstep. Until then, I wasn't sure that the power was real. Once I saw you, I wanted to keep you for my own. So I dabbled a bit more—some violet petals, a love charm under your pillow, a moonstone in my pocket. I bound you to me by way of your dreams, even though I knew it was wrong. Love must be freely given. And as much as I adore you, I cannot in good conscience deceive you any longer." Her voice cracked with emotion and he could see that she was on the verge of tears.

"Come here, sweetheart," he said, gently guiding her onto his lap and enfolding her in his arms. "I know you believe that magic played a part in what happened between us, but it's simply not true. I came to Marblehead quite by accident, Desirée. I got turned around in a snowstorm, that's all. And as for my dreams—" he smoothed back her hair as he spoke "—they are nothing more than a natural result of my being attracted to you. Over these past few weeks, I've come to see you as a lovely, gentle woman whom I respect and admire. Sure, there is a certain mystique about you that intrigues me, but I respond to you as a man in love, not a man possessed. Your amateur dabbling is nothing more than coincidence, Desirée. It had nothing to do with our coming together. The trouble with you is that you know more about love potions than you do about love itself. No outside influence can produce the condition. It's something that occurs inside a person and grows stronger with time. Trust me on this one.'' He cupped her chin and tilted back her head. "It's you, not some ritual, that's aroused my passion."

"But you don't understand—"

He stilled her reservations with a searing kiss. "Let's forget about all this sorcery stuff and make a little magic of our own," he suggested, standing with her still cradled in his arms.

She linked her arms around his neck and cast him a beguiling smile. "In broad daylight, Mr. Malone? Is it proper?"

"Perfectly, Miss Warren," he assured her with a roguish grin.

CHAPTER THIRTEEN

THE DAYS CAME and went in Marblehead, and two pivotal forces—love and jealousy—steadily gained momentum. Mackey was no meteorologist but he knew the result when a hot and cold front converged: a major atmospheric disturbance. Ominous rumblings were in the wind. The direction Malone's life had recently taken placed him directly in the path of the storm. Mackey worried that his charge's character was not strong enough to withstand the turbulent days ahead. The man seemed to be functioning in a delusive haze—so did the little lady for that matter. The pair of them weren't merely sleepwalking at night; they were sleepwalking through their days as well.

Unlike Mackey, the two were oblivious to the ill will swirling through the streets of Marblehead. Desirée did not notice that her business had fallen off considerably in the past few weeks. And he, though slightly aware of being treated aloofly whenever he ventured into public with his landlady, attached no special significance to the drastic drop in the social barometer. Neither did he think it especially strange that Patsy James no longer carried on a flirtation with him. He'd assumed that since he hadn't encouraged her, she'd merely lost interest.

Archie Hooper had the same gloomy suspicions as the guardian angel. He knew Patsy hadn't suffered any pangs of conscience or a change of heart. She was merely biding her time, was all. He'd heard from Nathan Pritchard that she'd been successful in attaining the two-hundred signatures required to bring a warrant for a special town meeting before the Board of Selectmen. Whatever slim hope he'd held out that old Nathan's information was incorrect vanished when he saw Patsy tack up an official notice of warrant on a lamppost right outside his shop.

"I can't believe she'd post it directly across the street from Desirée's shop. What a spiteful thing to do." Marilyn Estes was duly appalled.

"I can believe it. Patsy's got a mean streak. You just haven't been exposed to it. But you're about to be, Ms Estes." He shook his head glumly as he stacked a bunch of clean mugs and then stored the load in a sliding rack beneath the counter. "Uh-huh, this is only the beginning. Things will get a whole lot nastier before it's all over."

"I really don't understand how a special town meeting works." She quickly turned on her stool and faced Mr. Hooper so as not to have to acknowledge Patsy when she traipsed by the window.

"It's a fairly simple process. Patsy's taken care of the mechanics. She's collected the two-hundred signatures necessary to get a warrant to air a grievance before the town. She's posted the official notification in ten prominent places thirty days prior to the meeting so's anyone interested in the agenda can attend. The meeting is held in the high-school auditorium and conducted by a moderator. It's an open forum. Since Patsy sponsored the warrant she'll present her side first. Any voters can debate the issue, so long as they confine their remarks to the subject at hand. Once everyone has had their say, it goes to a vote, which is generally signified by a show of hands.''

"Good grief, Mr. Hooper! That means Desirée Warren will have to show up to speak on her own behalf. I don't envy her the task.''

"Uh-huh, Patsy's caused a hell of a stink this time.''

The newcomer gathered her shopping bags in preparation for leaving. "I only met Miss Warren once. She seemed to me to be a rather meek soul. I fear that by the night of the town meeting, anarchy will reign, and poor Miss Warren won't even be allowed to plead her case.''

"Oh, folks will let her speak her mind,'' Archie assured her. "It's just that most of them will have already made up theirs and won't much be listening to anything she has to say.''

"Then why bother to go through all the motions?'' Marilyn fumed. "Why not just shut down her shop and have the constable escort Miss Warren across the county line?'' Rarely did Marilyn Estes fly off the handle, yet she was dangerously close to doing precisely that very thing and making a royal fool out of herself in the process. For some crazy reason, she wanted to rail at Archie since she couldn't rail against the petty prejudice that she found offensive and intolerable.

"We believe in the democratic process here in Marblehead, Ms Estes. We're not a bunch of vigilantes. Desirée will get a chance to speak her piece."

"The bastille and guillotine were part of a democratic process, too," she reminded him. "Did you ever read *A Tale of Two Cities* by Dickens, Mr. Hooper?"

"Uh-huh. Had to read it as a kid in school, but I don't remember much of it."

"Maybe you and everyone else in Marblehead should refresh your memories. Maybe you'd see some similarities between eighteenth century Paris and modern day Marblehead—between Madame DeFarge and Patsy James. It's a good example of what can happen to the democratic process when reason escapes us and chaos reigns." She could see that Archie was distracted. "Oh, what's the use in debating it." She sighed, clutched her packages to her and swiveled on the stool.

"I'm listening, Ms Estes." The old shopkeeper looked back to her. "Jacob Malone's making his way across the street," he explained. "I wanted to see if the notice caught his attention."

She turned to look too. He walked right by it and into the Mug and Muffin Shoppe.

"Morning," Jacob greeted the pair as he strolled through the door.

Marilyn vacated her place at the counter as he sat down. Behind his back, she mouthed to Archie, "Tell him'' and pointed to the notice of warrant tacked to the lamppost.

The old shopkeeper nodded as he set Jacob's coffee on the counter. "So long, Ms Estes."

"Good day, gentlemen," she bid the two men before slipping out the door.

"Nice day, huh?" Jacob said chattily.

"Well, I suppose it will be for some folks," was Archie's low-key reply.

Jacob grinned and took a sip of his coffee. "That's a rather ambiguous statement. Is your day not off to a good start, Arch?"

"Mine? No, my day's going about the same as usual. I was referring to somebody else." He didn't know quite how to lead the conversation around to the matter of the warrant.

"And who might that be?" The proprietor's odd behavior aroused Jacob's curiosity.

Archie peered at him through the lower half of his bifocals. "It could be that Desirée's day might go downhill in a hurry."

Jacob could tell by the older man's troubled expression that something serious was weighing on his mind. "You sound pretty certain of that. How come?" he asked pointedly.

Archie slung his dish towel over his shoulder, left Jacob sitting at the counter and went outside to collect the notice from the lamppost. "Something like this could tend to ruin a person's day," was all he said when he came back in and laid the warrant at Jacob's elbow.

Jacob quickly skimmed the contents, then raised his eyes to Archie's. "Does this mean what I think it does? There's going to be a public hearing to decide whether or not Desirée can continue to conduct business at her present location?"

"Uh-huh. That's about the size of it." Archie poured himself a cup of hot coffee.

"Do you know anything about these zoning restrictions cited as cause for warrant?"

"All I know is that the Old Town is a designated historical area and there are certain requirements that are strictly enforced. The street out front is the boundary. The restrictions don't apply to me, but Desirée has to comply with 'em. Somebody's contending that she's in violation of the Certification of Appropriateness Act."

"What the hell does that mean?" Jacob knew enough linguistic legal tricks to smell a rat.

"It's just a fancy way of saying that the Warren family didn't obtain the necessary permission to convert the place into a shop. So technically, The Magic Herb Hut is ineligible to be designated a historical site. The bottom line is that Desirée will either have to obtain special dispensation to continue trading in Old Town, which most likely won't be granted, or restore the place to its original look, which puts her out of business."

"But her family has been doing business in the same spot for years. Why all of a sudden is a conversion that took place a quarter of a century ago an issue?"

Archie was impressed by how quickly Jacob had
zeroed in on the crux of the matter. "Probably because it's just a roundabout way of accomplishing
what some folks have wanted to do for a long time."

"Which is?" Jacob pressed.

"Make it impossible for a Warren woman to stay on
in town," was Archie's frank answer.

"I know Desirée is not the most popular person
around here, but I still find it strange that these
charges have just been leveled against her." He studied Archie, noticing the small signs that meant the old
man knew more than he was telling. "Come on, Arch.
You know what's really behind this. Tell me the truth.
I want to help Desirée but I can't unless I know the
whole story."

"I don't generally like to mix in other people's affairs. I learned a long time ago that it caused more
trouble than good. But I'm going to make an exception this once because I like Desirée and I think you're
an honorable young fella."

"Don't endow me with too much character, Arch.
I have on occasion resorted to less than noble methods in order to get my way." Jacob polished off the
coffee and shoved his mug toward the old man for a
refill.

"Uh-huh. Well, I hope it doesn't come to that."
Archie wondered if he was doing the right thing.
Meddling was not something he did lightly. He filled
Jacob's mug and said nothing for a moment.

"It's important that you tell me, Arch. I'm a good
lawyer but I'm out of my element. I'm not familiar

with your local statutes and I certainly don't understand the small-town mentality. I promise you that I'll keep whatever you say to me confidential.''

He sounded sincere. Archie decided he owed it to Chelsey to apprise him of the facts. He hadn't stood up for her as a young buck, but maybe it wasn't too late to redeem himself as an old man and help her daughter. "Patsy James is the one who started digging into the records and brought cause for warrant before the Board of Selectmen," he said. "She circulated the petition and got folks fired up about the inappropriateness of Desirée's shop. And you, young man, are the reason that she started the whole damn fracas.''

"Me?" Jacob blurted, spraying coffee all over the counter in his surprise.

Archie took the dish towel from his shoulder and wiped up the mess. "Uh-huh," he reaffirmed. "She wasn't coming in here every day to moon over me. She's smitten with you and she's gotten it in her head that Desirée is an obstacle to her future happiness. Patsy's never been one to let things fall to chance. She doesn't lack initiative or nerve when it comes to something she wants. And you're the prize she's after, Jacob. Of course, it didn't help matters any that she's got an ax to grind when it comes to the Warren women anyway. You're all the incentive she needed to act on a long-standing grudge.''

Jacob muttered. "I should've set the woman straight right off. I'm not some prize in a grab bag. Ever since I came into town, the craziest things have been happening to me. Maybe I should go back to Boston. Desirée would probably be better off if I did and perhaps I would be, too.''

''It's for you to decide,'' Archie said with a shrug. ''Course your presence in Boston won't have any bearing on the town meeting. It'll still take place in thirty days. Your presence here might make a difference, though. Who else is there to speak on Desirée's behalf? Me? I'm no talker. I'm just an old man nobody listens to anymore. It's a short ride to Boston, my friend, but when you have to swallow your pride in order to return, it'll be the longest drive of your life. I'd give it some serious thought before I acted hastily. Like I said, you're an honorable young fella. In the end, you'll know the right thing to do.''

''And what if, like *I* said, you've endowed me with too much character?'' Uncertainty was revealed in his green eyes.

''Then we'll both have been guilty of exercising poor judgment,'' was all Archie offered in answer to his customer's soul-searching. ''More coffee?'' He started to replenish Jacob's mug.

Jacob shook his head. ''Give me a glass of milk. I feel an ulcer coming on.''

Archie did as he was instructed.

Jacob drank the milk in a couple of gulps and wiped the white moustache from his upper lip. ''Okay, now what about this grudge you mentioned?''

Archie's worries disappeared. He'd done the right thing in telling Jacob Malone. He suddenly had complete faith that the young lawyer would do the right thing with the information he'd entrusted him with.

JACOB HAD KEPT what he had learned earlier in the day to himself. Since Mr. Hooper had removed the notice of warrant posted across the street, Desirée was not yet aware of the impending town meeting concerning her livelihood. Jacob hadn't the heart to tell her until later that night when they lay cuddled together in bed.

"Did you mean it when you said that sometimes you wished you had left Marblehead, Desirée?" He pretended it was just an offhanded question.

Something in his tone gave him away. She scooted closer to him and brought the quilt up over her breasts. "Something's wrong, Jacob. I can tell. You've been in a strange mood all day. Why are you asking me this?"

"Because I wonder why you stay here." He rolled onto his side, propped his head on his hand and gazed thoughtfully at her.

"Where else would I go? I've spent my entire life here. It's my home," she answered.

"But you yourself said that the people here are unfriendly to you. Why continue to subject yourself to the abuse?"

"For one thing, my roots are here, and they run just as deeply as those of other Marbleheaders. My grandmother and mother overcame a lot of adversity in order to make a go of The Magic Herb Hut. For another, what else am I equipped to do but sell herbs and roots and magic trinkets?"

He could see that she was fast becoming defensive. Desirée had a sixth sense when it came to anything that threatened her Wicca heritage. By now he knew the small warning signs of her guardedness: the slight lift of her chin, the stiffening of her slim shoulders, the feisty flick of her red-brown hair. He treaded carefully. "There's plenty of work in Boston, or—"

"Boston! That's it, isn't it?" She sat straight up and turned to him with a look of alarm. "You want to return and you don't know how to tell me." Even in the dark, he could see the betraying quiver that traveled the length of her body.

"No, sweetheart. That's not what I'm trying to prepare you for." He reached out an arm and pulled her down against him.

"Then what is it, Jacob? Please, don't keep anything from me. I can always sense when something is troubling you," she murmured against his chest.

He snuggled closer to her, idly stroking her temple with a thumb. "Your neighbors are plotting against you, Desirée, especially Patsy James." At her attempt to lurch from his embrace, he calmed her with a commanding, "Shhh, it's all right. Hear me out, okay?" At her mute nod, he continued. "I saw an official notification of warrant posted on a lamppost across the street. A complaint has been lodged against your shop on the grounds that you're in breach of the zoning code. It's all legal crap and just another way of trying to get rid of you. If they take away your livelihood, they figure you won't linger in town much longer. There's going to be a special town meeting held in thirty days to decide the future of your shop. I just thought it would be simpler to spare yourself the ordeal and relocate elsewhere.''

''No!'' She adamantly rejected the suggestion.

''Why not?'' he argued, still holding her tightly in his grasp. ''Be reasonable, Desirée. There's no reason to subject yourself to this sort of prejudice when you could just as easily—''

She wriggled free and sat up. ''I may walk away from Marblehead, but I won't be run off. I've done nothing wrong except to have committed the unpardonable sin of being different. Do you really believe anything will change for me just because I take refuge somewhere else? I'm me, Jacob. Unusual would be a polite way of phrasing it. And I'll still be the same unusual me in Boston or wherever I go. Changing where I live won't change who or what I am. And what do you propose that I do in Boston or wherever I might happen to seek asylum? Sell lingerie in some exclusive boutique that caters to socialites? I don't know about such things. I know herbs and roots and—''

''Magic trinkets.'' He sighed.

''Yes,'' she said with a proud lift of her head. ''I'm a product of the Old Ways. I act differently and react differently because of it. And you must be able to accept that about me if we are to be anything more to each other than warm bodies to lie next to through the lonely nights.'' She bent back down and brushed her lips across his. ''I love you, Jacob, just as you are. I don't expect perfection, or for you to conform to some rigid pattern that doesn't suit you. I only want your happiness. If my 'differentness' causes you embarrassment, I will understand if—"

He lifted his hand to the back of her head and brought her mouth to his, kissing her deeply. "Shut up, Desirée," he whispered, sliding his body over hers. "You're my dream lover...." He kissed her again and again and again until she was breathless and heedless of all else but him—heedless of the fact that the moon beyond the bedroom window was in the last triad of its cycle. It was the time of the waning moon—a time when all things had to end to fulfill their beginnings. The waning moon—the sum of the whole, the symbol of all things seen and unseen, of all that went before and was yet to come....

CHAPTER FOURTEEN

THE COUNTDOWN BEGAN twenty-nine days before the town meeting. Soon it was twenty, then ten, then five. The date crept ever closer and tension mounted. Even Patsy James suffered a moment or two of misgivings. Nerves were on edge, and while the days grew increasingly warmer, the emotional climate in Marblehead grew cooler and cooler, especially toward the proprietress and her star boarder.

It was getting to Jacob. Though he'd always considered himself to be a free thinker and inner directed, a trait was surfacing in him that he neither liked nor wanted to acknowledge. It bothered him to be set apart—to be viewed as a *persona non grata*. He was unaccustomed to such treatment and it wore on him.

In spite of the loyalty he demonstrated in public, he harbored secret doubts about himself and his relationship with Desirée. He started taking long walks alone. For miles and hours on end he would be deeply introspective. Not to a soul—especially not to her— did he dare voice his misgivings. How could he admit to another what he could hardly admit to himself: that he was not the liberal fellow he'd once believed himself to be—a champion of basic freedoms, an advocate of individuality so long as that individuality worked within the framework of the law. Had it all been rhetoric? Underneath the noble sentiment did there beat the heart of a conventionalist?

In essence, he was questioning his strength of character. The intense scrutiny and gossip his association with Desirée had caused had been more than he'd bargained for. In fact, a relationship with her was proving to be a hell of a strain. She wasn't merely unusual—unusual he could handle. A work of art could be unusual, but that only enhanced its appeal and value. Desirée was borderline eccentric and occasionally controversial. Would he or could he ever get used to her Old Ways? Did he really need this discord, this woman in his life? When it came right down to it, were his needs shallow and his values superficial? Maybe in all honesty he preferred the standard, no-hassle beauty-queen type to a strikingly different woman who would forever provoke whispers wherever she went.

Cripes! What was he really all about? What did he want out of life? *Desirée and desire/desire and Desirée. Once in a blue moon. A dream lover who could make magic.* But did he love her? And if so, did he love her enough? Life would never be easy with Desirée. But then again, it would never be dull.

Through the winding streets of Marblehead at dusk, he walked and thought, walked and thought.

No answers came to him.

DESIRÉE STOPPED PACING and went to the shop's window again. Her eyes scanned the dark streets in search of Jacob. A storm was blowing in from the sea. Lightning crackled in the night sky and a clap of thunder resounded in the distance. Jacob had been gone for such a long time. It was the latest he had ever returned from his nightly walk. Desirée had respected his need for privacy these past days. She knew he was waging an inner battle with himself and she sensed the outside pressure was becoming too much for him to deal with.

Mew-Sinh and the invisible Mackey sat perched on the steps, watching and waiting, too.

"Oh, God! Where is he? I feel something is terribly, terribly wrong," Desirée fretted aloud. She left the window and resumed her nervous pacing. "He's pulling away from me. I know it. I have to do something. I can't let this happen." She hugged her midriff to stave off the icy dread coiling in the pit of her stomach. "I mustn't lose Jacob. I mustn't lose the shop. But how do I stop what has already been set in motion?"

A gust of wind blew open the shop door—a gust so strong that it ruffled Mew-Sinh's fur and caused the brim of Mackey's bushman's hat to flap wildly. The sudden whoosh of salt air also ruffled the yellowed pages of the old volume lying open on the table.

Desirée pushed the door shut, and when she turned around, her eyes fell upon the old volume.

The hair on the back of Alistair's neck prickled. *Uh-oh!* he thought. *No, little lady. Don't do it!*

Slowly she crossed the room to the table and looked down at the passage the wind had chosen. She was just desperate enough to resort to summoning the power of the Old Ways one more time.

She dashed around collecting the items necessary to cast yet another spell: a black candle, incense, a bowl of saltwater, a bit of red ribbon, a small poppet made of wax, and most importantly, the old volume from which to recite the ancient words.

When all was assembled, she began the ritual of binding her enemy. She lit the candle and incense, then sprinkled the poppet with saltwater, looked to the book, memorized the passage, closed her eyes and chanted.

"Blessed be, thou creature made by art. By art made, by art changed. Thou art not wax but flesh and blood. I name thee, Patsy James. Thou art she, between the worlds, in all the worlds. So mote it be."

She opened her eyes and took the poppet in her hands. Closing them again, she concentrated with all her might until she could visualize a silver net falling over the poppet and binding the one it represented.

Mackey was certain she'd gone into a trance. His own heart lurched in his chest at hearing the door open. Where was the announcing tinkle of the bell? *The wind must've jammed its clapper*, Mackey surmised. What rotten luck! Even before a flash of lightning confirmed that it was Jacob standing in the doorway, Mackey knew it was. He wanted to warn the little lady but she was too deep in concentration to be aware of anything except the poppet she cradled in her hands. He saw Malone ease the door shut and blend into the darkness. Now there were three watching her.

In a moment or two, her eyes flicked open. She took the red ribbon and wrapped it around the poppet, then tied it firmly. Glancing over at the old volume once more, she again memorized the ancient words, then charged the binding with power saying,

"By air and earth; by water and fire,
So be you bound, as I desire.
By three and nine, your power I bind
By moon and sun, my will be done.
Sky and sea, keep harm from me.
Cord go round; power be bound,
Light revealed; now be sealed."

It was done. Hopefully Patsy James would behave herself henceforth and the havoc she'd caused would end shortly. Desirée exhaled a sigh and bent to blow out the candle.

"Let it burn," a voice commanded from the shadows.

She started and peered into the darkness. "Jacob?"

He stepped from the darkness into the light of the candle. "The candlelight is becoming to you, Desirée." His tone was harsh. "It enhances your mysteriousness. Who is the recipient of your spellbinding this time?"

She could not lie to him. "Patsy James," she said in a low, tremulous voice.

His features hardened. "I suppose the wax image is her?"

She nodded.

"I'm curious. What do you intend to do with the poppet now that you have it all neatly tied up?"

"Bury it under a heavy rock," was her soft reply.

Jacob wanted to snatch it from her hands and throw the repugnant thing against the wall. He had never been angrier or more rattled than he was at the moment. "What in the hell do you think you're accomplishing?" he ground out.

"I just wanted to stop Patsy from taking my shop and driving you away," she cried. "I did her no harm, Jacob. It's only a protective spell."

He raked a hand through his hair and looked off, saying nothing for what seemed like an interminable amount of time. Finally he looked back to her and she could see the resignation on his chiseled face. "I thought I could handle it," he said tiredly. "I really did. But I can't, Desirée. It's too much for me. I have to be honest with you and myself. It won't work between us. I can go along with the herbs and roots and magic trinkets. But this? Finding you in a trance and chanting a bunch of crap over a damn poppet...." He threw up his hands in disgust. "It's too crazy. Too damn much. I can't deal with it. I thought I could but ...." He couldn't even think straight, let alone express himself.

The storm rolled in, releasing its fury. The wind blew harder, lashing the rain against the window. The staccato sound was magnified in the gloomy silence.

A lump swelled in Jacob's throat at seeing the tears stream down her cheeks. A part of him wanted to take her in his arms and soothe her tears away, but another part of him wanted to shake her senseless.

He backed away from her and hurried out the door. Something inside him urged him to get out from under her spell while he still could. He knew if he didn't go quickly he might do something really crazy, like swoop her up into his arms and carry her upstairs to make magic. He really was bewitched by her. *Don't look back!* an inner voice warned. He ducked his head and dashed through the pouring rain to his car.

Mackey could not stand by and allow Jacob to flee. For once Malone had to be true to his heart and convictions, because the guardian angel knew that only then would his soul be at peace. Besides, the little lady was sobbing as if her heart were broken.

He hoisted himself up from off the step and came to the window as Jacob climbed into his car. There was no time to go through proper channels, Alistair decided. He'd have to risk breaking the first and foremost rule in *The Angels' Handbook of Ethics*: thou shalt not alter the destiny of a charge without first obtaining Divine permission. The Fisherman would just have to understand.

The guardian angel focused on the hood of the BMW and did a bit of concentrating. He visualized the wiring beneath the hood until it was smoking and frayed. *That ought to do it,* he said to himself, feeling rather smug. Mew-Sinh came to sit at his feet and observe. He winked at the puss, as if to say, "No worries, mate."

Jacob tried and tried to start the BMW but the engine refused to turn over.

He let loose with a string of expletives, then climbed out of the car into the downpour to check under the hood. At touching the hot and frayed wiring, he cursed again. The only garage in town had been closed for hours. Like it or not, he was stuck in Marblehead for the night. He slammed the hood shut and charged back into the shop.

"You think you're pretty clever, don't you?" he yelled at Desirée.

She sniffed back the tears and stared blankly into his flashing eyes. "I don't know what you mean. What have I done now?"

"Don't play innocent with me, Desirée." He stood in the center of the shop, dripping wet and hopping mad. A small puddle began to form at his feet. "You think I don't know that you zapped my car. Well, it won't work. Just as soon as I can get a mechanic out of bed in the morning, I'm gone."

She nodded dumbly as he headed for the stairs.

"And no sleepwalking," he said as an afterthought. "We each keep to our own room. Agreed?" He shot her a black look.

His surly indifference was an affront to her pride. "Don't worry, Jacob. You're perfectly safe. Anything that occurred between us only happened because you wanted it to. Since you no longer wish it, nothing more will transpire."

He went up to his room.

Alistair shook his head. Sometimes he wondered why he bothered with Malone. Couldn't he see that the little lady had done what she did only because she was terrified of losing the things that mattered most to her? Mackey was getting fed up with playing nursemaid. His mission on earth was fast becoming a bloody drag. Were it not for the inevitability of incurring the Fisherman's disfavor, Mackey would have been sorely tempted to let the devil take Malone's soul.

DESIRÉE COULD NOT sleep. All she could think of was Jacob and the fact that by tomorrow he would be gone forever. How briefly but how profoundly he had touched her life. She could not bear the thought of his leaving, and yet, had she not promised him that she would never hurt him? Told him that she only wanted his happiness? Look what distress her dabbling had caused. The disbelief in his eyes at catching her would haunt her always.

"Oh, if only you could see into my heart, Jacob." Dejected and drained, she fell across the bed and buried her face in her hands. "I love you so much. Oh, so much," she choked. "I swear it by all that's holy and the power of three times three." She cried until she was limp. Mercifully, sometime during the night she finally fell asleep.

When she opened her swollen eyes it was daylight. Her first thought was of Jacob's whereabouts. She sprang from the bed and flew to the bedroom window. The BMW was no longer parked on the street outside. Her star boarder was gone—without offering so much as a goodbye or a cent of rent. Perhaps he was not the gallant paladin she had wished for. She crumpled into the rocker near the window and sat staring numbly into space. The Magic Herb Hut would not open for business today. If Patsy James had her way, in a few days it would be permanently closed.

Mew-Sinh jumped onto her mistress's lap. "It's just us two again, Mew-Sinh," Desirée whispered. The cat nestled closer as Desirée rocked and reminisced, rocked and wept.

CHAPTER FIFTEEN

ANXIOUS ABOUT HER summation, Addie had arrived early at the courthouse. She sat alone, studying her notes at the barristers' table. Her mouth fell open when she looked up to find Jacob standing over her.

"Well, if it isn't the Marblehead mariner come home from sea." She took a long, slow account of him. "You look awful."

"It's nice to see you, too, Addie." He perched himself on the edge of the table and glanced pointedly at her notes. "Today's the big day, huh?"

"I've been rehearsing. Something I picked up from you." She grinned at him. "So why are you here? Did you think that the star attorney might have a case of stage fright and the understudy might have to go on?"

He donned a wounded expression. "I just wanted to catch your act."

"Come on, Jake. You didn't drive back here for grins. Geez! Look at you. Your clothes are a wrinkled mess. You haven't shaved. There are dark circles under your eyes. And in spite of your devil-may-care pose, I recognize the symptoms of a grand funk. So give. Tell Addie all." She leaned back in her chair and pushed her hair from her eyes.

"Yeah, well, a funny thing happened while I was searching for the meaning of life in Marblehead," he told her, standing and rubbing the back of his stiff neck. "I fell in love." He carefully avoided making eye contact with her.

"Not with the bizarre little creature that runs the spook house?" she said, her face puckering as if she'd just bitten into a sour lemon.

"Have a heart, will you, Addie? We're talking about a woman I care for very much." His shoulders sagged as he thrust his hands into his pockets and walked to the tall windows overlooking the street.

"Sorry," she said. "I can be crass at times. How do you know it's love, Jacob? I mean, it's not a condition that either you or I have much experience with."

"Trust me, Addie. When it happens to you, you'll know it."

"I thought when you fell for someone it was supposed to be a 'many splendored thing.' You look like you've been run over by a truck."

He smiled ruefully at her accurate assessment of his wrecked state. "Mostly it is a 'many splendored thing.' But every once in a while it's hell, especially when the lady is out of the ordinary. Desirée marches to the beat of a different drummer."

Addie swallowed the flip retort on the tip of her tongue. "I noticed," was all she said.

"Yeah, well, I thought I could handle it, but then something happened to make me think I couldn't. So I left. I just packed up, got in my car and drove back to Boston."

"So it's over." She lifted a brow and snapped her fingers. "As simple as that, huh?"

"Hardly. I'm going out of my head thinking about her. I almost drove off the road twice. I can put Marblehead behind me. I can put her physical presence behind me. But I can't put the feelings I have for her behind me."

"Give it time, Jake. Everything is still too fresh. You're tired and—"

"Yeah, I know." He sighed and shrugged his shoulders. "But I'll tell you something, Addie. You can change your mind but you can't always change what's in here." He put a fist to his heart. "There's not another woman like her in the whole world. She was it for me."

"Then if you're that sure, go back and try to work out whatever is wrong between the two of you," Addie advised him.

"It isn't that easy. I want to go back. I do. But only if I can accept everything about her. And what if I try and I can't do it? Then what? We go through this swan song scene again? It's too damn hard." A muscle ticked in his cheek. For the first time since he'd left Boston, he fished the trusty gold toothpick from his shirt pocket and clamped it between his teeth.

Addie got up from the table and came to stand beside him at the window. "You'll get some perspective on this in a day or two, Jake. Then you'll know the right thing to do." She patted his shoulder consolingly.

"Archie Hooper told me the same thing."

"Who's he?"

"A local character," he answered in a thoughtful voice.

"Are you planning on sticking around long enough to hear my summation?" she asked, hoping that he was.

He blinked and looked over at her. "Sure. When's showtime?"

She checked her watch. "Forty-two minutes from now."

"But who's counting, right?" He pinched her cheek.

"Okay. So I'm a little nervous. It's my debut."

"You've got the right stuff, Addie. It's a piece of cake," he reassured her. "I'll swing by the office, change shirts and shave."

"You promise you'll be in the wings?"

"Same old Addie—always the worrier," he teased. "Save me a front-row seat."

"Not at the table, Jake. I'm doing a solo act this time." Something in the way that she said it made him take note of the change in her. Addie was coming into her own and today was her coming-out party.

"You don't want the understudy hogging the lime-light or taking any undeserved bows, is that it?"

"Do you mind?"

"Not at all." He shot her a wink and walked through the swinging gate.

As JACOB SAT in the rear of the courtroom and listened to his partner make her closing remarks, he was impressed—really impressed. Addie was wonderful. Direct but eloquent; confident but relaxed; aggressive but not ruthless. She'd laid the groundwork beautifully and now she only needed to coast over the finish line.

"I don't mean to be harsh or unsympathetic in my treatment of the wife or the mistress," she told the entranced jurors, "for it is a very delicate matter that we are debating in this courtroom today. Matters of the heart always are. There are, however, certain extenuating circumstances that must be considered in order for you, the jury, to render a fair judgment. Consider my client's beloved wife, who has been for many years only a shell of a woman. In the clinical context, what does a contract of marriage imply? I think most of us here would agree that, loosely defined, it implies a viable mate, companionship and occasional copulation, none of which my client has experienced in the past years."

Jacob put a hand over his mouth to wipe the smile from his face. The little minx was stealing his lines— reciting him verbatim.

"I ask you, was he, therefore, truly married?"

He noted the jury's attentiveness. She had them in her back pocket.

"Technically, yes; realistically, no."

Jacob sank down in the pew and rolled his eyes.

Addie continued with *his* summation.

"Was he committing adultery? Technically, yes; realistically, no. Did he then, deceive the plaintiff? Technically, yes; realistically, no."

Jacob wondered where she would go from here. Would she improvise or continue with the original

script. If it was him doing it, he thought, he'd stick
with what was working.

"If you agree that legal technicalities must be tempered by reality then you will also have to take into
account that my client was a man trapped between
love and loyalty, lust and honor, desire and divorce.
And when you make your decision you must consider
the irrefutable fact that my client was a man who never
shirked his responsibilities, no matter how painful and
unfulfilling those responsibilities may have been. His
actions prove that he does take his commitments seriously and does not make promises lightly."

Jacob heard himself and yet something inside of
him rejected the whole concept Addie parroted. He
wasn't the same man who had strutted before jurors'
boxes and scored big wins for fat clients, as Addie was
doing now. No . . . he'd changed. And seeing his partner playing his part in the legal arena only drove home
the point. He missed the law and he wanted to argue
cases, but not this way. He wanted to practice law, not
perform. He wanted to represent the small folk in the
right, not the big shots in the wrong. Suddenly it
seemed so clear to him. The time away had given him
a fresh perspective. Maybe the same would hold true
in regard to his dilemma with Desirée. Maybe given a
little time and distance, he'd gain a new perspective
and see things more clearly concerning the two of
them. God! He hoped so.

"And so, ladies and gentlemen of the jury, the outcome rests with you. I know this is not an easy case to
decide, but I am confident that you will be fair and

compassionate when rendering your judgment. I thank you for your patience.''

With a respectful nod, Addie took her chair.

Jacob had to restrain himself from jumping up and shouting, "Bravo! Encore! Encore!"

The jury filed out and the spectators began to dribble from the courtroom. Jacob waited in the back until Addie and her client had conferred and the smiling jerk had exited through the big, double doors to begin delivering a statement to the eager press hounds congregated in the outside hall.

He approached the barristers' table. A flushed and beaming Addie looked to him for a second opinion.

"You did good, Miss Addie. Your boy won't have to cough up much money, if any. I hope you charged him a mint."

"The services of Malone and Van Cleve are never cheap," she reminded him.

"Yeah, I remember," he said with a wry smile.

"Sorry about stealing your material. It was a good angle, Jake." She began stuffing papers back into her attaché case.

"It wasn't the content of the summation as much as the delivery. You wowed 'em today. You made the incredible sound credible. The jury believed in your portrayal of the client, and he's damn lucky you did."

She braced her hips against the table and leaned back on her hands. "It was a high. I never knew it could be so exciting. I thought I'd be scared witless and fumbling all over myself. But as soon as I stepped in front of that jurors' box, something came over me. I felt in control. Powerful, you know?"

"Yeah, it's addictive," was all he said.

She gave him a long, hard look. "You're not coming back in with me, are you, Jake?"

"You know me pretty well. It's not personal, hon. I hope you understand that. It's just time to take my name off the door."

She did know him well and she did understand. "Well, it was swell while it lasted."

"You'll be fine, Addie. You proved that today." He flashed her a dazzling smile.

"So are you giving up the law altogether?"

"No, I just want out of the big leagues." He glanced around the deserted courtroom. "Come on. Let's celebrate your debut with a drink. I'm buying."

"No can do, Jake." She turned and clicked her attaché case shut.

"Addie, Addie, Addie," he teased. "Will you ever change? As soon as one case is done, you're fretting about another. You have to learn to relax. Let go a little. The legal books can wait."

She looked amused. "I have an appointment to keep."

"Oh," he said. "You don't waste any time. You could take a few minutes to savor your coup before rushing off to woo another client."

She put a hand on her hip and slanted him a smug look. "I have a date, Jake."

"You're kidding. As in with a man?" He couldn't resist the dig.

"You needn't act so stunned, smarty-pants. After you rejected me, my bruised ego needed a boost, so I started accepting invitations that I'd declined earlier.

I've become something of a social butterfly in your absence.''

"So it's your second date, huh?'' He ventured a guess.

"Third.'' She laughed. "I met Douglas at a political fund-raiser. He's tall, good-looking and heavily into commodities.''

"Well, well. Then he should certainly appreciate you, since you're somewhat of a precious commodity yourself.''

"Why, thank you, Jacob.'' She feigned demureness while grasping her attaché case in one hand and looping her other arm through his. "I think maybe the relationship holds promise,'' she said brightly as they walked from the courtroom. "Of course, I thought we did too, once. Who knows?'' She shrugged her padded shoulders. "Maybe my only real love is the law.''

"Have you had sex with him yet?'' he pried.

"Jacob!''

"Well?''

"No,'' she admitted.

"Well, take it from me, if you start dreaming about it, it's him, not the law that's turning you on.'' He held open the door for her.

"I'll keep it in mind. Give me a rain check on the drink?'' She kissed his cheek. "We'll need to iron out a few details about dissolving the partnership.''

"Yeah. I'll be in touch. Tell Douglas I said that he's a lucky guy,'' he called after her as she walked away.

"So is what's-her-name.'' She gave him a backhanded wave.

"Desirée," he mumbled beneath his breath. "You spell her name the same as desire, only with two e's."

FOR THE NEXT several days, Jacob rambled around in his house. The place felt strange to him now: too big; too lavishly furnished, too damn empty. He hated the taste of what he cooked, and he couldn't stand the ordered-in stuff. He tried to read, but the words kept running together. He tried watching the sports channel on television, but he lost interest quickly. Napping was impossible, and when he went to bed late, he still couldn't sleep. He even tried smoking again, but tobacco had lost its appeal. There was only one thing he was successful at focusing on: Desirée, every waking minute of every passing day.

She preyed on his mind, haunted his dreams, stormed his senses. Oh, how he missed her! He'd kept track of the days. Tomorrow night was the town meeting. The thought of Desirée having to endure the ordeal alone was driving him to distraction.

And you, young man, are the reason. Archie's voice echoed in his head. *'Course your presence in Boston won't have any bearing on the town meeting. It'll still take place in thirty days. Your presence here might make a difference, though.*

Jacob poured himself a stiff drink and walked out onto the terrace. It was a starry night. He took a swig of the expensive scotch and focused on the silver sliver of a moon in the black sky above. *Who else is there to speak on Desirée's behalf? Me? I'm no talker.* Archie's words came back to him. *I'm just an old man nobody listens to anymore.*

Archie was too modest, Jacob mused. His insights were persuasive. They left an impression—a lasting one. *It's a short ride to Boston, my friend, but when you have to swallow your pride in order to return, it'll be the longest drive of your life.*

Jacob wondered if Desirée was having as bad a night as he was. *I just wanted to stop Patsy from taking my shop and driving you away.... I did her no harm, Jacob. It's only a protective spell.* Her voice, her face, crystallized in his brain. *I'm a product of the Old Ways. I act differently and react differently because of it.*

Had he overreacted? Was it so much that he was appalled by her behavior or that he was afraid of making a commitment? *You must be able to accept that about me if we are to be anything more to one another than warm bodies to lie next to through the lonely nights.*

God! He was miserable without her.

I love you, Jacob, just as you are. I swear it by all that is holy and by the power of three times three.

He glanced back up at the crescent moon. A shudder ran through him. He drank down the scotch and strode purposefully back into the house.

Mackey was bored and hungry. He was foraging for tucker in the kitchen when Malone breezed past him. Luckily Jacob was too preoccupied to notice the bag of potato chips levitating in thin air. Mackey pushed back his bushman's hat and let out a relieved, "Whew!"

He stuffed his mouth full of chips and pondered while he crunched. "Now what's he up to?" he muttered. The guardian angel was still miffed with himself for allowing the trip to Boston to have occurred. He'd underestimated Malone's resourcefulness, something an old croc poacher should never have done.

Mackey was almost as miserable as Jacob in Boston. There was nothing tasty to eat and Malone kept him up all night with his constant rattling around. Alistair missed more than just the little lady's leftovers. He missed the sheila herself and he missed his mate, the puss. He was seriously considering scruffing the mission and going back to Heaven to report his failure.

At hearing Malone's footsteps, he quickly stashed the bag of chips in the microwave oven and stood quiet as a mouse as Malone made his way back through the kitchen with a suitcase in his hand.

Could it be? Was he returning to Marblehead? Glory! Hallelujah! And Amen! Mackey followed him to the BMW and ensconced himself in the back seat. He stretched out, tucked his hands behind his head and smiled cockily. It was going to be a loverly ride back. He had no bloody worries. He could just enjoy the pleasant jaunt by the light of the silvery moon.

The angel did not know it was a waxing moon—the symbol of beginning, of growth and generation. It was a time for ideas and plans, time for life to be written upon the blank page.

CHAPTER SIXTEEN

IT WAS MIDNIGHT by the time Jacob eased the BMW to the curb outside of The Magic Herb Hut. He shut off the engine and sat thinking for a moment. *Okay, you're here. Now what the hell do you say?* Suddenly he felt fourteen again—infatuated, insecure and inarticulate.

Alistair sat up and took stock of the situation. They'd arrived but Malone wasn't making any move toward rectifying the situation. *Come on mate! She'll forgive you for acting the fool. That's it,* he silently coached as Malone reached for the door handle.

Jacob's hand and heart froze.

Alistair's impatience almost got the better of him. It took every ounce of self-control he possessed not to reach over the seat and give his charge's thick head a good cuff.

"Do it, Malone!" Jacob set his jaw. He yanked on the handle and sprang from the car in one agile motion.

"Thank you, Lord," Alistair whispered, rubbing the crick in his neck.

Jacob strode to the front door and banged on it before he lost his nerve.

Mew-Sinh was the first to respond to the summons. The feline bounded down the steps and sat at the shop's door, awaiting her mistress's lagging presence.

Jacob pounded more forcefully, then stepped back and looked up to the second-story window to see if a light had been switched on. It had. Desirée was coming down. His palms were sweating and his heart was hammering. What if she slammed the door in his face? What if...

The door swung open and she stood silhouetted against the dim interior light. Her hastily donned robe was open and half hanging off a shoulder. She wore nothing but a lacy teddy beneath it. He experienced a tightness in his throat and his groin simultaneously. God, but she was a lovely sight to behold!

"Hi," he uttered dumbly.

"Hi," she said softly.

He stepped closer to her. "I, uh, didn't get turned around this time. It's no accident that I'm here."

She opened the door wider and gestured for him to come inside.

Unlike Mackey, he did not realize that when he crossed the threshold his destiny was sealed.

Mew-Sinh slipped outside a split second before she closed the door. "Over here, you pesky puss," Mackey hissed, bending down to give the cat a playful ruff behind the ears. "What say we give those two some time alone and take us a walk, eh?"

He and Mew-Sinh set off on a moonlight stroll along the bay, the cat meowing in tune with the ditty he whistled: his sweet Flo's favorite, *Waltzing Matilda*.

THE STAR BOARDER was back for good. The vacancy
in the shy proprietress's life was permanently filled.
The love they had for each other was stronger than any
adversity and beyond any magic but what they themselves weaved. As Desirée lay snuggled in Jacob's
arms, she knew that no matter what transpired in the
days and years ahead, Jacob would always be her
champion, her lover, her one true friend. But whom
did she have to thank for the wondrous gift—the fulfillment of her deepest desire? She hadn't dabbled this
time. No spell had brought him back to her doorstep.
The who and why of it puzzled her.

As daylight crept through the window, she eased
from the bed and tiptoed to the window. Though her
heart was full, her mind was troubled. The town
meeting loomed before her, like the black clouds rolling in over Marblehead. As she watched the morning
dawn she worried over what the day's end had in store
for her.

She did not realize Jacob had awakened until she
felt his arms slip comfortingly around her waist. "It'll
be all right, sweetheart," he said soothingly, drawing
her back against him with a reassuring squeeze.
"You're not alone anymore. We're going to put our
heads together and figure out a way to beat Patsy
James at her own game." He nestled a cheek in her
hair.

"It seems so hopeless, Jacob." She sighed.

He gently turned her around by the shoulders and
gazed unwaveringly into her troubled eyes. "You forget, forums are my forte. I've been known to pull off

a litigious upset or two in my day. For your information, Miss Warren, I'm a damn good lawyer.''

She slid her arms around his neck, tilted her head back, and smiled warmly up at him. ''I'm sure you are. And you are most definitely a damn good man.'' She rose up on tiptoes to brush his lips with a kiss.

''And if all else fails, you can put a whammy on the whole town,'' he said jokingly.

''I don't know, Jacob.'' A look of misgiving flicked across her face. ''Such a spell would be very complicated. I'm only an amateur.''

''I'm only kidding, Desirée. For God's sake, don't try it unless you want to risk us being tarred and feathered and run out of town on a rail.''

''I knew that,'' she said in a way that made him wonder.

He took her firmly by the shoulders again and held her from him at arm's length. ''We're going to do this by the book—and I don't mean by that old volume downstairs. I want you to look up every document pertaining to the shop—anything and everything having to do with The Magic Herb Hut from day one. Hopefully we'll find something pertinent among the papers. I also want to get a look at the town records. Where are they kept?''

''At Abbot Hall,'' she informed him.

''Okay, that's a start.'' His hands slipped down her curvaceous torso and cupped her fanny. He pulled her hips into him and kissed her soundly. ''That's my retainer. I'll collect the balance later. A cup of coffee would be nice,'' he hinted with a wink.

"The policy of the house hasn't changed. Breakfast is included with the lodgings." She smoothed some hair back from his forehead and drank in his handsomeness for a lingering moment. "I don't know by what power you came to be in my life, my love, but I am grateful—so very grateful," she murmured.

He started to respond but she put a finger to his lips. "We've a great deal to do before nightfall. I'll fix the coffee while you get dressed." She collected her robe from the end of the poster bed and slipped it on before she left him. So much for lace teddies and thoughts of crawling back under the covers and making magic. He sighed to himself. "Abbot Hall. Abbot Hall. Keep focused, Malone," he muttered, reaching for his pants.

ARCHIE, flanked by his old cohorts, Nathan and Sidney, stood outside the high-school auditorium, watching the early comers trickle in and take their seats.

"It's going to be packed tonight," Nathan surmised.

"Uh-huh," Archie concurred. "I imagine most everyone will turn out."

"Bad night for it," Sidney noted, looking up at the sky. "We're in for more rain."

"Uh-huh." Archie seconded the dismal forecast as he, too, glanced up at the thunderclouds. "It won't matter, though. Bad weather or no, folks will still show up."

"Why'd we come? I'd sooner not have been a part of it," Nathan grumbled, straightening his suspenders.

"The girl's got little enough support as it is, Nathan. If the three of us stayed home soaking our bunions, she'd have no one to lend a voice on her behalf. We agreed on it. Remember?" Archie shot him an impatient look.

"I ain't Amos. My memory is just fine. I just don't see how we can do the little gal any good, that's all. We're only three old men against hundreds. No one's going to listen to anything we have to say," was Nathan's pessimistic prediction.

"Oh, I don't know about that." Sidney spoke up. "What about the time they were going to tear down the old firehouse to make way for some park or such as that? We argued against it pretty damn good that meetin'. The old landmark is still standing, thanks to us. Besides, you don't know that we're the only ones showing up in support of Desirée. You ever heard of a thing called the silent majority?"

"Sure I have." Nathan was sorry he'd brought up the subject of their attendance. "But I don't think the majority's sentiment is running in Desirée's favor or that they'll be silent about their views."

"Nathan's right on that, Sidney," Archie chimed in. "I don't think we can count on many of our neighbors siding with us tonight. Patsy's done little else for weeks but throw fuel on the fire. If she had her way, we'd adjourn the meeting and hold a witch burning instead."

"Speak of the devil . . ." Nathan warned the other with a jerk of his silver head.

Patsy, dressed in red polka dots and pumps, was making her way toward them. "Nathan-Sidney-Archie." She greeted the three as if they were one.

They mumbled a homogeneous hello as she flounced past.

"She looks pleased with herself," Sidney pointed out. "Kind of like the cat that swallowed the canary."

"Uh-huh," Archie agreed. "My guess is she's feeling mighty smug at the moment." He shook his head sadly. "It's a shame what spite can do to a person. Patsy could've done something positive and productive with her life instead of wasting her best years on some petty grudge. I wonder, if Steven was to show up here tonight and fall at her knees to beg her forgiveness, would she really want him back? Something makes me think not. Love was the excuse, not the reason for what she did. Uh-huh, it's a shame what spite can do to a person," he reiterated, glancing at the activity around him. The trickle of people had turned into a steady stream. "What time is it getting to be, Sidney?"

The old gent pulled a gold watch fob from his vest pocket and checked the hour. "Seven straight up," he informed him.

"Thirty minutes more." Archie exhaled a troubled sigh. "You boys want to take a seat or stretch your legs a little longer?"

"Too stuffy inside," Nathan grumbled, snapping his suspenders.

"Let's wait a while. I get stiff if I sit too long," Sidney complained, slipping the gold watch fob back into his vest pocket.

"Fine with me. I wasn't in any hurry. I was kind of hoping to see Desirée before the fireworks started," Archie said. "I thought it'd be encouraging to her to know that there were a few friendly faces in the crowd tonight." He spied Marilyn Estes and waved. "Now there's four against hundreds, Nathan. The odds are getting better." At the old man's scowl, he broke into a grin. Archie knew something the other two did not. He'd seen Jacob's car parked out front of The Magic Herb Hut. The capable young fella was back in town and Archie was counting heavily on his contribution at the assembly. If anyone could turn the tide tonight, it was he. Five against hundreds. Uh-huh, the odds were improving, he mused.

JACOB CHECKED his appearance in the mirror. It had been a while since he'd donned his court duds. He wanted to look especially impressive tonight. He'd chosen his wardrobe carefully: a gray suit, a pale pink dress shirt with his initials monogrammed in rose stitching on the cuffs, a Countess Mara silk tie with tan, rose and navy stripes of twill and satin, and burgundy calfskin loafers. He took a moment to study his reflection, deciding the finished ensemble presented the image he wanted.

"It's getting late, Desirée," he called, snapping off the bedroom light and proceeding down the hall to her room. "Are you about ready?" He eased open the door and peeked in.

"Almost," she answered from inside the closet. She stepped into a pair of high heels and bent down to fasten the straps around her slim ankles.

He sat on the edge of her bed and tapped his toes. He was anxious to get on with it. The prospect of arguing something as critical as an inalienable civil right had the old adrenaline pumping again. "We need to get a move on, Desirée. It would be impolite for the guest of honor to be late. What are you doing in there?" His mouth fell open when she emerged from the closet.

"What do you think?" She twirled for his inspection.

Yards and yards of soft-knit black fabric swirled. She was attired in a long-sleeved, mock-turtleneck dress that snugly hugged her torso to midhip, then flared into gores and gores that hovered just above her ankle-strapped shoes. Her hair was lifted high on one side and held with a clip. She had crimped it, and it looked fuller and wilder than ever. She looked stunning, but positively wicked.

"Haven't you something a little less..."

"Provocative," she finished for him.

He noted the telltale lift of her chin. "Black," he said, trying a different tactic.

"I thought the color black suited the occasion," she stubbornly contended.

He raked a hand through his hair. "Not a smart move, Desirée. You walk in the auditorium dressed as you are and you know what a reaction you're going to incite."

"They're expecting to see the town witch tonight, Jacob. I don't want to disappoint them. I'd venture to say that many people will be wearing black this evening, but I'll be the only one of whom they'll take special note and the only one of whom they will disapprove. Let them. I'm tired of their silly suspicions and fed up with their censure." She tossed her head defiantly. "Tonight may be the last time they ever see me and I want to leave them with a lasting impression."

He couldn't blame her. And, actually, he thought she looked sensational. "Okay," he gave in, rising from the bed and coming to stand before her. "Then let's let it all hang out tonight." He slid his fingers inside the high collar of her dress and pulled out the necklace she kept tucked from sight. Fingering the moon charm for a moment, he was reminded of his dream—the blue moon and the gift the lagoon maid had placed in his hand.

He raised his eyes to Desirée's and winked. "Wear your moon charm tonight. Be proud of your heritage," he told her, bending and kissing her rosebud mouth.

"I really don't care anymore what others believe. Only your opinion matters." She looked searchingly into his eyes. "I have to know, Jacob. Deep in your heart, do you think I am what they say?"

He cupped her pixie face between his large hands. "No, Desirée, I know the real woman beneath the black trappings. I know the goodness in her heart. My love cannot be undermined by innuendo. Not tonight, not ever. You must trust in that love always."

"I just had to hear you say it." She smiled shakily.

"Don't worry, sweetheart. Everything is going to work out as it should. The gods will be kind," he quoted with a wink. "Come on—" he clamped an arm around her tiny waist "—let's go give 'em hell."

THE AUDITORIUM WAS packed to capacity. Archie, Nathan and Sidney stood in the back, periodically exchanging worried glances as they took in the chatter and motion.

"It's worse than I thought. I never heard so much commotion. Look at 'em milling about and trading gossip. They remind me of a bunch of ants at a picnic," Nathan spat.

"Uh-huh." Archie shot a look at Patsy James. She reminded him more of a polka-dotted praying mantis, the way she was hopping from row to row in a last minute spate of politicking.

"Looks like the moderator's about ready to begin. Where's Desirée?" Sidney spoke louder than usual to make himself heard above the drone of voices.

Archie was wondering the very same thing. He glanced beyond the auditorium doors once more. A big smile broke on his wrinkled face upon seeing her enter the lobby on Jacob's arm. "She just came in, Sidney. Turn around and feast your tired old eyes."

"Hot diggity!" Nathan hooted. "Wait'll folks get a gander at her. Patsy's going to keel over."

The three old gents in the back were the only ones to have any advanced warning. When Desirée stepped through the auditorium doors and walked down the aisle, a stunned hush fell over the assemblage.

"Will you look at her?" Patsy gasped to a neighbor seated next to her. "I can't believe she'd have nerve enough to come here dressed in her witch's garb. The woman has no shame."

"Hear ye, Hear ye!" The moderator struck his gavel just as Jacob and Desirée took a seat up front. "This special town meeting is hereby called to order. Take your seats, folks."

While the notice of warrant was read aloud, Jacob bent his head and conferred with Desirée. "We'll do it as planned. I know it's hard to sit silently by, but I really think it's in your best interest if I do the talking. Okay?"

She nodded and settled back in her seat.

"The assemblage is now ready to hear any citizen who wishes to express him or herself on the issue under debate," the moderator announced.

Patsy James stood and waved her hand.

"Since you lodged the complaint, it's only fitting that you speak first, Mrs. James." The moderator recognized her.

She cleared her throat and read from a prepared statement. "It was I who circulated the petition and brought this matter before the Board of Selectmen. I did so because I felt it was my civic duty to bring to the town's attention certain facts that have gone unnoticed and do not adhere to the strict Marblehead codes of zoning and decency."

"A bunch of rubbish," Nathan grunted. "Since when did she become so community minded?"

Archie motioned for him to be quiet.

"The shop in question does not legally qualify to be located in the historical district," she went on, "and certainly has no right to receive the economic boon that such an advantageous location gives. The Warrens neither sought nor were granted permission to renovate the premises in question—renovations which, I might add, made it possible for them to set up shop in the most lucrative section of town."

Desirée sat stone faced as Patsy continued citing her grievous offenses.

"The restrictions as set forth by The Old and Historic Districts Commission is quite clear on the point. A Certification of Appropriateness must be granted by the commission before any structure may be erected, reconstructed, altered, restored, removed, or demolished. They, and only they, determine whether or not any exterior modification to any structure located within the district and subject to public view from a public street or way is appropriate for the preservation of the district," she recited. "I submit that the Warrens contemptuously circumvented procedure in a greedy quest for profit. I further contend that the pagan wares sold out of the unauthorized shop are an affront to the Christian community. The Magic Herb Hut is an eyesore that attaches a distasteful stigma to our town. I urge each and every conscientious citizen here tonight to support my petition. We must enforce the existing zoning and close down The Magic Herb Hut immediately and evermore."

Her gaze panned the assemblage, then came to rest on Desirée. "Both the shop and its owner are in violation of the high standards that we, Marbleheaders, have embraced for generations." She turned up her nose, as if catching a whiff of something repugnant, then sat down, straightening the folds of her polka-dot dress.

Spontaneous applause broke out in the auditorium. People nodded their heads and leaned to whisper in neighbors' ears. Everyone was amazed by Patsy's passionate eloquence. A few of the ladies from the Women's Old Town Beautification Society went so far as to compare her to the likes of the patriot, Patrick Henry. No one knew she'd been working on the speech since the first day she'd posted the warrant.

The moderator hit the gavel again. "Is there anyone else who'd like to voice an opinion?"

Randomly people stood and voiced their support of Patsy's recommendation.

Desirée grew nervous. She kept slanting uneasy looks in Jacob's direction. He appeared unruffled by the onslaught of adverse opinion. He just sat there, taking in every word and now and then jotting down a pertinent note.

"What's Desirée waiting on?" Nathan fretted. "Why don't she speak up for herself?"

Archie shushed him as Jacob came to his feet.

"I respectfully ask to be heard," he petitioned the moderator.

"And who might you be, sir?" the man running the show inquired.

"My name is Jacob Ryan Malone and, though I am not a member of the community, Miss Warren has retained me to speak on her behalf," he announced.

"It's highly irregular," the gentleman on the stage stated in an uncertain tone.

"But, I believe, within the framework of the town meeting format. It is an open forum, is it not, sir?"

"Yes," the moderator conceded, looking over at Desirée. "You are in accord with this, Miss Warren?"

She nodded.

"Proceed then, sir," the moderator told Jacob.

Jacob stationed himself mid center aisle, unbuttoned his suit coat, put a hand in his pocket and began his defense of Desirée. "First of all, I would like to address the legal aspects of Mrs. James's complaint. I have in my possession irrefutable proof that the conversion Mrs. James cites as being in breach of the zoning restrictions took place before the boundaries of the Old Town were extended to include The Magic Herb Hut. The renovations were completed on the twelfth of June, 1960, and according to the official records at Abbot's Hall, the historical district's boundary was not extended until November twenty-first of the same year. Therefore, the Warrens were not bound to seek permission and so, they were not then, are are not now in violation of the zoning code. A Certification of Appropriateness does not apply."

An astonished murmur ran through the auditorium.

"Based on the evidence of the documents I will produce for your inspection, the warrant is null and void. Of course, if you should not agree with our interpretation, we are prepared to debate the issue further in a state court." He directed a steely look at

Patsy James. "I would welcome an opportunity to argue the point on appeal."

She squirmed in her seat.

"But even if we can agree to dispense with the local warrant against The Magic Herb Hut, we can not so easily dismiss the constitutional ramifications of the persecution that has been waged against Miss Warren herself. Something much larger than a simple violation of local zoning codes is going on here tonight, my friends." His eyes scanned the suddenly quiet assemblage. "Oh, yes, there is another, much more insidious and foul violation taking place. What we are really debating, what is really at stake, is the most basic and precious of rights guaranteed to all citizens under the constitution—the right of religious freedom," he informed them in a loud, clear voice.

He paused for a moment to let the full impact of his words hit home. "Miss Warren has been brought before this assemblage on a pretext. I know it, and you know it. She's sitting here tonight and having to exonerate herself for only one reason—because she does not conform to a set standard. Whether those standards are high or not remains to be seen." Again he leveled a pointed look at Patsy James.

She fanned herself with the paper on which was written her prepared speech.

"The strangest part is that such a travesty of freedom should take place here, in Marblehead—the very cradle of democracy. The worst part is that you people do not even know for certain what Miss Warren's religious beliefs *are*. You *assume*, but you do not know—just as you *assumed* that the renovations took place after her shop was deemed to be within the boundaries of the Old Town. Perhaps it is time to consider the effect of your hasty assumptions. If you deprive one citizen of her right to exercise her individuality, you jeopardize the whole concept upon which our country is founded. What harm has Miss Warren's individuality done you? None!" He answered the question for them. "Now ask yourselves, if Mrs. James's attitude prevails, what harm is done you? When will it be your turn to be persecuted because you do not comply with a set code of behavior? Who sets the standards? You?" He pointed to a gentleman on his left. "Or you?" He pointed to a woman on his right. "Who gives you the right?"

Jacob removed his hand from his pocket and rebuttoned his suit coat. "Before you put it to a vote, I suggest you take a moment to consider the long-range consequences of your actions. Because, my friends, I think that you are good and fair people, and if individual freedom can be lost here, in democratic Marblehead, it's my belief that there can be no place in this wide world where it can be guaranteed. I thank you for letting me speak my mind."

As he walked to his seat, Archie began clapping. Nathan chimed in with a whistle, Sidney with a hoot. Then, Marilyn Estes joined in, and slowly but surely the applause built until the auditorium was alive with resounding acclamation.

Patsy James was mortified. She broke out into a rash of splotches. By the time she fled the auditorium, she was one big red polka dot from head to foot.

"Put it to a vote," Archie yelled out, tipping his cap to Patsy as she whooshed past.

"He's some talker, ain't he?" Sidney crowed.

"Uh-huh," Archie agreed. "The fella's got a knack for words."

The moderator banged the gavel, trying to restore order. Desirée slipped her hand in Jacob's and squeezed it hard. "You were wonderful," she whispered.

He winked at her.

"Quiet please," the moderator boomed. The din died down. "We'll take a vote by a show of hands. I remind you that a two-thirds majority is required either way when the vote pertains to zoning bylaws. Please keep your hand high until the tellers can get an accurate count. All right, those who are in favor of pressing warrant against Miss Warren and The Magic Herb Hut, raise your hand high."

Out of the three hundred and thirty persons present, only fifty some odd raised their hand. The members of the Women's League of Voters moved down the aisle, counting hands. When the tally was taken, they nodded for the moderator to continue with the vote.

"Now those who are in favor of dismissing the warrant against Miss Warren and The Magic Herb Hut, raise your hand high."

Again the tellers traveled the aisle, taking a count. The outcome was handed to the moderator.

"The vote is as follows—two hundred and seventy-two for dismissal of the warrant; fifty-eight opposed. It is decided that Miss Warren is not in violation of the zoning restrictions and The Magic Herb Hut will continue to be located and operated within the confines of the historical district. This special town meeting is adjourned." With a final whack of the gavel, it was over.

Desirée could not contain herself any longer. She stretched over the arm of her chair and hugged Jacob. "Oh, God! Jacob. You did it! We won!"

He was delighted with the end result, too. The gods had been kind. "I save your shop and reputation and you're giving rise to rumors again." He laughed, unable to resist a circumspect kiss of her neck. "Let's get out of here so we can be alone," he whispered, taking her hand and leading the way up the aisle.

People were actually smiling at her as she passed. A few even offered congratulatory handshakes and shoulder pats. Of course, it was Jacob who received enthusiastic slaps on the back and high praise. As he should, she thought. She was so proud of him.

Archie worked his way through the throng of people and stationed himself at the lobby door. As Jacob and Desirée approached, he made a circle with his finger and thumb and gave the young fella the "okay" sign.

Jacob grinned at him, then whisked Desirée out the door. He was sure he'd get a full critique of his actions in the morning when he made his usual pit stop at the coffee shop. He liked the old gent. In fact, right now he liked the whole damn town.

Once they were out of range of prying eyes, he looped an arm around her waist and pulled her behind a tree to steal a kiss. "You do look sexy as hell tonight, my little sorceress," he teased, suggestively nipping her earlobe.

She leaned back against the wide tree trunk and gave him a seductive look. "Maybe you're just bewitched," she purred.

"No maybe about it." He smoothed back the wild wisps of burnished brown hair from her face. "I was from the first."

"No, you weren't," she insisted. "If it wasn't for my dabbling, you'd never have taken any special notice of your landlady."

He shook his head amusedly. "What am I going to do with you? Dabbling had nothing to do with it, I tell you."

"Then how do you explain the dreams?" she asked of him, twining her arms about his neck and pressing nearer.

"Subliminal attraction," he reasoned. "It's as simple as that."

"Mmmm," she murmured, sliding her hands through his hair and drawing him to her in order to extract another kiss. "If you say so, Jacob."

"No more dabbling. Okay, Desirée?" At the contact of her lips, the request faded from his mind. If she answered him, it didn't register.

LATER THAT NIGHT, after hours of making magic with Jacob, Desirée eased back the covers and slipped from the bed. She quietly stole down the hall and then down the stairs to the shop below. Making her way by the dim glow of the lamplight outside, she moved to behind the counter and slid open the back panel of the glass case in which she stored her lucky stones. She plucked the new moonstone from its velvet niche and dropped it into her robe pocket.

"A little insurance," she whispered to Mew-Sinh with a pat of her pocket. Soundlessly she slid the panel closed and tiptoed back to bed before Jacob discovered her missing. She never saw the grungy bushman's hat draped on the hat tree in the corner.

EPILOGUE

"You did well, Alistair." The Fisherman bestowed a pleased smile upon the guardian angel, second-grade.

"Thank you, Your Eminence. It was a tricky assignment, but me instincts proved correct again," Mackey bragged. "The little lady was just the ticket to get Malone's soul straightened away. It's me considered opinion that all will be fine with him from here on out."

"I notice that you are not wearing your hat, Alistair. Did you forget and leave it behind on Earth?" the Fisherman asked.

"In a manner of speaking." Mackey did not want to admit to his superior that he'd left the old bushman's hat on Earth on purpose. During his stay below, he'd come to realize that his assignment in Heaven was a permanent arrangement. His Marblehead stint had given him the insight he needed to understand the greater purpose of which the Fisherman was always speaking. The life of a croc poacher had been exciting, but guardian angeling was a much more rewarding vocation.

"You look thoughtful, Alistair. Is there something troubling you? If it's the matter of your promotion, your good deeds have not gone unrecognized by the Almighty. I'm sure the angelic tribunal will award you first-class status soon."

"Oh, no sir, that's not it," Mackey responded. Then, the impact of what the Fisherman had just said hit him. "First-class status, eh?" He stuck out his chest. "Will there be a grand ceremony and such?"

"Most definitely," the Fisherman informed him.

Mackey preened like a peacock. "I thank you for putting in a good word for me with the mate up above."

"It was not I, but your own efforts that brought you to His attention."

For the first time the Aussie angel looked truly humbled. "Actually, Fisherman, what I was wondering about was Malone. I know that you have access to the full picture. I was hoping maybe you could give me a hint as to what lies ahead for him. The bloke's kind of grown on me."

The Fisherman pondered the unusual request for a moment. "As a rule I never reveal—"

"I know, but as a favor to an old croc poacher, couldn't you break the rule just this once?" Mackey wheedled.

The Fisherman smiled. "I will tell you one thing. Mr. Malone is destined to argue a landmark case concerning civil liberties before the Supreme Court."

"But does he win, Your Eminence?" Mackey pressed.

The Fisherman nodded.

"That's me boy!" Mackey whooped. "And what about him and the little lady? Do the pair of 'em stay together? And what's in store for 'em if they do?"

The Fisherman held up a hand. "I can't tell you everything you want to know, Alistair."

"Please, Fisherman. I'd give up me first-class status to know."

The superior could see that he was in earnest. "Their souls are connected. They will remain together and be happy."

Mackey was almost satisfied. "Any little sheilas or mates?"

At the Fisherman's tight-lipped expression, the subordinate decided the private audience was over.

"I just thought I'd ask. I'll be running along now, Fisherman. I should probably take a look-see at the printouts and make certain none of me other charges are floundering. G'day, mate," he chirped, swaggering out of his superior's chambers. Alistair whistled as he walked the sunlit corridors of Heaven.

The Fisherman smiled to himself at hearing Mackey's puckered rendition of *Waltzing Matilda*.

Harlequin Superromance

COMING NEXT MONTH

#358 MIDNIGHT BLUE • Nancy Landon
Their families had been feuding for generations. And
things got worse—Caroline McAlester tried to stop
Luke O'Connor from developing his theme park in
their town. Then, with one look into Luke's
midnight-blue eyes, Caroline forgot their feud. One
kiss and Luke remembered he'd loved her forever.

#359 AIRWAVES • Suzannah Davis
Chattanooga deejay Summer Jones was number one
in town—until the station was sold to Ryder
Bowman. He joined Summer in the control booth,
and radio's hottest new duo was born. The public
loved it . . . all but one mysterious fan.

#360 A PRIVATE AFFAIR • Kelly Walsh
Ever since Laurel Davis—personal manager to a
famous actress—had walked into the office of
private investigator Nick Malone, his life had felt like
a particularly confusing adventure film. There was
everything from blackmail to mysterious deaths to a
beautiful, aloof heroine. . . .

#361 PLAYING WITH FIRE • Risa Kirk
Cal Stewart and Mary Nell Barrigan were two
Tacoma-based engineers competing for the same
contract. Each needed desperately to win it.
Determined to remain apart, they refused to see
that by antagonizing each other they were only
tempting fate. . . .